LOVE HER EVERMORE

SHERI SHELDON

To my sweet husband, Philip. Thank you for your unwavering love and support, especially while I spent countless hours working on this novel. It isn't easy being the partner of a novelist.

To my mother, Marilyn, for her lifelong love and guidance, and who was the inspiration for Gram.

And to my children, their spouses, and my grandchildren, who fill my life with joy and happiness, I am grateful for you all.

·❤·❤·❤·❤·❤·

Acknowledgements

Editing: Doretta Pirollo Martelli

Thank you, Doretta! Your guidance was invaluable, not to mention your patience! You are a rockstar! I had no idea it would take over a year to complete this novel! Thank you for sticking with it and seeing it through.

Cover Design: BookDesignsbyShae

Playlist

https://music.youtube.com/playlist?list=PLyMn2dm
meyFQ0Q5ODEhw6Nh-CSa11Cr82&si=LwZZosqI
1IJjBT6

Nocturne in E-Flat Major Opus. 9, No.2 Frederic
Chopin
Only You The Platters
An Affair to Remember Vic Damone
The Way You Look Tonight Fred Astaire
The Blue Danube Johann Strauss II
Maria (West Side Story) Leonard Bernstein Sung by Larry Kert.
Something's Coming (West Side Story) Jim Bryant
Rock Around The Clock Bill Haley & His Comets
Rockin Robin Bobby Day
Mr. Sandman The Penguins (Originally) The Chordettes
Unchained Melody Les Baxter
Cheek To Cheek Fred Astaire
The Nutcracker Grand Pas de Deux Tchaikovsky

FILMS:
The Captain's Paradise Alec Guinness and Yvonne DeCarlo. An Affair
To Remember Cary Grant and Deborah Kerr
Sayonara Marlon Brando. The Prince and The Showgirl Laurence
Olivier Marilyn Monroe

Contents

Chapter 1

THE FATHER'S SON

SURREY, ENGLAND MAY 21, 1956

THE ROLLS ROYCE SILVER Dawn, a gleaming, sleek contrast to the vagrant-plagued neighborhood, crawled past countless shuffling feet and incoherent voices as Dane Wellington sat in the back seat waiting for George to park. Dark wisps of hair hitting his long black lashes, twenty-four-year-old Dane sighed and brushed them back impatiently, eager to see Frankie, the only barber he allowed to touch his thick, lustrous asset.

"I'll wait right 'ere, sir," George said.

Inside the barbershop, Dane noticed Frankie attending to a forty-something, balding gentleman.

Frankie nodded at Dane. "It'll be just a few minutes, Mr. Wellington."

As he waited his turn in the crowded shop, Dane couldn't help overhearing the boisterous gentleman in Frankie's chair bellowing. "Do a good job, Frankie. I'm to wed a young beauty tomorrow."

Dane chuckled to himself. The gent's expensive embroidered waistcoat and gleaming shoes spoke of prosperity, yet his stature reminded Dane more of a nervous insect than a powerful man.

Cheers erupted from the other men in the shop as the homely customer boasted about his upcoming marriage to a young girl from Leatherhead.

The mention of Leatherhead, a town where his father owned several properties, intrigued the normally unaffected Dane. He found himself drawn in as the stout geezer described his future bride.

"A beguiling and delightful creature with silky blonde hair cascading in soft waves, a deliciously slim figure, and seductive blue eyes, who already has the skills of a wife and mother! Plays the piano intuitively!" he blustered, proudly.

Leatherhead? Wavy blonde hair? Blue eyes? Piano? It could not be. Sounds like he's describing Katie Clarke. No, she is merely a child!

Bolting from his chair, Dane confronted the crass buffoon, struggling to stay calm while he prepared for the worst. "Pardon me, sir. I'm Dane Wellington. May I ask her father's name?"

"Mr. Wellington," the man nodded. "I'm Edward Barclay. Father's name is Clarke, Lenny Clarke. A sorry bloke, he is!" Laughing heartily, the other men echoed his glee. "An unlucky gambler forever in debt."

Dane, acutely aware of his racing heart and the pressure mounting, took a breath and inquired, "Your fiancée is Katherine Clarke?"

Surprised that Dane knew her, Barclay grinned victoriously, then wheezed and gasped when Dane seized his collar, pulling him off his chair. Barclay's stumpy legs wobbled as Dane released his grasp, and Barclay crumpled to the floor.

Dane growled. "Are you not old enough to be her father?" Dane dragged his hand over his uncut hair, now wet with sweat. Staring threateningly at the eccentric, he charged, "You cannot wangle yourself into marriage to that innocent girl! Is she even eighteen?"

Silenced by Dane's intensity, the men in the shop regarded one another, then watched as two brave souls helped the miscreant to his feet. Straightening himself, Barclay yanked his finely made trousers up over his plump midsection and tugged at his ill-fitting vest. Raising his double chin and his fist, he snarled indignantly. "This is a perfectly bloody legal and religious marriage! She is eighteen, and her family will be there to give consent! We will be married by half past ten on the morrow. I suggest you wind your neck in, man." Barclay stood his ground; his henchmen were just outside the shop.

His teeth clenched, not waiting to hear more, Dane bolted from the shop to the Rolls, startling the slumbering George into action. "Take me to the Clarke's at once!" he yelled, instantly regretting his tone. "Forgive me, George. I didn't mean to shout at you. I have just learned of an outrageous scheme involving the Clarke girl and a monstrous bugger. And you know how my father feels about her!"

"Indeed, sir." George, a thirty-eight-year-old ex-boxer with a heavy Irish accent, had been Ellis Wellington's driver for over sixteen years. "I 'ad jus' started workin' fer 'im the day yer father saved 'er life an' was dere all the times 'e came to 'er rescue o'er the years."

As they drove, Dane's agitation grew, the round man's words echoing in his ears; he dug his fingernails into the underside of the finely tanned leather seats. *She couldn't have agreed. Surely not. But even if she did, I bloody well cannot let her marry that fool! Father will be furious!*

In a flurry of hurried steps, Dane knocked harder than he intended at the Clarke's door. Katie's younger brother answered. "Hello, Paul. I don't know if you remember me, I'm–"

"Mr. Wellington! 'Ello. Yea', I know who ye are! Come in."

Noting Paul's schoolbooks spread on the table and the younger Clarke children cheerily playing marbles nearby, memories of himself, his father, and Katie in this cramped but tidy cottage came gushing back. The daisies he had brought her, his teasing about her unkempt hair, the lemonade she had made, and her dislike of his pet rat. *When was I last here?* Although he hadn't seen her in a while, he was well aware his father had.

Dane tried to control his frenzy and managed a polite smile. "Pardon the interruption. Where are your sister and mother?"

"They working a' the Atwood r's'dence, sir. I ca' show ye if ye like," Paul answered.

"Please."

Paul nodded, kneeling quickly to the children to inform them he would return shortly.

While waiting, Dane caught sight of the piano his father had purchased for Katie. He moved closer to the papers on the stand. He examined the impractical, self-created music sheet: a sketch of the keyboard with numbers marked on it. The next line held the numbers for the song she had learned. *She's created her own method of writing music. How remarkably resourceful.*

Paul, eyeing the interior of the Rolls with a grin, directed George to the stately home where Katie and their mother worked.

Dane pulled some coins from his pocket. "Thank you, Paul. This is for you." He turned toward the front door, once again dragging his fingers over his unruly mop before ringing the bell.

·❦·❦·❦·❦·❦·

T HE SOFT GOLDEN RAYS of the afternoon sun streamed through the paned window of the servants' break room, illuminating the minute dust particles dancing in the air. Standing before a heavily carved Victorian mirror, Katie Clarke trembled, her chin quivering, tears welling in her eyes. The musty scent of old lace hung in the air as she studied her slight frame, swallowed up by her beloved deceased grandmother's wedding dress.

"Tis not how I pictured me wedding," she said. "I imagined it bein' more like me novels. Me 'andsome beau on 'is knee begging for me hand."

Taking the straight pins from between her lips, her mother Norma said, "Come now. Ye agreed, 'tis a good match. Ye'll be rich an ye'll have a 'usband an plenty o'quid to care for ye babes. What more ye want?"

Katie, angry at herself for consenting to the marriage, wiped the tears from her face, resisting her mother's nudges to turn as she worked on the dress. As Katie and her mother exchanged a glance, she hoped she saw regret in her mother's eyes.

Norma hastily lined the pins along the sides of the garment. Since there remained only thirty minutes on their lunch break, and the wedding was the following day, she concentrated on the task. "Mr. Barclay is moneyed. Life's easier when dere's coin, an ye father and I'll relax knowing ye taken care of."

Living near the factory had made it easy for men to approach their daughter, and lately, the incidence of rape of young girls had increased significantly. The Clarke's recent discovery of a neighborhood cad in their home with Katie while she supervised the younger children convinced Norma and Lenny that she needed to be wed.

With a gambling debt to Mr. Barclay of nearly five hundred pounds hanging over him, Lenny Clarke seized an opportunity to satisfy his wife when the family attended a church function that Mr. Barclay sponsored.

Barclay's keen interest ignited, he immediately offered marriage, along with the courtesy of wiping the debt. "We would be kin, after all," Barclay had told him.

Lenny did all he could to persuade his wife. "'Tis the optimal solution."

Although she'd only spoken briefly to Mr. Barclay the day they all met at the church, Norma liked the idea. "'e's moneyed? Devout? Schooled?" Norma questioned her husband. "An 'e has land an a large 'ome? Sounds too good t'be true. She'd be the proper wife of a posh gen'leman an 'ave sufficient sums for 'er children."

"What more do I want?" Katie yelped. "I want t'love the man I wed."

Norma placed her hand on her daughter's shoulder. "Ye don't know what it's like t'not have 'nough quid for feeding ye babes, or to see 'em with no shoes on their feet. Consider what ye'll have. Tis a dream, girl. Tis a good life. An ye'll children 'ill have the things ye don'. Piano lessons', an' fine schoolin'."

Katie shuddered, her face wincing in disgust. "But, Mum...Mr. Barclay," she said under her breath. Her mind wandered as she listened to the rhythmic thump of a bouncing ball and the laughter of her employer's children coming from the courtyard outside the servants' break room. Through the window, she watched them giggling and taunting one another, a stark contrast to her plight. Katie yearned for days past when she was carefree and ignorant of the harsh realities of life. *Why'd I agree?*

The melodic ring of the doorbell echoed through the break room. Katie pushed her mother's hand away and looked her in the eyes, a desperate, hopeful thought occurring to her. "The doorbell," she gasped, bolting up the stairs, barefoot.

Opening the sizable door, she stumbled back, eyeing the strikingly handsome gentleman before her. No immediate signs of recognition between them, her baby blues stared into his soulful browns. Each momentarily forgetting her looming fate, they stood frozen on opposite sides of the doorway, the seeds of attraction planted.

"Pardon me. Can I help you?" she finally managed, feeling her heart fluttering. With recognition returning, she poked her head out of the door, spotting the Rolls-Royce. Her eyes widened with uncontainable delight, a breath escaping her lips. "That's Mr. Wellington's car! He's 'ere?"

"Katie." Dane said. He stared into her blue eyes. "Good Lord." His eyes traveled to her slim figure, then back up to her red, swollen eyes as his hand covered his heart. "I mean, you are so—" He followed her gaze. "Father is not here, it's just me. You remember me, of course? I'm Dane Wellington."

Katie gulped. "Oh! O'course. Mr. Wellington's son. What are ye doing 'ere?" her voice, barely a whisper.

"Hmmm ... Hello. I ...I was at the barbershop." He pointed away, then stopped and looked at her dress. "An interesting gentleman was bragging about his nuptials tomorrow to a rather remarkable girl. From his description, I ... I thought it might be you. And, I was wondering if, perhaps, it was true? I see the dress, so I guess you are to wed tomorrow? You have agreed to marry him?"

Tears immediately burst from her eyes, and her face contorted into a grimace of silent pain.

Dane sighed. Her tears and the look on her face told him what he wanted to know. "Does my father know?"

"No. I don' know what t'do," she said, her Cockney accent rising with every word. "Me mum wants me wed, and I 'greed. But I don' want to wed 'im. Mr. Barclay. He's so ..." She grimaced at the thought of the man. "Ah, I din' want to. Should 'ave said no. I did a' first, but then, I agreed." She paused for a moment, wringing her hands. "I thought of leavin', even packed me things', but I 'ave nowhere t'go. I wanted t'speak to ye father but didn' know 'ow to reach 'im. I prayed 'e would come." Katie blotted her eyes with both hands. "Me mum just fittin' me dress during our break," she said, wiping her damp hands over her dress, accidentally sticking herself with one of the straight pins. "Ouch!" she yelled, shaking her hand.

Dane instinctively reached for her. "Are you alright?" He pulled a monogrammed handkerchief from his pocket and wrapped her finger tightly. Holding her hand, he bit his lip. "I must speak with your mother. Surely, there is another solution."

She nodded. "Me mum is 'ere, sir. Won't ye come in? The misses' won' mind. But I'll check with 'er an get me mum."

Dane waited in the foyer for Katie to return.

Norma Clarke came up the stairs and gasped. As still as a statue, her eyes wide and fixed on Dane. "The son?" she breathed.

"Mrs. Clarke," Dane said, nodding to her.

When Katie returned, Norma, not taking her eyes from Dane, said, "Did ye ring for 'im? How is 'e 'ere?"

Katie stared at Dane and shrugged. "No, I didn'. He just came. I don' know 'ow."

Dane looked from the daughter to the mother. "You intend to marry her off? To that ridiculous rake?"

Norma sucked in her breath, cowering shamefully for her part in the scheme. She swallowed hard. "I cannot defy me 'usband, sir," she choked. "It's all arranged. She'll 'ave a good life, a 'ouse of 'er own. Dey'll be plenty quid for babes an food, an clothes. An, the debt'll be gone."

"What debt?" Dane asked.

"Pop owes Mr. Barclay quite a sum from gambin'. Five hun'red pounds. Mr. Barclay owns a grand 'ouse and land, 'e does." Katie looked at her mother. "Me mum's afraid I'll be an unwed mum. Wants me wed proper."

"Five hundred pounds? A bloody fortune. And what do you mean by 'an unwed mother?'" Dane shot back.

"The men from the factory comin' around. She too pretty for 'er own good," Norma quipped, eyeing her daughter. "She often alone minding the young ones, and dere's no one dere to protect 'er. I 'ave come 'ome an found men in me 'ouse! Mr. Barclay seems a good bloke. Schooled. Monied." Norma reached out to her daughter, but Katie, still angry at her mother for pressuring her to agree, pushed her hand away.

Katie understood her mother's reason, though. Her father was lacking in all the ways Mr. Barclay was not. Her parents did not own a home. They barely had money to put shoes on their children's feet each year. Everything her mother wanted for herself and her children, Barclay would provide. Her mother had told her *'Love will grow. And if no love, then maybe friendship or companionship.'* Her mother had none of those things either.

"Dere was a man," Katie said, remembering the incident." 'e asked for Paul. I let 'im in, but t'was a mistake. He tried t'kiss me. An me mum came in jus then. He frightened me."

"She needs t'be settled," Norma said.

"She does need to be protected, but this is not the answer. Father will be furious." Dane shook his head. "You know how he feels about her. He repeats the story of that day to anyone who will listen. How he bade George to stop at your home. He just knew something was terribly wrong. And, when he arrived, he said he found you frantic." Then, turning to Katie, he said, "You were burning up and gripping your stomach. You were but two or three years old."

"Yes. I remember all too well," Norma said. "'E thought t'was polio. I 'ad no idea, but 'e raced us to hospital."

"Thankfully, it wasn't, but she was gravely ill," Dane said, looking between the mother and daughter. "He dragged me to the hospital to visit a few times. I recall those blue eyes of yours and how you begged us to stay. Father engaged a private nurse so you wouldn't be alone. Do you know he says you are his 'special daughter?' Whenever I was home from school, and I joined him on his property visits, we always stopped to see you."

"I love Mr. Wellington," Katie said.

Dane's face flushed crimson. "If she needed protection, you might have spoken to my father about it! He would have gladly sent her to school. She cannot marry that absurd man! This is 1956! Not the 1800s!" He shook his head vehemently. "He is much too old for her. She'll be enslaved! Believe me, I heard how he spoke about her. He is not a good bloke, as you say. She cannot marry him." Dane took a breath. "Let's go see my father." He reached for her hand. "He'll have an answer."

Katie sighed with relief. "Yes, please."

Norma put her arm on his. "I canno' let ye take 'er, sir. She's t'be married tomorrow and properly set'led. If not, Mr. Barclay'll still be owed his sums, and me 'usband will be quite cross." She lowered her eyes and continued, "Ye 'ave no idea; Lenny, he's, well, 'e's no' nice when 'e's cross. Ye must leave 'er be. There is nothin' ye can do." She paused for a moment, eyeing Dane and then her daughter. "Unless ye marry 'er ye'self. T'would be a far betta' match, indeed." Norma crossed her arms; a barely noticeable smile crossing her lips.

Dane squinted at Norma and laughed. "Marry her? Me?"

"She loves ye father. Ye practically already kin. Ye father would be 'appy, too." She stood rigid, her arms still crossed, her determined eyes on Dane.

Dane shook with indignation, the color draining from his face just as Katie's flushed red, mortally embarrassed by her mother's suggestion. "She doesn't need to be married off. She just needs to be away from here. My father will send her to school."

"School? Wha' 'ill that do? Only delay 'er a year or two. Then what? She may never get such an off'r again. She 'as a chance t'be married an set'led with a 'ome of her own. No, sir. Either you marry 'er, or she'll marry 'im." Norma's eyes blazing with defiance, locked onto Dane's with unwavering resolve.

"School is the solution, ma'am. She will learn and grow. She will make something of herself."

Norma stood her ground. "She will make somethin' of 'erself when she's wed. Piano lessons right in 'er 'ome, if she wants. An, 'fore long, she'll be a mum. What else is dere?"

Squeezing the bridge of his nose as if in pain, he shook his head. "It's quite impossible, what you're suggesting."

Norma lifted her head. "Suit yeself. They'll be a weddin' t'morrow." She turned to Katie. "Don' let 'im ruin ye best chances."

Glancing at Katie's frightened face, Dane clenched his fists; perspiration flooded his temples, the situation tense. "I am a bachelor. I have a life …" His rugged features, his thick mane that complemented his dark, long lashes, and his charming manner disarmed even the most reserved women, leading to many romantic encounters. Taking steps that jeopardized his lifestyle was asking too much. But, more than that, his mother's infidelity reinforced his mistrust of all women and cast an unyielding lock on his heart. Marriage was the most offensive notion, the one thing he swore he would never do.

His eyes bounced between Norma and Katie. "I would like to speak to a vicar. Please, grab your things and inform the missus of the house that you must leave and may not return."

He waited at the door until the ladies reappeared, Katie clutching a small woven satchel and a sweater. "That's all you have?" Dane asked, eyeing the tattered bag.

"I just gather'd me most impor'ant thin's," Katie answered.

Chapter 2

SPECIAL BLOODY CIRCUMSTANCES

T HE CAR HADN'T FULLY stopped when Dane leaped out and sprint-ed to the rectory in search of the vicar. Katie and her mom hurried behind him.

At last he found Father Lionel in the flower gardens, introduced himself, and frantically explained the situation. "Father, please help me. We cannot let her marry that rake. He will use and abuse her. He is not a gentleman."

After a moment of contemplation, Father Lionel responded, "Good Lord, what a despicable situation. Most unusual and highly offensive. But if she doesn't want to marry him, her father cannot force her. She must agree, sign a contract. Then the banns must be read and so forth."

Katie and her mother approached. Dane gestured to them. "May I introduce Norma and Katherine Clarke. This is Father Lionel."

Father Lionel smiled. "Oh my! Yes, I know these young ladies. Good day."

Her father cannot force her. A glimmer of hope as a memory surfaced, father chuckling at her enthusiasm when they visited, always wanting a hug and his attention. They shared an undeniable bond, to be sure. Heat spread through him as he imagined his father's furious reaction. "Bloody ..." He caught himself before blurting out his overused expletive. "This wedding cannot take place. You said her father cannot force her. What must we do to stop it?"

The vicar massaged his chin before answering. "Who is her betrothed?"

"Mr. Edward Barclay," Norma said.

"Edward Barclay. Of Camberley? Oh dear. He is a valued member of the church, I believe. Not a member of our parish, but a significant donor, if I'm not mistaken." The vicar shook his head. "Have you agreed to the marriage? Has the contract been signed?" he asked Katie.

"I 'ave, and yes, the contract was signed. But, I don' want t'marry 'im."

"Oh, dear. A very difficult predicament, indeed. Especially after the reading of the banns," the vicar said. "And the banns have been read, I take it? Which church?"

"Yes, sir, a' St. Pet'r's Church. In Frimley," Norma answered.

"I'm sorry sir, but banns are read aloud in church on three consecutive Sundays so that people may raise these types of objections." Father Lionel turned to Dane. "You should have raised your objections with the church in Frimley."

Dane's heart lurched. "I just learned of this. The wedding is tomorrow, Father. I didn't have time to raise objections."

"After the banns are read, and with a contract signed, backing out is a breach. Although, a woman *may* back out without consequences most of the time, I'd guess Mr. Barcly will not take kindly to his reputation being soured. A last-minute cancellation by a woman leaves people wondering what happened, what wrongs he might have committed, what character flaws he might have demonstrated to cause this break. This will cause quite a scandal, even in these modern times. I'm sorry. I do not see how I can help you. No one has raised objections, and the parents and bride, I might add, have consented. She will have to tell her betrothed she's changed her mind and face the consequences, if there are any."

"She doesn't want to confront him, Father," Dane said. "I'm sure you are correct. He will be quite cross. I don't want to confront him again, myself." Dane looked at them all. *I need time to think.* He walked away, mumbling. While pacing back and forth, he thought of what his father would say. *Father would be furious if I didn't do all that I could to help her.*

He glanced at Katie. *She cannot marry him. That much I know. He is a brute. Life with him would be torture. What can I do? Perhaps marry in secret? And an annulment to follow when she turns twenty-one?*

He sighed. He had no choice. This was the moment. His moment. His father's lessons in his head. *'Do good for others; think of your fellow man; use your good fortune well.'* Dane motioned for the vicar to come closer, out of earshot of the ladies. "If I step in, is an annulment a possibility? I mean, with no consummation, of course."

The vicar's face flushed; he responded through gritted teeth. "I commend your honorable desire to help, young man. But marrying with the intent to annul is a sin. Marriage is a sacred sacrament with vows that should be kept and honored." Father Lionel and Dane stared at one another until the vicar, understanding the predicament, softened his tone. "To answer your question, I believe if both parties swear it is so, then, yes, I suppose you may petition the court. It would be up to the magistrate, of course."

Dane moved further away, motioning for Katie to join him. "May I speak with you, alone?" He took her hands when she approached. "You don't want to be forced to marry anyone, especially, Barclay. You should be educated and know your own mind before you wed. And I... I certainly do not wish to be married. I am a bachelor and wish to remain so. However, this situation is dire. As your mother will not let me take you to my father without marrying, I have a plan. If we marry, but do not consummate the marriage, I believe that is grounds for annulment. Once we are married, I will take you to my father's home, in Weybridge, where you shall have your own room. I keep a flat in Kensington. We will not be true husband and wife." Dane glanced at Norma, who was waiting with crossed arms for his decision. "My father will send you to a proper school, then once you are twenty-one, we will annul the marriage, and you may do as you please. What do you say?"

Katie stared at Dane. "We will marry?"

Norma approached. "Well?"

Dane, still holding Katie's hand, looked at his soon-to-be-wife. He had made his decision. This was what he must do. "She and I will marry, and I will take responsibility for any repercussions from Barclay." Dane noticed the smile crossing Norma's lips. He then turned toward the vicar. "And naturally, a sizable donation to the church will be forthcoming. Katie, would you prefer here in the garden or the church?"

Father Lionel laughed. "Are you suggesting you marry now? I cannot do that!"

"Father," Dane spouted, "these are special bloody circumstances. Pardon my language. I noticed Barclay had several muscleman with him when I met him. We cannot confront him. I'm quite sure the church would agree that this is the only resolution. Surely, you can see that."

Father Lionel's temper flared at Dane. "I cannot change the law. The banns must be read, and you must wait three weeks."

"The banns have been read," Dane said curtly.

The vicar cocked his head. "Not with your name, sir, and not in this parish."

Dane clenched his jaw, threw up his hands, and turned towards Katie. "Well, seems we have a problem I cannot solve. However, we must be on our way, post haste. After my confrontation with Barclay at the barbershop, well, let's just say he may very well be hunting for you. If the vicar won't marry us now, then we must be off to my father's home, where we will wait out the three weeks for the banns. And to appease you, Mrs. Clarke, I will sign a contract."

Katie placed her hand on her heart. "I 'ave loved yer father an 'ave wished 'e was me own since I was a babe. I would live in 'is home, then? With 'im?"

"Yes, when not at school. Father will insist you attend school," Dane answered, thinking that her speech pattern and formidable accent would be number one on the agenda to remedy.

A broad smile creased her lips as a wave of relief washed over her face. Dane smiled seeing the visible transformation in her bright eyes.

"Yes! I want to go! I want t'live with Mr. Wellington. It be a dream come true!"

Father Lionel's face brightened. "Wellington? Your father is Ellis Wellington?"

"That's right."

"Good Lord! Your father is a legendary and highly respected member of this community. Many of our parishioners are immensely indebted to your father."

"Yes, I'm quite sure that's true, and *she* is his very special girl, like a daughter." Dane pointed to Katie. "He will be furious to know I was prevented from helping her."

The vicar sucked in his breath, tilting his head to Dane. "You will not be, sir. I will contact the Archbishop of Canterbury and arrange for a license dated today."

All three sighed heavily. "Thank you," Dane said.

"One moment," Norma said, her finger pointed in the air. "What of the debt to Mr. Barclay? Mr. Clarke will be lookin' to ye for that, sir."

Dane's eyes narrowed. "I have agreed to marry your daughter, ma'am. You want me to pay off your husband's debt as well? A discussion for another time. Let's get on, then, we must hasten. Katie, the garden or the chapel?"

Katie glanced at her mother. "The chapel, if ye don' mind."

The apprehensive vicar scrutinized the couple. "I am against performing hasty marriages, but I see honor and duty in you, Mr. Wellington, and I see love and passion in your heart, dear," nodding to Katie. "Something tells me you two will find friendship, and with God's blessing and a good amount of patience; perhaps you will also find love."

Dane's eyebrows raised at that, for he couldn't imagine such a thing.

As they were leaving the flower fields for the chapel, Dane, spotting a patch of daisies, hurriedly garnered a handful, handing them to Katie. "I seem to remember your love of these." He smiled, seeing her face suddenly erupt into a sweet symphony of delight, and found himself conflicted between feelings of satisfaction and misery.

Vows recited, papers signed, cash exchanged, they were on their way within the hour.

In the car, Dane instructed George to take Norma back to her employer's home.

"Ouch!" Katie yelped, pulling a straight pin from the unfinished dress.

"Well, at least ye wore the dress for ye weddin'!" Norma laughed.

Katie glared at her mother until noticing her mother's sly wink and pointed glance toward Dane. Katie softened her gaze as her mother shrugged her shoulders and tilted her head just a bit. As a smile crossed Katie's face, the two women exchanged a quick squeeze of their hands.

Stepping out of the car, Norma said, "Thank you, Mr. Wellington. Ye done a good thing. Yer father will be pleased, indeed."

The awkward silence in the back seat hung heavily as both Dane and Katie contemplated the future.

Dane's clenched fists relaxed with a sigh, trusting that his plan would work and his life would not change. *There will be an annulment. This is temporary. It's not real. I've nothing to worry about.*

Chapter 3

REACH FOR THE STARS

1951, Five Years Earlier

"Mr. Forsythe, I must congratulate you on your expeditious action! You surely earned your keep, sir." Ellis Wellington patted his land manager on the back, nodding to his nineteen-year-old son triumphantly. "These are the finest buildings I have seen in a long time. I am thrilled to have acquired them. And so close to our other cottages. Good work." The three men were surveying the retail properties and introducing themselves to the tenants.

The block-long limestone buildings in the village of Leatherhead, Surrey, bustled with busy first-floor shops and second-story apartments adorned with stained glass windows and lush shrubbery, including colorful vines and flowers cascading over the railings.

Forsythe, having received a hefty spotter's fee for introducing Wellington to the previous owner, held his head high as Ellis's contentment shone on his aging but still handsome face. The group entered an apartment on the second floor, and Wellington smiled, testing the commode. "I'm thrilled to see this completed," Wellington said to Forsythe. "With over forty properties, we didn't need any more to renovate."

"No, sir," Forsythe said.

Recently, raw sewage had caused a cholera outbreak in England, prompting government grants for renovations. This left Ellis an overwhelming task of upgrading his numerous properties simultaneously.

As the men continued their tour, Wellington, hitting a pipe with his cane, said, "You must pay attention to the little things, son. If you let them go, a bigger problem will follow. Moisture is your enemy."

Stifling a yawn, Dane nodded, his mind already wandering. Acutely aware that he had every advantage, including the prospect of one day becoming the sole owner of his father's real estate empire, his mind was instead on Nina, a lovely brunette he had met the night before.

As they were finishing their visit, forty-two-year-old Forsythe said, "Let's stretch our legs a bit and walk to the cottages. Not too far." He pointed up the street to Ellis's six row-house cottages.

Dane, knowing where they were headed and angry that he had not thought to bring something, perked up upon spotting a bush of white daisies overflowing a brick planter. After gaining permission, he quickly clustered a handful, spending several minutes arranging them artfully, then carried them carefully along the winding cobblestone roads leading to the stone cottages where the Clarkes lived.

The uphill trudge from the busy street shops proved quite the undertaking, as the sun was bent on scorching the earth. Ellis, having gained weight and years, considered hopping into the Rolls-Royce following behind them.

Mr. Forsythe, who had been in charge of the properties in and around London and Surrey for over ten years, babbled on, "Clarke remains in arrears. His poor wife, with six brats to feed, works as a housekeeper, yet they remain broke from his boozin' and gamblin'."

Before they approached the Clarke home, Dane stopped to get his bearings, hardly recognizing the cottages. They seemed smaller and shabbier than he remembered from just a year ago, and he noted the front gardens behind the white picket fences were ill kept, except for one.

In the Rolls's window, he caught his reflection, placing the flowers on the ground as he straightened up his crisp white linen button-down shirt and brushed off his well-fitted slacks. As he picked up the flowers, he said,

"I should have thought ahead and brought her a book or something useful. She has nothing."

"She is an uncomplicated girl and will be touched by your gesture, surely. She will appreciate most anything you offer her," Ellis said. "Just hope she has finally forgotten that incident with your rat by now."

The incident. Anxious to show her his prized pet and all its tricks, a much younger Dane had pulled the white rat out of his pocket, and before he introduced it to her, she became hysterical. He had never seen his father so angry. "Yes, let's hope. It's been years. Time for her to let it go."

Several children and a few scruffy dogs were playing noisily in the cobblestoned street as they approached. Someone was attempting to play a piano.

"Ah, listen. One of my favorite pieces!" Ellis held up his finger, conducting what appeared to be Chopin's "Nocturne in E Flat Major," although barely recognizable and poorly played. Ellis glanced at Dane and they shared a chuckle over the erred notes.

Mrs. Smith, the Clarke's neighbor, opened her door to greet them, and they stepped inside.

Seeing Katie playing the piano, Ellis, sneaking a wink in Dane's direction, remarked, "That's quite good, young lady!"

Whipping around, Katie screeched. "Mr. Wellington!" She sprung into his arms and kissed his cheek, her brilliant smile illuminating her face.

"I like dat song! Mrs. Smith lets me play 'er phonograph, and 'er piano too. I'm trying t'figure the notes. Next time ye come, I shall play it correctly," she said, nodding with conviction, although she had no way of learning the complicated piece.

"It's remarkable that you can play it as well as you do with no instruction. Keep at it," Ellis encouraged.

Dane hadn't initially recognized the matured Katie. *Is she just thirteen?*

As the group walked to the Clarke home, Katie and Ellis, hand in hand, Ellis asked, "You remember my son, Dane, of course? You haven't seen him in a while."

"Of course she does. I was here last August. Every August, really. Well, other than when I went into the service, of course," Dane said, pursing his lips and bracing for the tirade.

Her face, void of the joy it had seconds ago, soured. "I 'member 'im and 'is stupid rat!" She pouted, crossing her arms.

Ellis eyed Dane with his eyebrows raised, and Dane grimaced. *Of course, she remembers.*

"Oh, come on! Albert Einstein was a terribly clever and well-behaved white rat. I raised him from birth and brought him everywhere. Even taught him several tricks. Everyone loved him." Dane shook his head in defense. "I have already apologized a dozen times, and it was many years ago. Won't you ever forgive me?"

She crossed her arms and scowled. "Ye were laughing a' me!"

"Well, to be honest, your reaction was rather hysterical." Biting his lip to keep from laughing again, he recalled her falling over herself, screaming bloody murder, and fleeing into the street. "Poor Albert Einstein was scared to death, too." *It* was *funny.* "Anyway, I have brought these for you. Sorry, they have wilted a bit from this heat." He handed her the flowers.

"For me?" Her cheeks flushed, and she instantly began combing her messy hair with her fingers and straightening her scruffy dress before accepting the flowers. Dane watched her face come alive with a smile that could make someone forget their name. Her teeth were white, too, he noted. A rarity, especially for the lower classes.

"Thank you. Me first time gettin' flowers." she blushed, adding, "Daisies! Me favorite."

"You are most welcome."

A look of contentment washed over Ellis's face as he beheld their interaction.

"Oh, me goodness!" Noticing Ellis drenched with sweat, Katie leaped into action, dragging over a chair, then disappearing briefly before returning with a pitcher of lemonade and glasses for the three men.

"Why, thank you, child. Much appreciated. You are a delight." Once refreshed, Ellis offered Katie the box of chocolates he'd brought.

"Thank you, sir," she grinned, passing it to her siblings. Ellis looked at Dane as they both noted she hadn't taken one for herself until her siblings each took theirs.

"Your garden is lovely." Dane said. "Who tends it?"

"I do, sir. I love flower gardens. An' I grew the lemons in your drinks too." Katie smiled, pointing to the small lemon tree. Eyeing the handsome young man, his dark, straight hair, drenched with sweat, falling to his eyebrows, she smiled.

"Well, you have the prettiest garden of all the cottages here. I shall purchase some tools and, perhaps, some seeds if you need them. I'll send them along with Father next he comes."

"That would be most 'elpful. Thank ye," she said. A sweet smile crossed her face as their eyes met for a few seconds before she looked away. She wiped her sweaty palms.

Ellis asked, "Are you still in that ridiculous excuse for a school?"

"Yes." She explained to Dane and Mr. Forsythe. "I passed the tests t'attend grammar school, but there wasn't 'nough room for the girls. I'm at the second'ry modern school."

Ellis's face soured, turning the color of beets. "I'll never understand the need for those tests. Everyone should be educated in academics. Secondary modern school is domestics and typing. You passed, but there isn't enough room? That is absurd."

As they were leaving, an unleashed neighborhood puppy snatched Dane's pant leg, shaking his head and Dane's leg along with it.

"Hey!" Dane yelped, trying to maintain his balance. "Let go of me!" The pup held on. "Don't stand there laughing! Get him off me!"

Katie crossed her arms, smiling at his predicament. "Serves you right for laughing at me."

"Come on! Please! He is going to rip my trousers!"

"Milo! Let go!" she scolded, shooing the dog away.

Dane inspected his trousers for damage. "Thank you."

"You are welcome. I wouldn't want 'im to 'ruin yer fine trousers. You do look rather dapper," she giggled.

He regarded her hair and pointed. "I think I shall purchase a brush for your hair too."

Grimacing, she combed her tangled mess with her fingers again. "I 'ave a brush!"

Dane laughed. "I'm quite sure you do. I was just teasing."

They burst into laughter.

While driving away, Ellis said, "Most unfortunate that our government doesn't think it necessary to educate the lower classes, especially the girls. She has intelligence, spirit, and compassion. She could go far if her circumstances didn't hold her back. I've often thought about sending her to school, but I cannot show favoritism to just one when there are five other children in that household."

·♥·♥·♥·♥·♥·

T HE FOLLOWING MONTH, WHILE Dane, Ellis, and Forsythe were out making rounds, Ellis spotted a yard sale in progress.

"What are you asking for that piano there?" he asked, pointing to a well-used upright.

Eyeing the Rolls-Royce and driver, the young man answered, "Only two hundred quid, sir."

"I'll give you ninety quid *if* you deliver it this afternoon."

"Righto, sir!"

Ellis scribbled a few words, along with Katie's name, address, and the quid for the young man.

Katie squealed with delight as two men removed the piano from the large metal truck. "A piano o' me very own!" she shouted, jumping up and down. Inside the bench was a note:

"Reach for the stars, young lady.
You might just catch one.
Ellis and Dane Wellington."

Chapter 4

WELCOME HOME
May 21, 1956

A T THE WELLINGTON ESTATE, George stepped from the Silver Dawn, opened the wrought-iron gates, and steered the automobile along the picturesque path, its tires crunching gently on the gravel. He stopped in front of the imposing, elaborately-carved double doors.

"Is this ye'r *house*? Looks like a grand inn. How many people live 'ere?" Katie peered intently at the exquisite limestone mansion, its wide cobblestone circular driveway, the lush landscaping, vibrant, colorful wildflowers, and the surrounding manicured gardens. A two-story, four-car garage stood separate from the main house. The matching impressive structures built with Old English stone and sweeping shingled roofs that shielded the iron-framed windows from the sun.

"It's just my father and our housekeeper, Mrs. Danbury, who has quarters downstairs, oh, and of course, sometimes, me. George lives above the garage, and Mr. and Mrs. Macklin, our cook and groundskeeper, live in a cottage on the property." Dane placed his hand over hers. "I realize this is bloody frightening for you, and I'm as gobsmacked as you, believe me. You are very special to my father. I know you care for him, too, and he will be pleased to learn you are safe, so let's see what he has to say about all this, shall we?" He exited the vehicle, turned, and offered her his hand.

Katie blushed and took it, impressed by the gallantry.

George opened the heavy doors, and Katie sucked in her breath as they entered. "Blimey!"

"Well, I suppose I'll take my swim now," they heard Ellis say from another room.

"Father," Dane shouted, leading his wife to the kitchen.

"Mr. Wellington!" Katie rushed to Ellis, startled to see him in a wheelchair. "What 'appened?" She searched his bearded face with worry.

Dane patted his father's shoulder. "He has had some heart troubles and is a bit weak, but we are working on getting his strength back. He doesn't really need that chair. Uses it just around the house."

"Oh, Mr. Wellington. I'm so sorry t'know it." As soon as she looked into his eyes, her face lit up. "Bu, I am 'appy t'see ye, sir!" She kissed his hands and hugged his neck, lingering, drinking in his familiar fatherly scent.

"My dear, is that my Katie? Every time I see you, you are prettier and prettier. And taller too. What are you doing here, child? If I can even call you that, anymore. Goodness. Are you wearing a wedding dress?" Ellis looked at Dane with suspicion.

Dane recounted the day's events, beginning with the barbershop, stopping just before their visit with the vicar.

"Good lord!" Ellis shrieked, his face turning red. "How dare your parents pressure you to marry a man you don't care for! To square a debt? For money? Not that women don't do that every day. But this wasn't your idea. You must be allowed your own decisions on who you marry. Good God. So, what have you done? I don't have all day, boy. I could expire at any moment! Why is she here?" He slammed his hand on the chair's arm.

"We went to the church, and Mrs. Clarke signed the consent." Dane slumped into a chair, throwing his head in his hands, mortified. "We are married, Father. I didn't know what else I could do!"

Ellis flailed his arms wildly. "Good God, boy! Brilliant!" he howled. "Of course, you did the right thing. What else was there to do? I am over the moon, indeed. I often considered how the devil I could send her to school, and now I have the answer!" He lowered his voice as he clasped both their hands. "And truthfully, this is the best thing that could have happened. For all of us. I have no doubt it was meant to be! Fate has lent a hand once again!" Ellis was as animated as a puppet on a string.

Dane did not join in his father's exuberance.

"Oh, Mr. Wellington. I prayed and prayed you would come an save me again. I believe God sent 'im!" She pointed to Dane, still sitting with his head in his hands. "He has sent ye every time I needed ye. Oh, I'm ever grateful!" she cried, hugging Ellis's arm.

Ellis placed his hand over hers as she hugged him. Studying both Dane and Katie, he asked, "How old are you now, my dear?"

"I am eighteen, sir. Nineteen in October."

"Good God! Where has the time gone? You were three when I took you to hospital. What a lucky day that was, my dear. So pleased you recovered completely. Seems so recent. Eighteen. Very well." He pointed at Dane. "This marriage shall not be consummated until a year has passed. Is that clear? You will get to know one another first."

Dane smacked his hand on the desk. "Sir, I have no intention of consummating the marriage. Not ever. Nor will I act as a married man. I agreed to marry her to save her from that fool, but I like my life just the way it is, thank you. No one must know. We will annul this marriage as soon as she comes of age." Dane sighed. "Two and a half years!" he said under his breath. Dane's life, a bachelor's dream that included a swanky London flat, enabled him to entertain in privacy, and he took full advantage of it.

"Very well," Ellis said. "We will find a suitable boarding school straight away. I shall be thrilled to have her company when she is home on holiday." He patted her hands, smiling eagerly.

"I'm t'go away, then? I jus' got 'ere!" she said, squeezing her brows.

Ellis laughed. "Well, for one thing, you must learn your numbers, grammar, and diction, poor girl. You must learn to speak proper English. And Katie, I know you love music. You will learn to play your piano, and you will love learning, indeed. I'm thrilled we get to send you to a proper school! You are a bright girl. You will become an extraordinary woman. It is your destiny," he said proudly.

"Am I not too old t'attend school? I wish I didn' have t'go 'way. I'm so 'appy to be here with you, Mr. Wellington. Oh," she sighed. "but, I do want t'learn, and I should like to speak propa, an learn to play me piano too."

"School won't start until September," Ellis said. "You will have the summer here, at least. We must get you ready. Choose a school and get you enrolled." He patted her hand again to reassure her. "Lots to do! We mustn't waste a moment!"

"Thank ye, sir, bu I 'ave one question." Katie looked back and forth between Ellis and Dane. "What's consummatin' mean?"

The men looked at one another and roared with laughter.

"Hum...Well, unfortunately, governments want to make sure people marry in truth. Not just saying it is so. They want babies, you see. That creates more taxpayers! So, for a marriage to be legal, the marrying couple must share a martial bed," Ellis explained, eyeing his son.

"Consummatin' means sleepin' in the same bed?" Katie asked.

The men looked at one another again, pursing their lips.

"To consummate a marriage is to have ... relations. Sex," Dane offered, holding his grin.

"WHAT?" She looked at them both, astonished. "Who made that rule? Prob'ly men, no doubt! I don't see who's business 'tis! Blimey!" She eyed the two men. "Are you pulling me leg?"

"No, dear. It's quite true," Ellis said. "In almost every country, a marriage must be consummated to be legal. And in many cultures, the wedding guests are present while it is happening! Shockingly."

Katie's eyes widened. "Blimey! An annul? What's it mean?"

"It means the marriage shall end," Dane said. Biting his lip, he turned and called for the staff.

"This is Katherine Clarke," he said when they gathered. "Or, as we call her, Katie. You certainly have heard her name over the years, although only George actually knows her. She is like a daughter to Father, as you may know. Her parents are tenants of ours in Leatherhead, and now she will live here and likely attend boarding school as soon as we get that sorted. I needed to step in and stop an unfortunate situation from ruining her life. We have wed but only temporarily and in name only. I implore you to keep this to yourselves."

They welcomed Katie to her new home as Dane introduced them. The housekeeper held out her arm. "Come with me, child. We will get ye situated."

With her eyes darting in every direction, Katie admired the magnificent home as she followed the housekeeper. Heavy cranberry velvet drapery hung over the oversized leaded windows. A brilliant chandelier spiraled from the second-story ceiling over the curved stairway, its prism crystals glimmering in the sunlight. As they climbed the wooden staircase, she noticed another room on the first floor, which appeared to be almost all glass and bathed in light. Dark plank wood flooring covered the entire first floor, with thick area rugs scattered about. Red flowered wallpaper climbed the stairwell walls, contrasting beautifully with the dark wood paneling in the hallway. The stairs, hallway, and bedrooms were awash in a sea of coordinating dark red floral carpeting.

Following Mrs. Danbury down the hallway, Katie squawked when she eyed her elegant bedroom. "This is me own room?" At home, she and her three sisters shared a windowless room less than one-third the size, with one bed, one desk, a dresser, and a chair. "Blimey!" she said, smiling widely. "I must be dreamin'. 'Tis beautiful. So bright." She grinned, eyeing the frilly white curtains trimmed in red that adorned the three iron-paned windows and the white sheers that hung from the mahogany four-poster bed. Elegant white linens and bed covers with coordinating red pillows trimmed with white lace dressed the bed. A similar brocade fabric covered the window seats. Two stately red velvet chairs, facing one another with a small table between them, looked like the ones in Buckingham Palace she'd once admired in a magazine.

"Did ye bring any belong'ns, night clothes?" Mrs. Danbury asked.

Katie shook her head. She had nothing.

"Oh dear. Well, nothing t'fret about, m'dear. We have plenty of items 'ere. Why don ye relax in a bath, an I'll round up some things for ye?"

"Thank you. I'd like that."

Mrs. Danbury hurried to the adjacent washroom to run the water in the cast iron tub, then helped Katie avoid the remaining pins in her grandmother's dress, turning around as she slipped it off and stepped into the warm water.

Resting her back against the tub, Katie allowed her body to relax, taking a deep breath of the bath salts and enjoying the peace. Never before was she able to take a leisurely bath. *'Tis 'eaven!* As she unwound, her thoughts drifted to Barclay. Overcome with relief and gratitude toward the Wellington men, tears leaked out the corners of her eyes as she thought of how close she'd come to a life of submission and humiliation.

Enjoying the fragrance of the scented soap, she cupped her face with wet hands. *School. I'll be much older than the other girls.* How she had wanted to attend grammar or boarding school where she could learn to read and write and about the world instead of having to take typing and sewing classes. *I don fit in. I don speak propa.* She sank into the tub, holding her breath under the water to soak her hair.

Mrs. Danbury surveyed the items in the bedroom closet where she stored clothing and accessories that guests had left. She chose a few dresses and undergarments, then came back to the washroom with her arms full, bringing Katie back from her thoughts. "I found a few things that'll suit ye 'til we can get ye some decent clothing. Ye'll be comfortable enough, m'dear."

Katie sighed, noting the oversized dresses, wondering who they had belonged to. After drying her hair, she followed Mrs. Danbury downstairs for a bite to eat. The aroma of chicken pie, warm rolls, and sweet jam wafted through the air, filling Katie with mouth-watering anticipation. Starving, her stomach a painful knot after two days of near-fasting, as she had worried about her impending nuptials.

"Sit down, child. The tea will be a moment longer," Mrs. Macklin said.

Dane and Ellis came in and joined her for a bite.

"Do you like your room, Katie?" Ellis asked.

She nodded. "Oh, yes. Tis fit for a queen! Thank ye, Mr. Wellington, sir. I'm very 'appy to be 'ere with ye. Hope I won' be a burden. I can earn me keep. I'm good with 'ousework; can cook, sew, iron."

"Nonsense. I am very pleased to have your company and a chess partner." Ellis smiled.

She turned to Dane. "And thank ye, sir, Mr. Wellington, for what ye did. I hope this don't ruin ye life."

"Don't you fret about that, love. It will all work out, I'm quite certain. We can say that my father is educating you as your benefactor. And we wouldn't exactly be lying." Dane flung his hair back once again. "And tomorrow, perhaps, I can try again for a haircut! Although I hope there are no other damsels in distress to save." Everyone laughed. "And please, call me Dane. It gets quite confusing with two Mr. Wellingtons in the house."

"Thank ye, Dane," she said shyly.

Mrs. Danbury looked at Dane. "She 'asn't any garments t'all, sir. We will 'ave t'get 'er some suitable clothing, indeed."

"Yes," Dane nodded. "Of course. Tomorrow."

"Thank you," Katie said, stuffing the last bite of the roll and jam into her mouth.

"Slow down, girl! The food isn't going anywhere!" Dane burst out laughing. Soon, they were all laughing again.

Katie grinned with love in her heart. "Thank ye, all. F'makin' me feel so welcome. I'm very grateful."

Dane excused himself and retreated to his quarters, too exhausted to do anything more than plop onto the bed. "What a bloody mess!"

Chapter 5

SPRINGTIME DOES HER WONDERS

*P*LEASE, TELL ME *I was dreaming.* He lifted his arm over his eyes to shield them from the bright morning light. *No, not a dream. Married. Bloody hell.* With his arms crossed behind his head, he considered his actions. Never in a thousand years would he have imagined himself not only married but having not consummated his marriage on his wedding night. He shook his head. *Surely, this is God's way of punishing me.*

Dane found his father in the sun-drenched conservatory, enjoying his Earl Grey tea, freshly baked scones, and newspaper. "Morning son," Ellis looked up over his spectacles, searching his son's face. "You did well yesterday, my boy. Mark my words, you don't realize it now, but she will be the perfect wife for you. She has a good head. She is sensible, grateful, loving, and quite beautiful. One day, you will be joyful about this. Don't be so quick to let her go, son. Bide your time. Let her grow. Go have your fun, if you must. But none of them will match her in the end."

Dane leaned against the desk nearby. Not wanting to argue, he held his tongue and nodded instead, knowing he would never agree to remain married. This is temporary. He'll live his life, and she'll live hers.

Ellis picked up a sheet of monogrammed paper and handed it to Dane. "A mate from my club has provided me with the names and numbers of some of the finest boarding schools in the area. Let's start with the schools on this list."

A knock at the front door interrupted them, and Mrs. Danbury announced Priya's arrival. Ellis looked towards the door, then back to Dane with furrowed brows.

"I asked her to come to take Katie shopping," Dane defended. Ellis nodded.

The five-foot-nine Indian beauty swaggered into the conservatory with a shopping bag full of items for Katie. Her pale pink v-neck dress was the perfect color to highlight her light brown skin. Dane marveled at her appearance, taking in her pink heels, her long, toned legs, the thick mane of black hair, sultry greenish eyes, and that stunning smile. *Springtime does her wonders*, he grinned; *the less she wears, the better she looks*. She had developed a lovely new habit of ringing him late in the evening, asking if he wanted company. He realized he hadn't seen her fully dressed in a while.

Beaming, he kissed both cheeks. "Look how beautiful you are."

Her green eyes sparkled at him. "Good morning, Dane. Good morning, Mr. Wellington," she said, glancing at his father.

Ellis nodded in her direction.

In a dress that more resembled a sack and threatened to slip from her shoulders at any moment, Katie struggled down the stairs.

"Good God, what are you wearing?" Dane chuckled, instantly regretting it and biting his lips to curtail the grin." Katie, this is Priya Reddy. Priya, this is Katie Clarke."

With her head down, Katie said, "I don't 'ave anythin' t'wear." Her eyes widened when she saw Priya. The woman's vibrant red lipstick, sculpted rouged cheekbones, and unexpected height were arresting, but it was the way her dress hugged her figure that held Katie's eyes. "Hello. Nice t'meet ye."

"Hello, Katie. Dane has arranged a most wonderful day for us! We are going shopping! My most favorite thing to do!" Priya giggled.

"Come have some breakfast before you head out. Please," Dane motioned to them.

As Katie gobbled some of Mrs. Macklin's spinach and egg quiche, Priya pulled out the items she brought. "Dane asked me to bring a few things for you to wear on our outing. Shall we go upstairs and see what suits you?"

Katie sighed deeply, picking at the dress she had on. "Oh, thank ye. I don' know who's dress 'tis, and I don' want to seem ungrateful, but I certainly don' want t'wear it."

A short while later, Dane's grin widened, observing Katie descending the stairs in a well-fitting dress, complemented by a smile to match. "Much better," he nodded to both ladies, handing Priya some cash. "I've made arrangements for credit at Selfridges. Here is some cash for a bite if you get hungry or for whatever bits and bobs she needs from the chemist."

Before they left, Dane pulled Katie aside and whispered, "Not a word about being married. Do you understand? She would be furious!"

Katie nodded, and Dane saw the worry on her brow, understanding her dislike of deception.

·❤·❤·❤·❤·❤·

Perched on the edge of her seat in Priya's car, Katie was awestruck by the bustling city, her eyes darting from the cars, buses, and trolleys to all the pedestrians rushing around.

The sales ladies in the brightly lit and magnificent department store were all dressed like Priya, with their sharp uniforms, coiffed hair-dos, and red lipstick. "Tis funny 'ow they try t'be so accommodatin'."

Before Katie had a chance to take it all in, Priya shuffled her up the escalator.

"Movin' stairs? Blimey!"

"Yes, quite a marvel. This way," Priya said, leading to the ladies' department.

Looking at the fine clothes on the racks, Katie asked, "Where I be goin t'wear such fin'ry?"

Priya handed a few items to the salesgirl for Katie to try on. "You will need a few comfortable dresses, skirts, and blouses for daywear, and perhaps a dress or two that are fancier for special events or stepping out. You will need a swimming costume, as there is a swimming pool at the house. Also, some night clothes and undergarments and, oh, yes, a variety of shoes and hats."

As they went from department to department, Katie couldn't help but get caught up in Priya's exhilaration, and in the dressing room, she stared at herself in the mirror, her mouth wide open in astonishment at the instant transformation a well-made dress made. Her eyes opened even wider, seeing the delicate pieces of lingerie the salesgirl brought, noting how full the bras made her breasts look.

Gulping at the pile of clothing lying on the counter, Katie said, "Perhaps we don' need t'get s'much t'day?"

"Nonsense, we will splash! Don't worry, dear. The Wellingtons have plenty of money, and this is a task I was born for!"

In the shoe department, Priya kicked off her high heels to relieve her red, swollen toes, choosing a smart pair of navy flats for the rest of their shopping. Then, eyeing the store's café, she said, "Let's rest for a bit."

Priya ordered egg salad sandwiches, tea, and a chocolate fountain shake after Katie said she'd never had one before.

"Delicious!" Katie giggled, her face full of surprise.

Priya shook her head, chuckling.

Katie smiled, then blurted, "Are ye Mr. Wellington's girlfriend, then?"

"Well, I am a girlfriend." Priya smirked. "We have known one another for quite some time. And I wish I could tell you I am his one and only girl. But... I know that I'm not."

"But, ye so lovely. Ye look like a model in a mag'zine. Why would 'e want more than the likes a' ye?"

Priya shrugged.

"Ye love 'im, then?"

"Yes, very much."

"An, ye'd like t'marry 'im? I mean, if 'e asked ye. Ye would?"

Stirring her tea, Priya said, "Well, yes. I would, indeed. Dane is, well, he is unmatched. I have been around the block some. I have met all sorts. There is no one—no one—that matches his...his..kindness. He gets that from his father, you know, although Mr. Wellington isn't always that kind to me.

Katie refrained from asking why.

"But, he is a bit of a rake, too." Priya paused, lost in her own head. "Some blokes can be dogs, indeed. Always wanting something different." She shook her head, regretting her words. "Oh, I should not say that. Dane isn't looking for someone better. He just runs away from anyone who gets too close. He will never marry, unfortunately; although, I do keep hoping he'll change his mind. We are very compatible. He doesn't want children, and I can't have any, so it's rather perfect."

"Ye can't? Why no'?" Katie asked.

"I've had a malignancy and surgery on my ovaries, so ..."

Katie held her breath, stirring her shake. "Oh, I'm sorry, really, am. But, 'e's a good man, then? I mean, b'sides 'e don't want t'marry?"

"Yes, a very good man," Priya said. "And like his father, tries to do the right thing. Extraordinary, truly. Even if it hurts his pocket. Most generous. Why, he once sent his doctor who doesn't do house calls any longer to my mother when she was ill with influenza, and naturally, she never received a bill. I've been with him to charity balls where he donated anonymously. You'll find very few who don't want the recognition these days."

Katie stirred her shake, trying to mask her guilt. "Blimey."

Priya studied the young girl, finally asking, "How did you come to be Mr. Wellington's ward?"

Katie told her about her family, her parents, and how Ellis had saved her life when she was three. "Mr. Wellington 'as always been s'kind t'me. An now 'e's sending me t'school in September! 'Tis a dream!"

Priya's tight-lipped smile relaxed as she studied the unpolished girl with poor grammar.

· ♥ · ♥ · ♥ · ♥ · ♥ ·

RELIEVED TO HAVE AVOIDED the shopping excursion, Dane enjoyed a relaxing day, finally having his hair cut, thankful that Frankie's shop was quiet. While in the car, he spotted Katie's satchel on the floor.

Curiosity overtaking him, he peeked inside, although he knew he shouldn't, and discovered a Bible, some photographs of her siblings, her birth certificate, and the note his father had left inside the piano bench. The Bible, he noticed, had something stuffed into the back. Goosebumps traveled up his arms when he saw the dried white daisies. *Good God. These are her most precious possessions?*

·❤·❤·❤·❤·❤·

BEFORE SHE SLURPED THE last drops of her shake, Katie asked one more question. "Priya, if men are dogs, why do ladies let 'em...you know? I mean, me mum, she don' like it when me pop is on 'er. I asked her why she don' just take a bat t'him. She needs his wages, I s'ppose." She squished up her face in disgust. "But why do ladies do it without bein' wed?"

Priya blushed. "Well, some men, some men...they are tender and sweet, and it's very lovely, dear. And Dane is...." She swallowed, stopping herself from saying more. "When you are with a man you love, you will understand."

"I want t'understand now! I don't know nothing 'bout love, or what truly 'appens 'tween a man an' a woman. Me mum was afraid I'd be caught by the blokes from the fact'ry coming 'round t'see me."

"I see," Priya said. "So that's why you're at the Wellingtons, I understand." She checked her watch. "Well, it's time to be off. We still have one more stop... at the chemist. You'll need an assortment of grooming and feminine products."

When the girls returned, Katie's happy face and all the shopping bags brought a chuckle to Dane. "Well, look at you. You look like a different person. I like the dress too," he said, eyeing the bright yellow sundress.

The women, including Mrs. Danbury, scurried upstairs to sort out and admire the purchases. Priya, pleased with herself, watched as Katie held each piece up in front of the mirror, not recognizing the lovely lady beaming back at her.

Supper in the dining room that evening was lively, with Katie and Priya chatting away like best friends, recalling the humorous moments of the day's outing. Katie described the sales girls as "full o' beans" and her amazement that the people on the street "were in a fury t'get 'ere 'n there."

Ellis ate his supper slowly, grinning at his daughter-in-law's antics. Dane and Mrs. Macklin exchanged a few glances, observing Katie's generous devotion towards Ellis, kissing his cheek and placing his napkin under his chin.

Katie caught a glimpse of Dane and Priya having a moment as well.

·♥·♥·♥·♥·♥·

Aﾠfter supper, Dane asked, "Katie, have you seen the gardens?"

"Ah, no. I 'aven't been outside a' all."

"Let's go for a walk, shall we?" Dane suggested. "Priya wants to rest a bit."

The well-tended gardens full of springtime blooms brought a smile to Katie's face. They passed the sweeping lawns and the mature woodlands that surrounded the three acres of the fully manicured property. Dane pointed out the meandering paths that led to quaint pavilions, each a surprise and delight to Katie, some covered by a pergola or gazebo where one could sit on a weathered bench and enjoy the tranquility. A bed of daffodils edged a flowing stream with lily pads, busy goldfish, and "Oh! so many tadpoles!" she giggled. They came to the well-planned rose garden that was surrounded by wild African daisies.

"The daisies," Dane explained, "are supposed to help keep insects away from the roses."

Pointing with one hand to a tiny cottage with a thick thatched roof, while gathering a handful of the daisies with the other, he said, "That's where the Macklin's live."

"I love daisies," she blushed.

"I'm aware," Dane said, handing them to her, chuckling to himself.

"This is the third time you 'ave given me daisies," she said with a sweet but shy smile.

Dane's eyes gleamed back. "And likely not the last. I hope you like roses too, as we have an abundance of them."

The path opened up to reveal a large pond where water lilies floated gently, surrounded by comfortable lounge chairs with royal blue and white striped upholstered cushions and three wisteria-covered cabanas.

Turning their attention toward the house, Dane said, "We have been busy here, just finished renovations. Through those doors is the indoor pool, a washroom, and the conservatory, and also Father's new bedroom."

"Blimey, that's costly, I imagine."

"Yes, it is. And a messy job, but I very much enjoyed the process. If I had my choice, I would have loved to have been a builder or an architect."

"Perhaps ye'll be able t'pursue that one day," she said, turning her eyes towards his. Neither was in a hurry to look away. She hadn't allowed herself to have a good look at him before this. "Looks like ye got your 'aircut," she grinned. She reached out to touch it, but stopped herself quickly. "There were no other girls t'save, I 'ope."

"No, thank goodness." Dane grinned.

Suddenly, she threw her arms around his waist tightly and murmured, "Thank ye. I know what ye 'ave sacrificed for me, an' I feel just awful 'bout it. But I'm grateful."

"What do you mean?" Dane pulled her arms from around his waist.

"I know ye never wanted t'marry. An now you've gone an' married me. I do no' look like Priya. No pretty like 'er. I'm awful sorry t'ave ruined ye life!"

"Nonsense, Katie. Our marriage, well, as I said before, it's our secret, and when the time comes, we will ask for annulment. Like it never happened. You haven't ruined my life." *I certainly hope not.* "And you most certainly *are* as pretty as she. More so, even," he said, touching her chin. *Perhaps I shouldn't say things like that. She'll get the wrong idea.*

"Mr. Barclay. He would 'ave wanted the consummatin' part? He'd 'ave wanted t'do it?"

Lord. She knows nothing about sex. "Let's pop our feet in the water, shall we?" He adroitly removed his shoes, then helped her remove hers. Sitting on stone ledges that doubled as benches, they dipped their feet in. "Yes, I'm afraid he would have wanted that. And not just that day. That's actually the point of the marriage, I'm afraid. That and babes, I imagine," he said, kicking his feet.

She nodded, then turning her flushed cheeks away and blinking back her tears, she asked. "Why? Why do blokes be wantin' to do it s'much?"

Dane laughed. "Well, Mother Nature plays quite a trick on all living things. She is brilliant, making it quite pleasurable. That ensures that lots of babies will be born, and life will continue, you see? Animals don't know they are procreating when they do it, actually. They just know they fancy it."

"Is that why Priya said men are dogs?"

Dane howled. "Did she say that? Well, yes, some men, I suppose." *Bloody hell*, he thought. *I am, surely.*

Her tear-filled eyes rested on the large lion fountain that spit water into the pond, and she dropped her head into her hands, sobbing.

As she cried, Dane felt a knot in his stomach, unsure of what to do next. He lifted his arm but refrained from putting it around her. "It's alright. You're safe now," he whispered.

She wiped her tear-soaked face with her hands. "I prayed. I prayed so 'ard for ye father t'come. 'E has done it before. Showed up when I needed 'im to. And then there ye were! A miracle." Unable to stay erect, her head fell onto his chest, and Dane's arm cradled her instinctively.

Dane gulped. "I'm aware of the many coincidences. Appearing quite literally out of the blue to find you in distress. Rather peculiar."

"Mum said I were foolish t'think Mr. Wellington would come. But it 'appened. Ye came."

Fate, Father said. He looked up to blink away the sudden flood in his eyes, spotting Priya watching them through the upstairs window.

He rose abruptly. "Shall we go in? I'm sure you are quite exhausted from your excursion today." She took his outstretched hand, wiping her eyes quickly. He led her, flowers in hand, back inside, where Priya was waiting for them.

"Priya, may I see you in my study before you leave?"

Priya smiled slyly. "With pleasure."

Dane turned to Katie and playfully performed a royal bow. "Good-night, M'Lady."

She forced a smile. "Good night." Turning toward Priya with a warm hug, she said, "Thank you f'all your 'elp today. I hope t'see ye again soon."

"Yes, dear, I am sure you will," Priya answered.

Katie dashed to her room, immediately noticing her satchel on the bed with a white rose atop it, letting out a breath and a whisper, "My 'usband." She carefully placed the daisies and rose into the small vase on her dresser, then put her hands together and prayed, "Dear God, thank you for sending both Mr. Wellingtons to me. Bless them both and keep them safe. Amen."

·♥·♥·♥·♥·♥·

DANE POURED BOTH HIMSELF and Priya shots of brandy. "Thank you for your tremendous help today, love. I know it was a trying excursion. I can't imagine what I would have done without your perfectly brilliant effort." Dane kissed her lips softly, then her neck, until she giggled.

She grinned at his gratitude. "Oh, sweet sir, you will pay for my effort. I intend to collect my due, have no doubt." A mischievous smirk played on her lips. Without another word, she downed the brandy and exited the study, her hips swaying seductively as she ascended the stairs. Dane trailed behind, his gaze locked on her tantalizing curves.

The doors to the dressing room blew open as Priya showcased her new silky, sheer, white teddy. "I'm not quite sure if 'you' purchased this today for you or for me. Do you fancy it?" she teased, twirling around.

Dane's eyes gleamed as he admired her enticing silhouette. "Oooh! Yes, very much. I made a wise choice," he joked, stepping closer and letting his hands glide slowly down her neck and over the sides of her breasts. As his lips met hers, she shivered with delight. His gentle hands skillfully brushing across her skin left a trail of goosebumps in their wake.

"Oh!" she groaned, closing her eyes.

"Remember, we are not alone here," he reminded her in hushed tones, following several throaty moans.

"I'll try, but I can't promise. I've missed you."

Chapter 6

ADJUSTMENTS

N^{OT READY TO EXIT} her comfortable bed, Katie studied every piece in her room, starting with the vanity, the rich floral brocade fabric on the seat, and the antique oblong mirror attached to it. Above the stone fireplace and mantle, she eyed the portrait of a mother and a baby boy, guessing it was Dane and his mother. The sight of the flowers in the vase on her dresser brought a fleeting smile, quickly erased by the memory of the groans she'd heard the previous night.

"Men are dogs," she whispered to herself. "An 'e is no different."

Hugging the pillow, she considered her new life. She looked at the wardrobe chest full of clothes and smiled. *My room, my new clothes. Blimey.*

Bouncing down the stairs and into the kitchen, a cheery "Good morning, Dane," accompanied a bright smile. Her new sleeveless white blouse and navy skirt swayed with each step.

Dane lowered his newspaper to take in her ensemble, nodding his approval with a grin. "Good morning to you. I trust you slept well?"

"I was up a while, but I slept well, fin'lly," she said, embarrassed to look at him, trying not to think about the noises coming from down the hall last night.

"Can I git you some more coffee, Mr. Wellington?" Mrs. Macklin asked.

"Yes, ma'am. And keep the pot close. It will be several cups this morning, I fear."

"Yes, sir." Mrs. Macklin brought the coffee, some cream and biscuits, and milk for Katie.

"I've made some eggs 'n beans, too, just as ye father likes 'em."

"Oh, thank you, but no," Dane said, shaking his head quickly.

As she turned her back, Dane stuck his finger in his throat and made a face to Katie, who giggled immediately. Both were laughing as the cook turned around and Priya entered the room.

"What's so amusing?" Priya asked.

Mrs. Macklin cocked her head at Dane.

"Nothing. Just a bit of fun." Dane clamped his lips together trying not to laugh; although, the second he and Katie looked at one another, they burst into laughter once again.

When Dane refused to explain their little "private joke," Priya straightened herself, abruptly switching her purse to her other arm. Dane and Katie exchanged glances, and another chuckle. Priya clenched her teeth.

Mrs. Macklin turned back toward the kitchen without a word, and Katie noted her dismissal of Priya.

"Well," Priya continued, "I have many things to do and must take my leave. Katie, it was lovely spending the day AND an ungodly amount of Dane's money with you. I enjoyed myself thoroughly. And I hope to see you again, very soon, indeed." She started towards the door, and then glanced at Dane. "Will you walk me out, love?"

When Dane returned, Katie said, "Thank ye fa all me new clothes. I like Priya. She were sweet. She loves ye. D'you love 'er?"

"You are very welcome. And it's 'she *is* sweet', not 'she *were* sweet.' We are going to have to correct your speech, young lady. And that accent...." He paused, biting his lip. "To answer your question, it's complicated. She is an independent and modern woman. I will say I am quite fond of her. She supports her mother, and that is a fine thing. She works hard as a secretary and is agreeable and easy to please. But we have little to discuss, unfortunately."

"So, ye wouldn't 'ave married 'er, then?"

"No. Not her, nor anyone else."

Katie nodded, relieved she wasn't adding to Priya's distress, then continued, "Why no'?"

"Well, I enjoy my life as it is. Uncomplicated. I have never met a woman I want to spend more than a few days in a row with. And I have met a good many women. I see no reason to marry. I think I would be terribly bored, being with the same woman for years on end."

"But, surely, later in life ye'll be lonely, with no wife or children t'care for ye."

"Well," he shook his head, "I imagine I will have staff to do that, as my father does." Dane stood, stretched his arms out, and then his neck, from side to side. "It seems Father is swimming, as he often does in the morning. Think I'll join him. How about you?"

"I canno' swim."

"Well, you must learn, then. Let's go change. I'm sure I can teach you."

Ellis, Katie, and Dane spent the rest of the morning frolicking in the pool. Dane taught her the basics of swimming.

"A humorous endeavor, indeed," Ellis said. "She will need much practice."

"Am I doing it?" she kept asking.

"No, your legs aren't moving!" Dane answered each time, he and Ellis laughing.

Mrs. Danbury, watching from the conservatory, shook her head. Once they were finished, she stopped Dane as he headed upstairs to change. "Mr. Wellington, may I 'ave a word?"

"Of course."

"I need to say me piece, sir, if ye don't mind. You did a fine thing saving 'er from a life she did no want. I commend you for that, sir. But, 'tis not proper for ye t'bring that trollop, Miss Priya, into your ... bedroom ... with a young girl jus' down the 'all! Scandalous! Do you want the girl t'assume that kind'o behavior is acceptable? You must make adjustments if ye truly want t'protect that child, and yourself, sir. Well, I've said it then."

Dane's eyes fluttered in embarrassment. "Mrs. Danbury. You are most correct. This is new for us all. Naturally, I am not used to having an innocent girl here. Thank you for your candidness, and yes, I hadn't considered the consequences of having Priya here, but I see now I must make adjustments."

"Bollocks!" he said, as he made his way up.

·♥·♥·♥·♥·♥·

KATIE SPENT THE FOLLOWING day reading, having found a most elaborate library equipped with a comfortable cushioned leather chair and a footrest. With the aromas of book leather and pipe tobacco lingering, she eyed the volumes of books in the floor-to-ceiling bookcases, everything from law and real estate, to novels and reference books. After perusing one interesting book she noticed hidden among the treasures, she wandered to the kitchen, where she found Mrs. Macklin preparing a stew.

"Please, Mrs. Macklin, allow me t'help. I'm curious t'see what ye do," Katie said, explaining that part of her job as a housemaid included preparing meals for the family's children and that she had done much of the cooking at her own family's home.

Mrs. Macklin smiled and eagerly put Katie to work. Soon, the young girl demonstrated that she had skills and intelligence to go with her beauty.

The scent of the warm rolls and the rich aroma of the savory stew filling the air, Ellis, the staff, including George, and Katie gathered outside for supper, enjoying the gentle evening breeze around the grand wooden table. Katie's new family and the low hum of conversation and laughter warmed her. She smiled and said, "I can't remember when me own family sat t' 'ave supper t'gether. Dere's no grand table or even 'nough chairs for all a' us." Katie leaned back, taking in the moment, enjoying the candles and lanterns flickering in the breeze and the way the crystal wine glass rims glimmered in the moonlight. She placed her hand over Ellis's and said, "Thank ye for making me feel at 'ome. This is lovely."

Ellis covered her hand with his other. "Happy you are here, dear."

·♥·♥·♥·♥·♥·

THROUGHOUT THE SUMMER, DANE kept himself busy, using his London flat as his home base. There was much to do regarding his father's properties, the bulk of which was now falling upon his shoulders. As he traveled around, he also allowed himself a bit of entertainment with his lady friends. One such girl was a long-time friend and occasional lover, Juliette Lefrak, who he had met during his year abroad in Paris. A French teacher, Juliette lived in Leeds, and Dane often called on her when he had meetings to attend.

Juliette and Dane shared a similar philosophy regarding commitment. She was uninhibited and skilled in the bedroom, which had significantly increased Dane's understanding of female pleasure; however, as strong as their physical connection was, their relationship never turned romantic.

Dane admired her perfectly straight, shoulder-length dark hair, an atypical look for women her age. She wasn't what he would call beautiful, but she was striking and quite polished. A thoroughly modern woman, dressing somewhat provocatively when not teaching, her skirts were shorter than most young ladies' skirts, and her blouses were sheer and unbuttoned, showing a bit of her very feminine lingerie and cleavage.

In the aftermath of their frenzied sexual encounter, Dane asked, "Why live in Leeds, of all places? Why not be closer to London, where you could enjoy the city more?"

Juliette took a long, slow puff of her filtered cigarette. "It's the only offer I received. I'll wait a year or so and apply to the schools in London again. Once I build experience as a professor, more opportunities will come, I'm certain. They are all adding more female teachers now, non?"

"Oui." Dane laughed.

A warm breeze stirred the sheer white drapery, billowing gently in and out through her tall wood-framed balcony doors, a hypnotic rhythm that held Dane captive as he relaxed shirtless against her headboard. The soothing melody of a French ballad on her record player, the aroma of her cigarette, the candles and the jasmine on her balcony sedated him further. *There is something soothing about French music.*

The next morning, on the two-and-a-half-hour train ride back to London, Dane closed his eyes and crossed his arms. The rhythmic rumble vibrating his skull, he drifted into a daydream about his indulgences with Juliette. He laughed out loud, recalling her moves, flashing his eyes to see if anyone nearby had observed the sudden chuckle and flush in his cheeks.

As the train clanked along, Dane made some notes about the things he would need to improve upon at the house now that Katie was there. A record player, for one thing, was a must. He loved the music Juliette had been playing. *I bet Katie would love that. Father loves the classics. Perhaps a few of those as well.*

George was waiting to collect him at the London station. "Home, sir?"

"No, George, I want to purchase a few electronics."

George, who spent his free time investigating all the technological advances that had been introduced, knew exactly where to go. "Mind if I go in with ye, sir? I do enjoy lookin' a'all the new inventions."

"No, not at all, George. Your brilliant knowledge of mechanics certainly makes you the expert. I'd appreciate your help."

As George carried the boxes into the house, Ellis, Katie, and Dane stood, looking over the purchases. "My, how fast things are changing," Ellis said. "An absolute technology boom. Look at this, an alarm clock and a radio in one. From what I read in the newspapers, I believe we will be ready for a television set soon."

"Oh, that I want t' see," Katie joked. "Mrs. Atwood, me 'mployer, said ev'ry household 'll 'ave'm in a few years. Blimey!"

"George and I looked at the television sets, but the sales clerk said there were very few reliable stations just yet." Grinning at the young girl sitting on the floor playing with the new purchases as though they were toys. *She is pleasant and joyous. And she livens the house. More than anyone else I know. Father is certainly enjoying her company.* He hated to admit he was also thoroughly enjoying coming home.

Chapter 7

FOLLOW THE PATH

Not long after Dane and Katie's marriage, Lenny sent word through Mr. Forsythe that he wanted to meet Mr. Wellington at the local pub. Dane suggested they meet at the Clarke's home immediately after work, hoping Lenny's drinking would not have left him relieved of all of his senses that early in the evening.

Dane brought George along in case there was trouble, and Lenny wasted no time confronting Dane. "Ye stole me daugh'er from me. We 'ad an accord, we did, with a right fine posh gentleman. Ye 'ad no right t'do what ye did, ye being me landlord or no, ye had no right. And I still owe the bastard four-hundred-eighty-five quid! What'ye intend t'do about that, sir?"

"Mr. Clarke, let me first say my father and I are appalled and disappointed in you, sir. I thought you a good man. Yet you intended to marry off your lovely daughter to that ridiculous fool? And all due to your splashing out at the pub, and betting on those damn horses? And you expected your daughter to pay with her life, giving up her future for your debts? Are you quite mad?"

Lenny's eyes widened, and he lowered his head, "I s'pose I had no' thought of 'er feelin's, only that she be safe, 'ave a home of 'er own, an 'nough to buy anyth'n'. An', 'e offered to clear th' debt, sir."

"That's disgraceful. Furthermore, sir, you are at least three months in arrears with your rent. If you fancy living here, you had better spend your free time working off your bloody debts, man. My father's generosity is surely limited, as is my patience. I am quite sure my father does not intend to let you live here rent-free indefinitely. Not while we are clearly aware that you are, in fact, employed, and your wages spent on foolery. Bloody Hell!"

Dane saw the thoughtful expression in Lenny's eyes and toned down. "As for the sums owed, Mr. Clarke, I could pay off your debt to that swine, but I prefer to educate, feed, and clothe your daughter."

"Dat bloke ain't no fool, sir. He 'as land and a right fine estate. An me daut'er would 'ave a respectable life. Now, he an 'is cronies are miffed. An he wants his sums dats owed him now too. He'll no sit by an by."

George stepped closer to both men, noticing Dane's tight fists and clenched jaw.

"She would not have been respected by that miscreant, sir." *I certainly don't need to make an enemy of Mr. Barclay, though.* "I'll tell you what, Mr. Clarke. There is work to do here. All these properties need maintenance, and if you are willing, I will pay off your ghastly debt to Barclay, and you can work it off each week. And, if you can stay out of the pubs until you have repaid your debts, keeping your current rent up-to-date, I will forgive your past-due rent. Now, that's a fine deal, wouldn't you say, sir? Mr. Forsythe will supply the paint and supervise. Do you agree?"

Lenny nodded. "Thank ye, sir. That's mighty gen'rous of ye. An what of me dau'ter? Ye have taken 'er as ye wife, then?"

Dane shifted uncomfortably and took a deep breath. *He won't like that I intend to annul our marriage.* "She is my wife. And she will attend boarding school in the fall."

Lenny nodded.

Long-term tenants had been a problem during the war years. Clarke was out of work until the factory converted to manufacturing ammunition, but wages were sparse, even then. Ellis's words were imprinted on Dane's heart: *"How can you evict long-term tenants you have known for over ten years?"* Most people had lost their jobs, and many men were at war, wounded, or dead. His father refused to evict anyone, instead shouldering the burden himself. There were even times when Dane had seen his father refuse to take money from several of the tenants, Norma included, shaking his head, pushing her hand away.

"Please give me regards to your father," Lenny said, interrupting Dane's thoughts. "He is a fine gentleman."

"Yes, he is. And he is appalled at your lack of concern for your daughter."

Lenny looked at the ground, put his hands in his pockets, and kicked his foot. "Please send me apologies to ye father and me dau'ter. I meant well for all of us. And, her mum, well, her mum just wanted her t'have the things we canno' provide. A house, fine clothes, piano lessons. We meant well." Lenny took in Dane's fine clothing, well-cut hair, and polished loafers. "You are provin' t'be a fine gent'man as well, sir."

"Thank you. Not sure you are entirely correct, but it is something I am working on."

As the Rolls ambled onto the roadway, Dane considered Lenny's last statement. His father's discipline, philanthropic nature, and honest values have served him well. Dane sighed, knowing his reluctance to reign in his romantic adventures was far from what his father would consider a fine gentleman.

Chapter 8

RAISING A WIFE

DANE BROUGHT HIS FATHER up to speed regarding the school system. "As behind as she is in academics, the independent schools, that don't rely on the government funding will be more flexible and better able to accommodate her. They also have music studies and sports. But they are costly."

Ellis replied, not looking up from his crossword puzzle, "I don't mind the cost of education. Good work, son. Time is of the essence. Find the best independent school you can. She must be tutored and ready to attend by fall."

For the rest of that week, Dane interviewed tutors, choosing the chipper Margaret Lipton, a graduate of Lady Margaret Hall, an Oxford University college for women, where she was hoping for a teaching position. "There are not yet many positions for women, unfortunately. In the meantime, I am building an impressive tutoring schedule," Maggie said. Miss Lipton, who was not much older than Dane, won him over with her witty personality, and Dane thought Katie would take to the scholarly brunette as well.

As time elapsed, Dane, assuming control of his father's enterprise, faced numerous responsibilities, including an imminent business meeting with his land manager in Bath. As it meant an overnight stay, a rendezvous with Michelle Dugan, a gal he had met years prior when she was secretary to one of the board members of the Bank of England, was on the agenda. She was striking and slender with shoulder-length red hair, hazel eyes, and flawless porcelain white skin dotted with freckles across her nose and cheeks. Their first meeting had been at a pub get-together with some of his business friends in Bath. Their playful banter led to more serious flirting, and throughout the meal, he could think of nothing else but putting his lips on her naked body. Ever since that night, she was happy to receive him whenever he was conducting business in Bath.

On his way back from Bath the next morning, Dane stopped at the office for a while, then met his half-brother Joel at a pub nearby. When their drinks arrived, Dane lifted his glass. "Father and I have decided it is time for you to join the business. What do you say to one third of the profits from the rents and a third of the equity value starting from this point forward?"

"Why on earth would your father want to hand me part of his business? I thought he despised me."

"No, he doesn't despise you. He's taking more of a back seat, and I need a partner. You are my brother. Who else would I trust?"

Recovering from his shock, Joel took Dane's outstretched hand and lifted his glass. "To E.W. Holdings!" The conversation turned to Ellis's deteriorating health and vitality, then to Priya, and finally, in hushed tones, to the story of Katie.

"Good Lord," Joel exclaimed upon hearing his brother was married. When Dane shushed him, Joel softly asked, "And no consummation? Will you be able to honor that?"

"Absolutely," Dane said. "It's a must. Now, we must go. Everyone is waiting on us for supper."

Neither Dane nor Joel noticed the thug sitting just behind them, well within earshot of every word.

When Dane and Joel arrived at the house, Ellis and Katie were already at the table, laughing at a story Ellis was relaying. *Probably about me,* Dane thought, watching the pair, his father's hand on hers. *A most affectionate gesture.* He often wondered why he felt no jealousy over their closeness, so unlike his own relationship with his father. "Look at you, two peas in a pod!"

"This young lady has brought me much joy." Ellis smiled at Dane.

"Katie, I'd like you to meet my brother, Joel. Joel, this is Katie Clarke."

As Joel sat, Mrs. Danbury whispered to Dane that Priya was on the telephone for him.

"Please excuse me, I'll be but a moment." Dane went to his study to take the call. "Priya, darling. How's by you?"

"I'm fine, Dane. I miss you. Can we meet tonight? I can come to you, and we can drive into the city."

"Tonight?" Dane plopped into his chair, exhausted. "Oh, well...I'm quite slumped, actually, my dear. Just returned from a busy business trip, and my brother is here. I'll have to pass on that, love."

As he returned the receiver, his thoughts turned to his recurring problem in his intimate relationships. Though the women he courted always started out tolerating his bachelor status, eventually, conversations regarding future holiday plans, and even children, became more frequent, until the inevitable ultimatum arrived, forcing an end to the relationship. In Priya's case, however, refusing her ultimatum hadn't ended their liaisons. She agreed to his terms, and as a consolation, he promised to spend certain special occasions with her.

He leaned back in the cushioned leather chair and poured a half glass of brandy. Taking a swig, Dane let the comforting warmth wash over him, melting away his tension. His thoughts drifted to Michelle. This time, while they'd been together, she had hinted about the future, and he'd felt his neck tighten immediately. He lusted for her, as his loins painfully reminded him, and he did like her, but he didn't love her. *What is love, anyway?* he wondered, downing the brandy. *Will I ever love anyone?* Deep in thought, he watched the rain pattering with a melodic rhythm on the patio table and then dropping to the ground before swirling down the drain. *No. I don't need love. My life is perfect just as it is.*

Back at the table, Dane poured wine into all their glasses and lifted his. "I want to say I'm thrilled to welcome my brother to the business, pleased to see your change, Father, and I look forward to Joel's help and presence, indeed."

Ellis nodded, a silent acknowledgment of the shift. Dane mulled over his father's change of heart, his mind replaying Ellis's years of rejecting Joel, the product of his mother's betrayal.

Joel was neither as polished nor as tall as Dane, but he was a good sport, well-mannered, and well-liked. He had attended college in Cambridge, studying finance, was sensible and more conventional than Dane. They'd make good business partners. Joel beamed and lifted his glass. "I'm most grateful for the generous opportunity."

With candlelight illuminating the grins on everyone's faces, the cozy dining room hummed with the cheerful sounds of laughter and the comforting aroma of roasted meat and warm bread. A tangible sense of joy settled on everyone sitting around the table as Katie's animated childhood stories came to life.

Following two bottles of wine and several shots of whiskey, including one for Katie, and after Ellis had bid them goodnight, the three donned swimsuits and played in the pool for a bit. Joel and Dane exchanged meaningful glances when Katie exited the pool, her swimsuit hugging her slim figure. It was hard to look away, and in fact, neither did.

Mrs. Danbury brought a few towels, wrapping one around Katie. "Come 'long, dear," she insisted, giving both men a nasty glance.

Joel and Dane chuckled. Each nursing a brandy and smoking cigarillos, they relaxed on the lounges, enjoying the quiet of the evening.

Over the years, the brothers had spent many nights downing whiskey, smoking pipes or cigarettes, and deciphering their mother. She had been well over fifteen years Ellis's junior and had married him not long after their meeting at a debutante ball they'd attended while she was visiting London.

"I was only two when she and her friends started following your father's band around town," Dane said. "Perhaps Father kicked her out after discovering she was with child, knowing you were not his."

"Well, who would blame him for that? I know she found your father a dull old man, even though he is neither dull nor old," Joel remarked. "My father was in no position to afford a wife and child. That's how we ended up in Pennsylvania with Gram and Pops."

"So, Mother had two unwanted pregnancies. Father's stern warnings about being careful not to get trapped into marriage due to pregnancy always caused me to suspect Father married her as his duty after discovering she was pregnant. And since she was out listening to music at clubs, which is how she met your father, I assume she was bored with mine. He isn't exactly the type to enjoy that lifestyle."

"And, now, raising your wife, are you?" Joel teased.

"Hardly. She's almost nineteen."

"And an annulment at twenty-one, you say? You had better get her into school, but fast, Mr. Wellington. Or you'll be consummating that marriage of yours before you know it. And that, my brother, will be the end of your bachelor days. I say, you won't make it. I will wager the marriage will be consummated before she turns twenty. Mark my words."

"I'll take that wager, you wanker!" Dane said quickly. "I promised Father I would wait a year until consummation anyway. And I bloody well intend to keep that promise. Besides, I like my women experienced. Pretty as she is, I'll not be married. Not to her or to anyone. Women cannot be trusted. I've not met one that would be useful to me other than in the bedroom. And I see no reason to settle when I clearly have no need."

"Well then," Joel said. "You must put time and distance between you. Eyeing her luscious curves is going to get you into trouble." Joel looked at his brother earnestly, then added, "Fifty quid, then?"

"Wanker," Dane said, shaking his brother's hand.

Chapter 9

WHOOPING AND HOWLING

DANE, JOEL, AND ELLIS spent each day attending to business matters, including property visits and meetings, while Katie remained at home, receiving instruction from Maggie Lipton. One day, while waiting for her tutor, Katie watched from the grand front window as a thunderous storm raged outside, remembering how she used to sit with her siblings, counting from when the lightning struck to when they heard the thunder. She missed them, wondering if they were all together now, counting.

Gazing into the distance, she noticed something moving in the bushes. She couldn't quite make out what it was. An animal of some sort, she guessed. Sneaking outside to get a closer look, sure enough, she discovered a little pup, shivering and cowering in a pocket under the bushes.

"Goodness! What are ye doin' out 'ere all by yeself?" Picking up the wet mop and tucking him inside her sweater, she scooted to the laundry room, grabbed a towel from a shelf, and yelled, "Mrs. Danbury, come quickly! Look! Is 'e not the most precious thing?"

Mrs. Danbury, seeing the wet, ragged mop and the white towel, roared, "What in the world possessed ye to bring that mangy thing in 'ere? Goodness me, girl." She grabbed the once-pristine towel away and offered a considerably older brown one to dry the pup's fur.

Katie then took him to sit by the fire, where the frisky pup licked her face and neck excitedly. "Oh, 'e is such a love!"

Once Miss Lipton arrived, Katie completed her lessons with the drying mop of brown curly fluff cuddled in her lap, her mind no longer on her arithmetic.

When the men arrived, Dane, upon seeing the pup in Katie's lap, cried, "Oh no! Where the devil did that come from?"

As Katie explained finding him in the rain, Joel laughed, "He's quite a little bugger, isn't he?" The pup bolted from Katie's lap, darting in a frenzy around the men. "He is probably a neighbor's dog. Perhaps you might see who is missing their pet," Joel offered.

Once the rain stopped, Katie and Dane set out to find the dog's owner, leaving the furball with Joel. "We will start with the young couple who just purchased the home next door. Perhaps the pup is theirs," Dane said.

A young woman answered the door, balancing a two-year-old child on her hip, tears glistening on the little one's bright red cheeks.

"Hello, can I help you?" she said.

"Hello. We are ye neighbors. I'm Katie, an' this is Dane Wellington. Are ye perhaps missin' a small brown puppy?"

"Well, we have a new puppy, but I don't think he is missing," she said. "Let me see if he escaped." The woman walked to the back of the house. "Buster! Where are you?" She was visibly upset when she returned to the front door. "Oh, my goodness, he is missing!"

"We 'ave 'im at our house. We live just next door," Katie said.

"Oh, perhaps the gate blew open when he went out to relieve himself. Thank you so much for grabbing him. My name is Lucy, and this is Lilian. Can you say hello, Lilian?" They chuckled as Lilian buried her face in her mother's neck.

Dane trotted back to grab Buster while Katie stayed to chat with Lucy. Once the pup was safely back in Lucy's possession, Dane said to Katie, "We need to get going. It's pouring again and getting dark."

Katie drew her inadequate sweater around herself, as the unusually cool rain had soaked her white blouse and chilled her.

·♥·♥·♥·♥·♥·

J UST AS THEY NEARED the gates of the house, three large black cars, engines revving, surrounded them, their tires spitting gravel as they screeched to a stop, stopping Dane and Katie in their tracks. The car doors flung open. Four hulky men in black, their black caps pulled low over their eyes, seized Katie and Dane, hurling them into the back seat of the largest car.

Dane shouted, "What's this, now? What do you think you are doing?" Dane's arms were being restrained by the brute who muscled his way into the seat next to him. Another of the men shoved in beside Katie, the four of them now squeezed into the back seat. The two other goons jammed in the front seat next to a portly gentleman in a tall black hat who turned around to face them.

"Good evening. I am Mr. Barclay," he said calmly. "Perhaps you recall our encounter at Mr. Frankie's barbershop?"

Katie gasped.

Dane's temper flared. "Yes, I know who you are. What do you want, sir?"

"I want what was promised me," Mr. Barclay said, his eyes fixed on Katie, who let out a short, fear-driven yelp.

"My bride, sir. Prettier than I remembered. I have new information: it seems your hasty marriage has not been... consummated. Therefore, it is void," he smirked, flashing his yellow, misaligned horse-sized teeth.

Dane, struggling to break free of his restraint, yelled through clenched teeth, "You are mistaken sir. This is disgraceful. You are speaking to my wife. In the name of God and the British Crown! How dare you? You will open this door and let us out of this bloody car this instant!"

The savage brute held Dane in a fierce grip, and as Dane fought back, a sudden elbow to the jaw left him dazed and gasping for air.

Katie shrieked, "Stop it! Leave 'im alone!" She gripped Dane's arm.

"As your marriage has not been consummated, I remain your rightful ... betrothed, my dear," he said, smiling willfully at Katie. "You may leave, Mr. Wellington." Mr. Barclay, not taking his eyes from her, snapped his fingers to the unsightly varmint beside Dane, who flung the door open, stepped out, and yanked on Dane's arm and shoulder to remove him from the vehicle. Dane held on to the front seat, desperate to stay in the car.

"Stop! Let 'im go!" Katie wailed. "STOP! Wait! Ye are mistaken. It 'as been consummated!" she said quickly. She had their attention. "It 'as, I swear it 'as!"

"I doubt that," Mr. Barclay said. "My man here overheard your husband speaking to his brother recently in a pub."

"That's righ," the lowlife next to Barclay chimed in. "I 'eard 'im tell 'is brotha there'll be no cons'mation. Dey hevn't done the deed."

Katie and Dane exchanged a terrified glance.

"So, you say the deed is done now? Well, how shall you prove that?" Barclay stared at her, his eyes threatening.

"I beg ye pardon?" Katie yelped.

"I'll give you a chance to prove it. If your marriage has been consummated, then tell us, girl...of your wedding night. Go on. We are listening. After you humiliated me in front of my friends and family by not showing up at the church, you owe me that much." Mr. Barclay crossed his arms and turned fully around to face her. His men were laughing, their dark, dangerous eyes fixed on her. The muscled beast next to Dane pushed his way back in and closed the door, keeping Dane restrained.

"Sir, tis most insulting. An I believe a woman 'as the right t'change 'er mind 'bout who she marries," she protested.

Barclay sucked his teeth, looking at his men. "Perhaps. But you agreed. I had no knowledge you were not coming. I looked the fool. And I don't take that lightly, miss. So, now you are going to tell me what I want to hear." After a moment of silence, he added, "I am listening but hear nothing. I must surmise you cannot answer."

"I can answer. But t'woud be humiliating an' downright insulting f'me t'do so. Ye are rude, sir. I will no' recount such an int'mate detail," she shouted.

Barclay replied with a menacing grin. "If you cannot or will not answer, I will assume your marriage to be void and assert my right."

Katie pursed and shot back. "I don't believe ye 'ave any rights." As she beheld the man's menacing expression, her eyes widened, filled with a rising fear. Seeng Dane's haziness and his reddened, swollen jaw, she relented. "Alright. I'll tell ye!"

She spoke slowly, as if she were trying to remember. Her head down, shaking from fear and cold, she began. The men, including Dane, were staring at her. She took a deep breath, swallowing down nervous bile. The stench in the car, the sweat and filth of the men, the heat and dampness, to the lingering cigarette smoke assaulted her head and lungs. "Please. I canno' breathe. Can ye open the window?"

The hound next to her cranked the window, and Katie leaned forward to take a gulp of the cool, damp air.

"We're waiting," Barclay barked.

She shot him a nasty look, then sat back and placed her eyes on her lap, pretending to recall the moment. Not lifting her eyes, she began. "The wedding were right quick. 'appened so fast. I knew nothin' ... 'bout relations ... 'tween a man an' a woman, naturally." She wrung her hands, keeping her head down. "I were shakin' really. Couldn't stop." An easy thought, as she quivered from nerves and fear. She pulled her flimsy sweater around her tighter, but it barely covered her breasts. "'E were sweet, an' we talked for a while, then 'e kissed me. That's all that 'appened that night. 'E didn' do nothin' more. It 'appened later, after we got to knowin' one 'nother. Please sir, this is most insultin'. Do no' make me continue, I beg o' ye."

Barclay and one of his men shared a glance. "You *will* continue," Mr. Barclay snarled, his dark eyes studying her.

She clenched her teeth . "'E took me to a pub, an we 'ad a nice supper. When we got 'ome, 'e kissed me. Me lips, me neck, an' me shoulda's. Further down too." She paused, still unable to raise her eyes. "'E took 'is time, kissin' me. A long time, actually. Then, 'e caressed me, further down." She crossed her arms over her breasts. "'E were so gentle. It felt nice. Then... Then 'e removed me nightdress." Her face turned beet red, and she covered her face with her hands.

The men shouted and whistled. They were lapping it up. She looked at her hands again, still wringing them nervously. Dane was listening and staring at her. His jaw, flaming red and swollen, arms secured behind him.

"Go on, you have proven nothing yet," Barclay snarled, shaking his head.

"'E kep' caressin me, me 'ead, me 'air." Her hands stroked her hair, her shoulders, and arms. "I 'ad some brandy at the pub, so me 'ead was spinnin' a bit. 'E kissed me 'gain, ever so... tenderly." She touched her fingers to her lips, thinking about what to say next. She had a hard time breathing between the car's odor and her constricted chest.

"'E took me 'ands an' massaged dem. An' then me feet." She had read this suggestion in a particularly interesting book about sex she had found in the Wellington's library.

A rising tide of guttural howls sent shivers down Katie's arms.

"This went on fo' a good bit 'a time, 'til I was, well... bit more a'ease. Then 'e got on top o' me. Just laid there for a tick, kissin' me. Kissin' was nice, real sweet, 'e was. Saying sweet thins and touching me face." She bit her lip, still wringing her hands nervously. "An' then ... ah ...there was, um, a bit o'trouble. He ... he... well... 'e took it dead slow." She closed her eyes, mostly trying to keep her stomach from heaving its contents.

There were a few more hooplas from the men.

She shook her head. "Sir, please. I 'ave said 'nough. You needn' 'ear more."

"Oh, but I haven't, miss. Go on," Barclay said, losing his patience. He scrutinized her every move, searching for signs of deception.

The men were whooping and howling like wild dogs in cages. Their frightening high-pitched yelps pierced the silence, leaving her even more jittery, interrupting her thoughts. Recalling the book she had devoured, she kept going.

"'E were gentle. Ever so. An I....I. I 'eard meself moan, I did." Remembering Priya's noises, she looked at her husband lovingly. "'E went ever slow, an' kept kissin' da whole time." She covered her mouth with her hand, and muttered, "An', after a bit ... it ... it didn't hurt s'much." Staring into Dane's fear-frozen face while shedding silent tears, she repeated Priya's words, "Twas nice, actually."

Dane stared at her in disbelief.

A deafening howl pierced the air, echoing like wolves surrounding their prey. Her body instinctively jolted and sent goosebumps up Katie's neck and more tears down her cheek. Defiantly, she continued, staring at Dane with determination.

"An' afta'wards, we lay t'gether, an' 'e stroked me, an kissed me, an' 'eld me close."

The men, their solemn faces fixed on her, seemed to buy her tale. Her breath heavy, as if she were experiencing the encounter for real, matched her whirling heart.

She gathered herself, lifted her head triumphantly, and managed a shy smile at Dane, quickly adding, "We love one'nother sir. Truly. I shan't be s'prised if I'm already with child." The look that crossed Mr. Barclay's face worried her. *'ave I gone too far?* "Please, sir. Won ye leave us be? We are truly wed." She nodded as she said this, adding sincerity. She and Dane shared a loving yet desperate glance as she held his arm.

They were all silent. Mr. Barclay looked at his men and then from her to Dane.

Dane took a deep breath, then leaned over and kissed her lips lightly. "Darling, I do love you, indeed." Their eyes locked, his arms still restrained by the odorous hostile beside him, his face and lips rested on hers.

His words danced in her heart. She wrapped her arms around him tightly and closed her eyes.

Barclay motioned to his men, and the door flew open to let them proceed.

Dane grabbed her arm and waist and ushered her out of the car and into the house. Once inside, they hugged tightly for several seconds. Katie did all she could to hold her tears.

"That was bloody brilliant. Well done!" he whispered, holding her face with his hands. "I don't know what I would have done had they taken you. I would have gone mad with worry. Father, too. Bloody hell!"

"I'm mort'fied that I said all that. Most embarr'ssin. 'e's an awful man. Worse than I imagined." She looked at him. "Dane, your jaw. Are ye alright?" She touched her fingers to the bruise forming below his cheek.

Turning to see Mrs. Danbury and Mrs. Macklin gaping at them from inside the kitchen, they both gasped then sighed. The whistling kettle had shielded their words, but the young couple's desperate embrace was most definitely witnessed.

"We should change out of these wet clothes before supper," Dane murmured.

Although she needed a warm bath, she changed quickly and hurried back down, the chill of the dampness clinging to her head.

Dane gulped down his meal silently, reeling from their violent encounter, while Joel and Ellis exchanged questioning glances. When Joel opened his mouth to ask, Dane subtly shook his head so as not to upset his father.

Katie ate one bite, and after thanking Mrs. Macklin, raced up to draw a bath, shaking and scrubbing her skin, wiping away Barclay's filth. Her knees to her chest, she rocked back and forth, trying to erase the violent, humiliating encounter. Reliving the sweet moment she felt Dane's lips on hers, she shook her head, knowing his words, *'I do love you, indeed,'* were not true. But the tender moment they shared set fire to her heart.

·♥·♥·♥·♥·♥·

AFTER ELLIS RETIRED FOR the evening, Dane, with Joel in the study, a bottle of brandy and two glasses between them, repeated the evening's treachery. He could not let it go. Unable to sit still, he paced the room angrily, going over the events, omitting the details of Katie's brilliant tale of their consummation.

"One of his henchmen must have followed me to the pub. Listened to our conversation. I was caught completely off guard! Overpowered! There would have been nothing I could have done had they kicked me out of the car and taken off." The thought of what might have happened turned his stomach sour as he pulled on his hair with both hands. "I'm extremely grateful we escaped unharmed."

"The pub? Oh no! Bugger! How did you escape?"

"We didn't escape, really. Barclay demanded an account of our consummation, and Katie recited it as if it actually happened!"

"Good God!" Joel yelped. "How dare he? And then?"

"Then they let us go. Her tale was believable. Remarkably so. Heartfelt. She even accounted for the fact that we did not consummate immediately, so it matched the conversation you and I had. I am gobsmacked! My wife saved us, not I."

"Hells Bells!" Joel lifted his brandy glass. "Good for her. To your most capable wife! I admire her more and more."

In his bed, Dane felt his male muscle stiffen as he recounted her tale of their consummation. He tried to put her out of his mind, but his body took over and he released himself with the soft touch of her kiss still on his lips.

Chapter 10

CURIOSITY

I N THE KITCHEN WITH Joel and Ellis, Dane fingered his third cup of coffee, ruminating over the previous night's events.

Mrs. Danbury rushed in to fill the kettle and turn on the stove. "Well, you and your gallivanting 'round in the freezing rain all evenin' has done plenty o' harm, indeed. She's quite poorly."

Dane's breath hitched. "What?" He bolted to the steps, taking two at a time.

"Mr. Wellington! You are no going into 'er bedroom!" Mrs. Danbury shouted.

Ignoring her, he barreled straight into Katie's room. Placing the back of his fingers on her forehead, he gasped. "Bloody Hell."

"I'll be alright. I just need t'rest," she whispered, closing her eyes.

Dane checked on her several times throughout the day, each time noting a slight fever.

Once Katie was awake, he stayed by her side, feeding and tending to her.

"You should get some rest, sir," Mrs. Danbury told him when she came to check on Katie. "She is much improved."

Dane meant to leave, but fell asleep in the chair next to her bed, and woke a few hours later. Seeing that she was awake, he reached over to feel her forehead lightly. "I'm glad you're alright, love."

"Oh," she said groggily. "Wha' time's it?"

Dane glanced at her clock. "Oh, Lord! It's about half past four in the morning. I hadn't realized."

"I slept the'ole day?"

"Afraid so," he said.

"I 'ad such strange dreams."

"You had a fever." He tenderly gathered the hair stuck to her forehead. *My wife.*

The next morning, he knocked before entering. "How are you feeling this morning, love?"

Still in bed, she looked at Dane. "Much better, thank ye. Ye best no' be in 'ere. You'll catch it next."

He smiled, daring to sit on the bed next to her. He instinctively took her hand. "We are very lucky, you know. I don't want to imagine what could have happened. They came upon us so suddenly."

She nodded. "Mr. Barclay is dreadful. Thank ye, Dane. So very grateful I'm not married to 'im."

He looked down at his hand holding hers. "The way you described our consummation. How did you know so much? It was quite detailed, so very intimate."

She bit her lip gingerly and grinned. "Priya told me some, an I found a most inter'sting book... in'ye library!"

He considered which book she might have read, guessing she had discovered *How to Attain and Practice the Ideal Sex Life* by Dr. Rutgers. "Good God, that book isn't meant for innocent girls! What were you doing reading that?" He turned away to hide his flaming cheeks.

"I was curious. I want t'know more."

"Well, as inappropriate as it is, I guess it was quite lucky you had read it, then. You did well. Very, very, well."

"Miss Lipton wants me t'read in me spare time, ye know."

He tapped her nose. "Well, I hope no one sees your reading material, indeed!"

Chapter 11

BE EXTRAORDINARY

O NE AFTERNOON, WHILE EXAMINING the chessboard with Ellis, Katie asked, "Why must I go t'boardin' school? I wan t'stay 'ere with you."

"Because you must learn. About the world, history, and music. We have the resources, and you have the brains to be anything you want. You might like teaching or nursing. Or even become a medical doctor! Why not think big, my dear?" He paused, placing his hand on hers. "You know, I have wanted to educate you since you were very young. Education is your destiny, dear. I know you can be…. extraordinary. But you must want it for yourself. Choose to be extraordinary."

After a brief reflection, he added, "Dane attended Tonbridge in Kent, a very fine school. He did quite well. Excelled, truly. Even took a year in Paris. My biggest regret, however, was sending him away so young."

"How old was 'e?"

"I'm embarrassed to tell you, he was eight. He had a hard time at first. The older boys were mean."

Katie gasped, picturing young Dane thrown into that lonely world.

"Dane's mother did not marry Joel's father," he continued. "Not long after Joel was born, the two returned to Philadelphia to live with her parents. I refused to allow Dane to leave England, naturally. I wanted him educated here. Boarding school was all I knew." Ellis's thoughts overcame him.

"Irony is, I encouraged him to go abroad when he reached seventeen to avoid military. Since the war, all boys, when they reach seventeen, must serve for eighteen months in military. As Dane's mother was American, he could have left for school in the States. But he chose to stay here and serve. That is Dane."

"My goodness," Katie said. *Priya had said he was a good man. He most certainly is. Married me against his own wishes, served in the Army though he could have gone to school abroad, and is stepping up to take over his father's business, even though he would rather be a builder or architect. When is it his turn to do what he wants?*

Ellis's words empowered her, planted the seed of ambition, and as she matured, instilled a blossoming confidence. "Katie, you weren't born to live a life of mediocrity. Society will try to restrain you, tell you who to be, what to believe, and how to act. You must think for yourself. Live your life with conviction and passion and never settle. Stay the course until you get what you set out for. No matter what it is."

"Yes, sir. I will try."

Ellis studied the girl so dear to him. "You are special, my dear. I have seen it your whole life. Many colleges and universities are now accepting female students. More and more women will become doctors and professors. You must take advantage of that."

He cupped her hands in his, and they shared a loving father-daughter moment filled with unspoken affection. "I've established a trust to cover all your school expenses, including clothing and transportation, for as long as you remain enrolled in school. It is my sincere wish that you stay in school forever! That you make something of yourself. Be the woman I know you can be."

"I don't think I can ever thank you 'nough, sir. But, more'an that, I'm grateful for our time t'gether. I'll miss these daily chats the most." Katie blinked back the tears welling up. She loved having him all to herself, listening to his passionate wisdom. She placed her head on his arm. "You 'ave opened me, ah.. *my* eyes to a world a possibilities I never considered b'fore."

Serious questions were forming in her head. *Why does a woman need to be a maid 'til marriage, but a man no? Why aren't all universities allowing women to study?* And the most important for a girl of her age, *What does kissing feel like?*

·♥·♥·♥·♥·♥·

ONE OF ELLIS'S BANKER friends arranged an interview for Katie at Roedean, an all-girls school an hour south in Brighton, near the English Channel. Dane liked that the independent school offered standardized academics but also provided each student a more personalized curriculum.

Having greeted them with considerable warmth, Mrs. Marjorie Hughes, the smartly dressed headmaster, presented the curriculum and stringent school policies before leading them on a tour of the school, which was once a prestigious estate.

Dane gave his father a thumbs-up upon their return, prompting Ellis to call the school and offer a substantial legacy pledge to be provided in his will, subject to Katie's graduation. Maggie Lipton accompanied Katie to the uniform shop, and not long after, Katie and Mrs. Danbury busied themselves sewing the emblems on the navy jumpers, jackets, and hats.

Passing by the parlor, Dane stopped to watch Katie and Mrs. Danbury. They both looked up at him. "Oh, I was just remembering my days in uniform, Mrs. Danbury. And how many times we were in this room, fiddling with my blazers." He stood for a few minutes watching, noticing how Katie filled out her uniform, trying to ignore the pangs of emotion that were bubbling inside him.

Mrs. Danbury smiled, "I 'ave fond memories, sir."

Finally, when all was complete, Katie came to show Ellis how she looked, twirling her pleated plaid skirt.

"Well, look at you, my dear! You look fine." Ellis said, nodding his approval. "You should be proud of yourself, young lady. I am proud of you. You have worked hard and deserve this. I don't want you to think you don't belong there. You do. You belong here, and you belong at Roedean. Never let anyone tell you otherwise." He took her hands and squeezed them.

"Thank you," she said, blinking back her sentimental tears. "I love you, sir. I don' know what I would 'ave done without ye all my life."

"Please, all of us in the kitchen tonight," Ellis told Mrs. Macklin. "My favorite room."

The cozy nook just off the large kitchen, a circular turret with large curved windows, boasted a custom-made round wooden table with curved half-moon cushioned bench seats on one side below the windows. Warm and inviting upholstered armchairs balanced the other side. Stained-glass chandeliers hung above the table, and rich drapery adorned the six curved windows. Most often, when Dane was away, Ellis ate in the kitchen nook with his staff. After twenty-four years, they were like family.

While enjoying their meal, Katie said, "Blimey, this 'as cost you a fortune, with the uniform, new clothes, an' school itself. So many r'quired pieces a'clothing. Of clothing," she corrected herself. "All my life, I've 'ad but two or three dresses, and they were me mums 'fore they were mine. Before they were mine," she corrected herself again. "I'm so sad to be leaving. You've all treated me so very kindly, and I've been so 'appy 'ere. Happy here." She laughed at herself, now able to hear the difference in speech. "I used t'dream about what it was like to live in a grand house such as this."

Turning to Ellis, she placed her hand over his. "But more than that, I used t'dream 'bout what it would be like t'be your daugh'er. I used to pretend you were my father, an you would take me to museums and fairs. Being 'ere with you 'as been more wonderful than anything I could 'ave imagined." She stood to kiss his cheek and hug his neck. "I love you. Thank you. A million times, thank you."

"Nothing would give me greater pleasure than for you to call me Father, dear. I have always considered you a daughter."

One by one, Katie walked around the table, thanked and hugged each of them, and their glances at one another revealed how deeply moved they were. As she moved around the table, Ellis said, "This is your home, dear. You will be away at school, but you will be home many weekends and on holiday."

"We will see you during your breaks," Dane added, disturbed by the tightness in his chest. "You are not leaving for good."

"Thank you, too!" she said, coming to Dane's seat. She hugged him tightly. "If you 'adn't done what you did, I'd be married t'that awful snake right now."

Dane hugged her back, glancing at Mrs. Danbury, who seemed to register disapproval of this display of affection.

"We'r ALL goin' t'miss you, m'dear. Your bright, cheery smile a'n all the chaos you bring us daily. I'm sure I speak fa' everyone when I say we loved ev'ry minute of it," Mrs. Danbury said, laughing.

Taking a deep breath, Dane lifted his glass. "Come now. Let's not make this a sorrowful evening. Let's be thankful for what we have. Wonderful family and I do mean all of us here. Let us toast to new beginnings."

"Cheers!" everyone said at once.

·♥·♥·♥·♥·♥·

D ANE DROVE HER TO Roedean the next day. When they arrived at the school, Dane turned off the engine. "Now, I want to have a word with you. There will be times when you will find yourself outside of school with other gals and, perhaps, even chaps. Knowing how most young men act and what is ever present on their minds, I want you to promise me to never be alone with a boy, especially if you have had anything to drink. You won't be able to control the situation. A boy can take advantage of any girl if she is a bit hammered. And you are quite inexperienced. Don't let yourself get into any sticky situations. Do you understand?"

"Yes. I'm a married woman! I won' be meetin' boys!" she laughed.

Dane's eyes widened in alarm. "No, actually, you are a soon-to-be unmarried woman with an unconsummated marriage that will be annulled, dear. I sincerely hope you are not hoping for any other outcome."

"No! O' course not!" she quickly answered. "I'm no' interested in being married, either. Certainly not t'you. When I marry in truth, I want me future 'usband down on his knee, beggin' me to marry 'im."

Dane relaxed and laughed. "Good God! You are quite the dreamer! I cannot imagine doing such a thing!" He laughed again and shook his head, ignoring her dismay. "Alright. Give me a squeeze before we walk in," he said. Neither broke quickly away from their heartfelt embrace, which lasted longer than necessary.

"I am proud of you, Katie Clarke. You have accomplished quite a lot since you first arrived, and your speech has greatly improved. Much better. Keep practicing. Speak even slower, and remember to pronounce every syllable." With a sly grin, he touched her nose, adding, And don't forget to have a bit of fun, too."

Mrs. Hughes welcomed them and completed the admittance.

Dane's strained smile touched Katie's heart. "I will see you soon. Good luck!"

She nodded, hugging him quickly. As he walked away, he paused for a moment to glance back, touching his chest lightly as he inhaled slowly. "Down on his knee?" he whispered, shaking his head.

Katie's roommate, Lizzy Green, a tall, thin girl with short brown hair, who, Katie thought, resembled a gazelle, had already been at school for two years. She quickly helped Katie adapt to life at boarding school. After a quick tour and an introduction to several other girls, Katie lay on her small bed, a sudden emptiness striking her heart, missing her peaceful, wonderfully comfortable room and both Mr. Wellingtons.

Chapter 12

FRIENDSHIP

"**H**OME EC IS ALL 'bout teaching girls how to be housewives," Katie said, while dividing the fish and chips onto their plates. "But I don't 'ave to take it. Grammar is more important."

Chomping on a chip in the Brighton pub, Dane mused, "You mean to tell me they teach the girls how to iron a man's shirt? You have got to be joking!"

She laughed. "It's true."

"You are not going to school to learn to be a housewife. Ridiculous! You will never be just a housewife if I have anything to say about it. And I hope I do."

"Oh, no worries there. I 'ave already had that job, taking care of me, my sisters and the cot'age. No, thank you." She stopped for a second to look at him, swallowing hard. "Thank you again for the flowers. They were beautiful. Daisies and white roses. Perfect." She recalled the note that was attached, *'Happy Birthday, darling. See you Friday. Warmly, Dane.' Warmly?*

They spent a few moments regarding one another until Dane broke away.

"Well, I'm happy to be off for a week for the Autumn break," she said.

"I'll bet. And I have some good surprises for you at home," he teased.

"What? Do tell."

"You'll see." They laughed easily. Dane, chuckling at her antics, watched her dance in her seat to the overhead music. And suddenly, they were back, their eyes locked on one another. "It is good to see your happy face."

A shy, blushing smile lit her face. "I'm happy t' see yours too."

Katie squealed with delight upon seeing all the new records and the mahogany-encased television set. Since there still wasn't much to watch, she turned to the records, playing some top hits by American recording artists Perry Como, Guy Mitchell, Tony Bennett, and others. "Rock Around the Clock," by Bill Haley and his comets, sparked her need to dance, and when Ellis came into the parlor, happy to see the girl, he pranced around with her for a few minutes, before plopping back into a chair. She snagged Dane's hand and danced around him for half a song before Dane excused himself, heading for his room.

"A moment!" Ellis said. "Perhaps something special for Sunday? A trip to London? A museum or such?"

"That would be lovely," Katie said.

"Of course, father. We shall decide tomorrow. Goodnight."

"Goodnight, Dane. And thank you," she said. "And goodnight, Mr. Wellington! I'm so happy to be home," she added, kissing Ellis's cheek. Disturbed by his weakness, she helped him hobble to his bedroom with his cane.

The next morning, after breakfast and swimming, Dane asked Katie, "I'm thinking of taking both you and Priya to a show and then a pub this evening. How does that sound?"

"I'd love that, if Priya would be willing."

❦ · ❦ · ❦ · ❦ · ❦

D ANE WENT TO HIS office to ring Priya and lay out his plan.

"Hmmm, well I suppose she is part of your life now," Priya sighed. "Alright, I'm sure we will have lots of fun. See you later then, darling."

Her curt tone told Dane that Priya was not too happy. And, in fact, he was sure he heard something crash as she hung up the phone.

Mrs. Danbury greeted Priya at the door with little civility. They stood in the foyer waiting for Dane and Katie, both hearing Dane's voice echoing from the hallway above.

"Don't you look absolutely lovely."

Priya and Mrs. Danbury offered each other pinched smiles. Dane's words were not for Priya, and as Katie descended the stairs, Mrs. Danbury's pinched smile broadened to fill her face.

In the pub, the other patrons' laughter, the clinking of glasses, and the lively off-key singing created a vibrant atmosphere that enhanced their supper and everyone's mood. Both Priya and Katie were sorry to leave, but the picture show awaited.

Her eyes wide upon entering the theater, Katie exclaimed, "My gosh, it's so grand!" Gold velvet drapery extended across the width of the sizable stage. Glimmering crystal chandeliers hung high above several tiers of seating.

Priya sat between Dane and Katie, leaning toward Dane. Her physical proximity and constant whispering demanded his attention, leaving Katie isolated.

But, as the curtain rose, *The Captain's Paradise,* starring Alec Guinness and Yvonne De Carlo, a romantic comedy about couples aboard a passenger ship, captured Katie's full attention. Several times throughout the show, Dane and Katie exchanged glances as Priya's's head rested on his shoulder. A wide grin spread across Dane's face seeing Katie's unadulterated joy. She watched, eyes wide, as the two main characters fell in love, and in the end, when they shared a passionate kiss, Dane caught Katie clutching her heart as a blush rose in her cheeks. He chuckled as she whispered, "How romantic!"

"Well, what did you think?" Dane asked when the'd left the theater.

"Oh, t'was brilliant! Remarkable! Romantic. I enjoyed it so. Thank you for bringing me." She skipped and twirled ahead of the couple walking arm in arm. Her enjoyment of everything he took for granted was brilliant. Even Priya grinned at her enthusiasm.

When they arrived home, Katie turned and hugged them. "Thank you both so very much. I had the most lovely evening. So much fun. I LOVE the cinema!" she shouted, dancing around and around, her arms lifted high.

They laughed and wished her good night. As she ascended the stairs, she heard the couple whispering.

"I'm afraid we cannot stay here," Dane muttered. "I've promised Mrs. Danbury I would refrain from entertaining when the girl is here. So, we must be off."

.♥.♥.♥.♥.♥.

ONCE SHE WAS SETTLED in bed, Katie listened closely, but heard no sound whatsoever. *Are they in his bedroom?* She and her silly friends talked a lot about boys, sex, and romance. But none of them had any actual knowledge. *Oh, how I wish I could be a fly on the wall in there.* She imagined herself and Dane on the passenger ship, kissing, as the curtains closed.

.♥.♥.♥.♥.♥.

"DID YOU ENJOY THE evening, darling?" Dane asked as he took Priya's jacket.

Priya smiled as sweetly as she could. "I did. It was lovely. And the girl is charming and getting prettier by the day, don't you agree?" she whispered, watching Dane's eyes. She bit her lip and rubbed her knuckles, waiting for his response.

Dane grabbed her waist, pulling her close for a sultry, demonstrative kiss, his hands placed on the back of her head, and his mouth demanding hers. "Is she? I hadn't noticed." His warm breath tickled her neck. She giggled and instinctively retreated. His fingers wrapped around her ears, under her hair, and his lips grazed hers as he spoke. "There was only one beautiful woman on my arm tonight. And there is only one I want right this minute. Why would I want to think about a mere girl when I have pure perfection in my arms?"

"Oh, Lord." Priya's breath hitched. Her body relaxed as his tender kisses consumed her, and her clothes melted off her body like warmed chocolate.

.♥.♥.♥.♥.♥.

K NOWING THE STAFF WAS off for the weekend, Katie surveyed the
cupboard, spying a loaf of freshly made bread. *Eggy Bread!* Soon, the
aroma of the cinnamon, sugar, and butter carrying throughout the house,
Ellis was summoned to the kitchen, anxiously awaiting the delightful pieces
of heaven about to decorate his plate. "It's even better with maple syrup,"
she said, pouring a few drops.

Dane arrived as Katie was finishing tending to Ellis. "What do we have
here? It smells wonderful."

"Please, sit. I 'ave some for you too. Will Priya be joining us?"

"No," he said, not offering more. "Thank you, love. Who needs Mrs.
Macklin when we have you?"

Ellis chuckled without looking up. While Katie was in the kitchen, Ellis
glanced at Dane and asked, "I wonder if the other one would have gotten up
to make you breakfast?"

Dane clenched his teeth. But as they chatted about the previous
evening's entertainment, Dane watched Katie whisking about the kitchen
with ease, and caught his father's glance that said, '*I told you.*'

"Father and I have a lovely day planned. So, let's be on our way within
the hour. You'll need your raincoat and an umbrella, Katie. Father, will you
be ready shortly?"

Finishing his tea, Ellis looked at Dane and pursed his lips. "You two
run along. I think I'll stay back and rest. Not feeling like heading out today,
actually."

Dane's brows furrowed. "Are you alright?"

Ellis waved his hand. "Of course. You go on. Have some fun."

Dane stared at his father skeptically. Ellis responded with an exaggerated
grin. Dane's face went pale. He leaned in and whispered, "I thought you
wanted me to stay away from her?"

Ellis shrugged.

Katie gathered her things and kissed Mr. Wellington goodbye.

Driving into London, Dane said, "We are going on an adventure. Are
you familiar with the Tower of London?"

Katie's eyes widened. "Of course. That's the prison where they held
Anne Boleyn?"

"Yes, the second wife of King Henry the Eighth. She didn't give him any sons, so he had her locked up in the tower three years after their marriage, beheading her later to marry Jane Seymour. Gastly man."

"What an adventure! I believe I went once with my class many years ago, but I don't remember much of it."

"After that, we will see how the weather holds," he said.

The chill of the cold stone seeped into Katie's bones as she imagined the agonizing pain of the medieval rack and the weight of the chains. They walked through the dark, musty tower, each step echoing eerily; Katie swallowed hard as the tour guide described the torturous punishments, instinctively holding Dane's arm as they climbed the narrow stone circular stairway. Moods brightened when viewing the crown jewels, but darkened again when they came upon the stark, barren chambers where Anne Boleyn was held before her execution.

Following their tour, they strolled towards Potters Fields Park, the bright sunshine warming their faces, and the sounds of clashing swords and excited shouts from the actors at the jousting festival filled the air.

Dane cleared a seat at a picnic table, and they feasted on the roasted meats the festival vendors offered while the musicians and costumed actors interacted around them. Two knights dressed in metal armor fought with shimmery steel swords. "God save the Queen," one knight shouted as the other fell to the ground.

"You know, my father and I met King George VI. Father was awarded an OBE. It stands for Officer of the Most Excellent Order of the British Empire, and it is the second highest order after, perhaps, Knighthood."

"What did 'e do to get such an honor?"

"Actually, he helped many people survive the war. He had acquired numerous properties during the depression and more during the war. Many were vacant. So, he went to the shelters, found women with young babes who had lost their soldier husbands ... and offered them a free place to live."

She touched her heart. "That's remarkable! What an extraordinary man 'e is."

"Yes, he is. But I didn't always appreciate him."

"What? Why?" she asked. "Well, I guess I know some of it." She frowned. "I know you were only eight when 'e sent you to boarding school." Katie reached out her hand and touched his arm. "He told me 'e deeply regretted sending ye to school so young."

"Hmm. He didn't know how to care for a small child, indeed. But it got easier. And later I had a companion. I stole Albert Einstein from the lab at school. His mother had several babies, and as soon as he was old enough, I took him. That little rat was splendid company. And he and I became quite popular with our little tricks. Changed everything. In hindsight, I should have prepared you before pulling him out of my pocket like I did that day so long ago. I'm sorry I scared you."

"It's alright," she sighed, wishing she hadn't told him she hated his pet.

"Of course, now I know my father is a wonderful man. Look how he's even embraced Joel."

"And your mother?"

"She was ill for quite some time. Liver failure, I believe. Didn't eat or sleep well. Lots and lots of liquor. And cocaine. Heroin. And cigarettes. Lots of cigarettes. Took its toll, I suppose."

"She died?" A quick gasp escaped before she covered her mouth with her hand.

"Yes, when I was about thirteen." They both looked away in silence.

"I didn't know. I'm sorry. That makes me think about my mother, I should write to 'er soon. Now that I've had time t' think about it, she was only trying t'see that I was cared for. She didn't know Barclay, surely. We all just spoke to 'im briefly at the church, the day we met."

"I like how you can see the forest through the trees. You have a good heart, love."

After a bit of silence, Katie said, "And you 'ave a glorious life, Dane. You are no' spoiled. You work 'ard, and you're a good person. You care about other people. You do the right thing." She smiled profoundly. "You are your father's son."

"Thank you, love. However, not everyone would agree with you. My father included. I need to do better. More charity. Perhaps build a school or a library wing. I do live a rather unconventional life. But at least I am honest about it all."

"You are talking 'bout women?"

He chuckled. "Yes."

She grinned back, biting her lip. "Dane. Are we friends now?"

Dane laughed. "Yes, of course."

"May I ask you a few personal questions?"

Dane's eyebrows shot up. He pursed his lips in anticipation of her questions. "Yes, go on."

"You are quite the rake, aren't you?" she giggled. "I mean, you court many women. 'ow do you do it?"

Dane laughed. "What do you mean?"

"'ow do you get them all to, you know. 'ow do you know they would be interested in *that*. Without marriage or love?"

"Ah. Well, they find me, actually. I'm usually not the one to make the first move."

Katie's wide-eyes, her slightly embarrassed, slightly excited smile brought a smile to Dane, amused by her obvious fascination.

"Men 'ave all the advantages," Katie pouted. "They can do whatever they want, marry or not. Women are expected t' be mothers and house-wives... and virgins until marriage. And you can court as many women as you want, and nobody cares! It's no' fair! Not fair," she corrected herself.

"It's good to see you correcting yourself on your speech. Well done! And good for you for thinking about these things. But to answer your remark, my sweet, no, it isn't fair."

"If I don't remain a virgin, I will be labeled a tart, no matter me, eh, *my* education. I don't see why it's anyone's business what I do with my body! But society has decided what I must not do, and t'isn't right."

"Yes, I see your point," Dane admitted. "But, now that birth control is becoming more commonplace, women will have options."

He cocked his head, grinning seductively. "Are you saying you want to have sex, then?"

Her eyes wide with embarrassment, "Oh, you!" she pushed him playful-ly. "No!" She buried her head in her hand and giggled. "I didn't mean now!"

"I'm just teasing you." They laughed, holding one another's gaze for just a moment too long.

"Do you visit your grandparents much?"

"Joel and I travel every year at Christmas to see our grandmother. She moved to Manhattan after Pops passed. Much more fun!"

"Manhattan! Oh! What a wonderful city. I should like to see Manhattan one day."

"You would love it."

Her smile vanished suddenly. "Christmas? So, you won't be here over winter break?"

"Well, no... But father will be here, and I had hoped that you would invite your siblings to the house. I'm sure you miss them?"

She sighed, "I do. That will be lovely. Thank you." They had another long moment, and Dane was sure his wife was indeed getting prettier by the day.

"We should be off," he said, gathering their trash. He stood, offering his hand.

"Won't Priya be angry that you won't be back for New Year's Eve?"

"I will be home by then, and yes, she would have been."

"You will miss Christmas with her, though. I'm sure that makes her sad."

"THERE!" he said. "That's what is extraordinary about you! Empathy. It's rarer than you know." It was no use. His eyes caught hers once again.

She smiled. "Thank you. And thank you for a most interesting day. I think you are as much as treasure as your father. I'm glad we are friends."

"As am I," Dane responded, their eyes locked. Pangs of heartfelt longing churned inside him as he wrestled to identify his feelings.

When they returned to the house, Dane marched into the conservatory. "Seems you intended us to be together, yet you made me promise to leave her alone! What are you after?"

Ellis, busy with his crossword puzzle, replied, "Friendship, of course."

"Friendship?"

AN AGENDA

SCANNING THE LUNCH MENU at the local café near their offices, Joel asked, "So, are you taking your wife to New York? I mean, Gram would love to meet her."

"No, not taking anyone," Dane replied. "I want to be free in New York, thank you. And sod off about it, wanker."

Joel grinned. "And what about Priya? Does she still have your attention as she did before?"

"I cannot give her up. She is beautiful. An easy lover. Pleasing her is easy, and she pleases me just as easily. And we have already been through the ultimatum. She is not going anywhere, and neither am I. And I need no protection. No worry about pregnancy. It's perfect, actually."

"You'll be missing Christmas with both your lovely women, then. Perhaps some sort of splash is in order? A holiday party, if you will?"

Dane thought for a moment, then pointed his finger at his brother. "That's a bloody good idea! We shall do that."

After ordering, Dane said, "I plan to ring up Elena while in New York. You remember her, no doubt?"

Elena, a cocktail waitress at the Stork Club nightclub, was a no-nonsense Cuban firecracker. Dane recalled watching her run the tables, manipulating the rowdy men who were forever trying to manhandle her. No one messed with Elena.

The night they met, both he and Joel were on dates. Dane, the ultimate gentleman, was polite and charming, and by the end of the evening, Elena slipped him her number. He hoped she was free this year, as last year she had a beau and wasn't available.

"Have you anyone special in New York that you'd like to see?" Dane asked.

"No, I don't. Nor am I interested in seeing anyone while we are there."

Dane squinted at his brother, wondering about that curt answer, finally shoving his brother's arm playfully. "Oh, bloody hell...do I have to wangle it out of you?"

"Alright. I've decided to get serious with Trisha," Joel blurted. "I think I love her. Oh, heck, I do love her, and am going to ask her to marry me. You going to give me hell about it, I suppose?" Joel crossed his arms, sat back, and waited.

"Good God! Well, that's brilliant! I'm happy for you." Dane reached over and shook his brother's shoulder. "Aces!" Dane laughed, shaking his head. "That's why you wanted to be home for New Year's Eve. Jolly Good!"

"Thank you for your support. It means a lot," Joel said. "Oh, and Happy Birthday, big brother!"

The server came with the lagers, and they toasted, "To Trisha Smith and many more birthdays!"

·♥·♥·♥·♥·♥·

THEIR EARLY CHRISTMAS DINNER, catered by one of the best restaurants in London, included Dane, Priya, Joel, Trisha, Ellis, Katie, Maggie Lipton, and their Oxford area land manager, Troy Anderson. The last two, Katie's idea, as they were both single, enjoyed the arts, had fathers who were barristers, and were Oxford grads. Maggie was still hoping for a teaching position at one of the Oxford colleges for girls.

Katie gave both Dane and Ellis cashmere scarves she had knitted. Dane's was ivory, with black edges, and Mr. Wellington's was black with white trim.

"These are quite lovely, my dear," Ellis said. "I'm sure this took you much time, and I appreciate all your hard work to make something so beautiful."

"I agree. Lovely. I shall take it to New York with me. Thank you. That was very thoughtful." Dane said, not holding Katie's gaze too long.

Ellis had a baby grand piano delivered and set in the parlor. It was exactly what the room needed, and Katie's high-pitched squeals would have scared an intruder. As she was already taking lessons at school, she immediately played the first ten bars of the Chopin Prelude in E Flat Major.

"That's all I know so far," she said as they applauded.

"Very well done, dear. Look how far you have come! I hope you are proud of yourself," Ellis remarked. "One of my favorite pieces of music. I remember you trying to play that when you were young."

She clapped her hands softly, and held them to her mouth, as if in prayer. How she loved Ellis, especially when he told her how proud of her he was. "Thank you. I cannot wait to learn the entire piece and play it for you. I'm afraid it will take me all year to learn it, though. It's quite complicated."

"Doesn't matter how long it takes. It's the accomplishment that matters," Ellis said.

Everyone left contented and in good spirits, everyone except for Priya, who went home alone. Dane's belly too full of food and, certainly, drink, he was in no shape for anything but a good night's rest.

After Priya left, Dane pulled Katie aside. "I'm afraid I have a bit of bad news. Seems your friend, Mr. Barclay has filed a motion against us. Claims we committed fraud, and is suing for Breach of Contract and damages. My barrister will handle it, but we may be required to go to court at some point."

"Oh, no." she yelped.

"Nothing to do just yet. We have to wait and see," Dane said.

·❦·❦·❦·❦·❦·

V ISITING GRAM IN NEW York was always a joy, and the brothers loved traipsing around Manhattan, seeing Broadway shows, and dining in fine restaurants with her. Much like their mother, she was a spirited and highly educated lady with a busy life.

Joel, however, was on a mission during this trip, eager to reach the bustling three-block-long portion of 47th Street, known as the Diamond and Jewelry District. The district hummed with excitement as the clinking of tools and the sparkle of jewelry and diamonds filled the crowded cubbies and workspaces. The jewelers, mostly male Orthodox Jewish immigrants who had fled the persecution of the German Nazis, dressed in black suits and tall hats, their religious garb poking out from underneath their garments. Dane found it humorous how the jewelers tried to lure patrons into their spaces like spiders trying to capture prey on their webs.

After a brief education on diamond grades, Joel chose a traditional, one-carat, round solitaire.

While Joel waited for the stone to be set in white gold and the ring sized, Dane set out to choose gifts for each of his ladies, including a pair of eighteen karat gold pearl and diamond earrings for Priya and a delicate diamond heart necklace for Gram.

"Will you purchase something for your wife?" Joel ribbed.

"Be quiet." But Dane knew he couldn't possibly leave without something for Katie.

It took him a while, but he found something quite remarkable. "My God," he breathed upon spotting the handmade eighteen-karat gold necklace, an artfully formed flower basket fashioned from intricate gold wire. A bouquet of daisies, marquise-shaped diamonds with yellow sapphire centers, cascaded on wire stems from the delicate basket.

Chapter 14

THE RISING SUNFLOWER

READYING HERSELF FOR HER sisters' arrival, Katie, exiting the loo, glanced toward Dane's room; the sun's rays illuminated the brandy glass left on his dresser. As no one was around, she crept through the open door, feeling his strong, masculine presence. The aroma of his cologne filling her head, her eyes darted around the room, landing on the large, ornately carved bed. At the head, there was a rounded canopy, with dark green velvet drapery tucked around it, just over the headboard. She caressed the rich velvety fabric of the bedcover, with colors of deep green, dark burgundy, and gold that coordinated with decorative pillows. Burgundy velvet covered the windows and two chairs.

Surveying the items on his nightstand, she peeked in the small drawer. There were tissues, a pen and pad of paper, and a Bible. She picked up the fine brown leather Bible, studying its bejeweled cover, running her finger over its sterling silver trim.

How magnificent! She had never seen one so beautiful. On the inside page, there was an inscription: '*To My Darling Ellis on our wedding day. Yours forever, Rachael.*'

Oh dear. His mother gave it to his father on their wedding day! How terribly sad... Tears welled in her eyes.

"What are ye doing in 'ere?" Mrs. Danbury yelped, her arms full of clean, folded linens.

Katie jumped, her eyes wide with fear. "I...I...Dane, oh, ummm... Mr. Wellington had given me this Bible, and...and I was just returning it." She dropped the Bible into the drawer, slammed it shut, and flew past the housekeeper.

Mrs. Danbury followed her to her room. "Dear, dear girl. Don't be fooled by the 'andsome face or the charm and grace 'e possesses. 'e will never marry, an 'e will never love just one. He will never be true to ye o' any other. Tha'tis his way. He won' be changin.'"

Mrs. Danbury's straightforwardness was shocking. Katie's heart pounded as the woman besieged her.

"He dailies wi' girls like Miss Priya, who gladly give 'im what he needs, and when 'e is done, 'e is off seeking pleasure from others. Each time 'e travels somewhere, 'e has another. Dere are girls willin to take 'im to bed everywhere 'e goes. You cannot tame 'im. Each of the girls prob'ly thinkin' they could too, but they ain' goin' ta." She shook her head.

"You, on the other hand, 'ave been given a great gift. You are a beguiling creature, the likes o' which most men will never behold, let alone possess. You are rising like a magnificent sunflower! You must stay untouched, girl." She took Katie's arms and shook her. "Twill be the mistake of ye life t'let yourself be taken 'fore you are wed, and especially by a man that'll never be true to ye."

Mrs. Danbury continued, her voice softening as she gently stroked Katie's hair, a calming rhythm on the girl's head. "Gentlemen in high society will want t'wed ye. I don think you realize 'ow rare a beauty you are! And the men, dear, they will wan' someone pure. No someone who 'as been devoured by 'nother man before them. Take 'old of yeself, girl. He's no' the one for you." She touched Katie's shoulder and left.

Covering her face with her hands, Katie sobbed into her pillows. *Everything she said... She is right! What am I thinking? He is very handsome and sweet, a good person. But I know Dane, and I know Mrs. Danbury is correct.*

For the next three days, Ellis and Katie entertained Katie's sisters. They danced, watched television, and played cards. The indoor swimming pool was a special treat, and Katie gave them swimming lessons in the warm, heated pool, while the cold outside air frosted the windows. They were grateful to Ellis for his chess tutorial and his efforts to make them think more about their futures. Along with the gifts Dane had generously provided, each of Katie's sisters went home with a greater understanding of women's roles, how important education was, and how to be as independent as possible.

Chapter 15

BLUE SATIN BOXES

Exhausted from nine hours of traveling, Dane arrived home in the afternoon of December 30th and slept until the morning of the 31st. Before dressing for New Year's Eve, he motioned for Katie to meet him in his study.

"You wanted to see me?"

Dane stood. "I'm sorry I cannot include you tonight. I'm afraid dear Priya wasn't keen on sharing me on New Year's Eve."

"That's alright, I understand," she laughed. "I do want to hear all about New York and your visit with your grandmother. Do you think you will have some time tomorrow, perhaps?"

"Of course, but not too early. I fear I may be quite spent until the afternoon."

She giggled as she caught his wink.

"I brought you something from Manhattan." He handed her a blue satin box adorned with red and white Christmas ribbons.

Her eyes opened in surprise. "You have already given me so many lovely things."

"Open it, please," he insisted, placing his shaking hands in his lap.

She unwrapped the box, opened it, and studied the necklace carefully, her mouth dropping open. "A flower basket," she whispered.

"It's eighteen karat gold, and the daisies are diamonds and yellow sapphires."

"Oh." She looked up at him, her tear-filled eyes wide, astonished that he would purchase such a lavish gift for her. "Thank you! It's absolutely beautiful." She laughed, "It has... daisies!"

"As soon as I saw it, I knew it was made for you."

Tears spilled from her eyes as she touched her hand to her heart. "It's... it's perfect! Thank you, Dane! How did you find this? I don't know what to say. I'm speechless. It's so beautiful. I will cherish this forever. My goodness, I love it so very much. Thank you."

His hands still shaking, he took the box from her, removed the necklace, and reached around her neck to fasten it.

Their faces close, Dane whispered, "I have come to care for you a great deal, love. You have many wonderful qualities I admire, and I am quite enjoying having you here." Deeply touched by her sentiment, he held her gaze for a bit too long, once again.

A wistful smile crossed her lips.

Dane, clearing his throat, broke the moment. "And now, I must get myself together for this evening." He stood, and she hugged his chest.

"Thank you."

He kissed the top of her head, desiring to hug her back, but refraining. Her reaction to his gift had warmed his body and brought an ache to his stomach.

Moments later, sitting on the edge of his bed, he considered his reaction. *This is ridiculous. I must get her out of my head. There will be an annulment.*

Dane dressed and came down to say goodnight to the group before leaving. Poking his head into the kitchen, he was pleased to see Katie, Ellis, and the staff enjoying a special New Year's Eve supper, complete with noisemakers and New Year's hats. They stopped to stare at him.

"Sorry to miss this wonderful meal. But I wanted to say Happy New Year to everyone before I left." he said.

"Happy New Year, Mr. Wellington! And my word, don't you look dapper!" Mrs. Macklin said, admiring his formal ensemble.

"Smashing!" Katie cheered, eyeing him from head to toe.

Dane caught Katie's eye and winked as he tugged the ivory scarf that was tucked inside his long black cashmere coat. She was grinning at him until she saw Mrs. Danbury raising her eyes. She turned quickly, fingering her necklace.

George asked, "Would you like me to drive this evening, sir?"

"No, George, thank you. I will collect Priya and head into the city. Going to the ballet, you know."

"The ballet? The Russian ballet? Oh, The Bolshoi?" Katie asked excitedly. "*The Nutcracker?*"

Dane sighed. *Of course, she knows the name of the ballet, the origin, and the troupe! Bloody hell, I am most definitely taking the wrong lady to see this fine production.*

"Yes, of course," he said. "Every year at this time of year. I should have known you would have enjoyed it," he said, hitting his head. "I should have taken you as well, but I'm afraid I would pull my hair out if I had to sit through the entire production twice in one month."

Everyone laughed. Dane placed his top hat on his head and said, "Well, I'm off, then! Good night, everyone! Happy New Year!"

·❦·❦·❦·❦·❦·

"Y OU ARE RAVISHING, MY dear," Dane said, admiring Priya's elegant attire. Inside The Royal Festival Hall, Dane helped Priya remove her coat, handing it and his own things to the coat check gal, but not before pulling something out of the coat's pocket. "Here is a little something to make you even more so." He handed her the elegant blue satin box, and she opened it without hesitation.

"Oh, they are lovely, Dane. How thoughtful you are."

"I purchased them on 47th Street in New York City. Diamonds and South Sea pearls. The very best for you, love."

"Thank you." She kissed him on the cheek. "I shall put them on straight away."

He couldn't help but compare her reaction to that of Katie's a few hours ago, watching as she replaced her earrings. *How different they are.*

Fingering the earrings lightly, he admired his choice, and her face in them. "Beautiful earrings for a beautiful lady."

"What else, I wonder, did you purchase? Something for the girl, no doubt? You didn't go there just to purchase a gift for me, surely."

"Well, I purchased something for my grandmother, of course, and yes, a little something for Katie as well, but the reason we went to the Diamond District was for Joel to purchase an engagement ring for Trisha."

Priya's face transformed into a ghostly-white, miserable mask of agony. She did not even try to hide her anger.

Oh, Lord! What did I say? "Now, darling, don't go acting like someone just died. I know what you are thinking. Stop it. We have an agreement. There is no reason for you to be upset." *Me and my big mouth.*

"I know we have an agreement. It just gets to me, sometimes. I can't help it. If you weren't such a wonderful lover and so good to me—." She hesitated for a moment. "I know you will never be mine. It's hard to walk away, but I fear I will have to someday, you know."

"Well, I hope not. I so enjoy your company, darling. If it comes, I shall be sad to see that day."

They settled into their seats without another word. Dane could feel Priya seething, but she looked towards the stage and said nothing more.

The orchestra music filled the hall as the dancers brought the story to life. Although he had seen this ballet many times before, he had never paid attention to the story. Nutcracker dolls are given to children at a Christmas party, and as she sleeps, a young girl dreams that her Nutcracker comes to life and fights with the Evil Mouse King and his army. At the last second, as the Nutcracker is just about to lose the fight, Katie picks up her slipper and throws it at the Mouse King, killing him! *Katie? No... Good God. Well, yes, it would be Katie who saved the day, wouldn't it?* Dane shook his head and chuckled.

At intermission, Dane tried to kiss Priya, but she pulled away. *Bloody hell. Why did I mention Joel's engagement? Stupid. Bloody Stupid.* "Are you going to be pithy all night, then? Over what, exactly? You know our arrangement doesn't include an engagement ring. Come now. You look stunning in your new and very expensive earrings. Look how well they bring out your beautiful smile and the white collar of your dress. And set against your dark hair, you are magnificent." He fingered her hair, gathered loosely off of her neck. "Are we not having a wonderful time? And, of course, afterward, we shall have a spot at The Gargoyle Club, where we will dance the night away! Come on now. Where's my lovely Priya gone?" He kissed her cheek.

Taking their seats for Act II, Dane grasped, for the first time, the rest of the story. The Nutcracker turns into a prince, whisking the girl away on a magical journey.

After much celebratory dancing, including some very slow and sultry swaying on the dance floor, Priya was once again her lovely, feminine, tantalizing, willing self. Back in his flat, his warm mouth on her cool, damp skin made her shiver with goosebumps. Heavily intoxicated and sweaty from dancing, his deliberate pace abandoned, he took her mouth with hungered fever, and easily slipped off her dress and his clothes. Lost beneath his skillful hands, she drew him closer and whispered, "My goodness. I want you."

Chapter 16

SUBCONSCIOUS MINDS

THE NEXT MORNING, WHILE she and Ellis were watching television in the parlor, Katie heard Dane enter the house. Wondering why he hadn't come in to say hello, she rose and went to investigate. He was stumbling out of the kitchen.

"Were you looking for coffee? Mrs. Macklin is off, you know. I can make you some, if you like. Are you alright? You look awful."

"No coffee. Just need sleep."

Katie assumed his condition was the result of his long night and returned to the parlor, where she and Ellis spent the morning playing chess and watching television.

After preparing lunch for Ellis, with still no sign of Dane, she climbed the stairs and listened against the door of his room. She heard something. *Is he moaning?* She tapped on the door. "Dane? May I come in?"

Cracking the door, she peeked in. He was lying face up on the bed, still in his trousers, buckle and zipper opened. He had unbuttoned and partially removed the top half of his shirt, while the bottom remained buttoned. On closer inspection, she gasped—the bright red cheeks and drenched hair could only mean one thing. Confirming this with a touch to his temple, she said, "You're burning up! Oh, no!"

She rushed to the phone to ring Joel. "Joel? This is Katie. Dane is ill. Terribly ill. A fever. Delirious! And everyone is gone for their holiday. I'll light the fire in his room and bring the fever down with warm compresses, done this many times in the past. I just wanted you to know, in case he needs to go to hospital."

"Right. Probably flu or pneumonia," Joel said. "I am up in Edinburgh now with Trisha's family. Sorry love, you are on your own. Make sure he doesn't get chilled. Cover the skin immediately after wetting it."

"Yes, I will; that's how I've cared for my brothers and sisters."

"Also, can you make some soup for him? Our gram has a wonderful, healing recipe that I think she shared with Mrs. Macklin. Can you find it, do you think? I know it has plenty of salt, celery, parsley, onions, and garlic. Our grandmother uses chicken feet too, in her soup, but I doubt you will have those handy. I'll call you back in a few hours, love."

"Brilliant thought! I think I know where it is. I'll find it and make the soup, of course."

What to do first? Should I tell Mr. Wellington? No, not likely he can help. Light the fire. Piling the wood into the fireplace, she concentrated, blowing lightly...*finally!*

"Dane?" she shouted. "Help me get you out of these clothes. Please." No use; he was too delirious to understand. She started tugging at the trouser legs, lifting his torso while pulling the trousers off his buttocks. Inching them down over his hips, she was making some progress. Then, with one good tug from the bottom of the trouser legs, finally freeing them, she lost her balance and hit the floor. Already exhausted, she pulled herself up, leaning her arms on the bed. Taking a moment to rest, she studied him, happy to see he had his briefs on. His legs were long and muscular. Unbuttoning his shirt, she turned him each way to get his arms out, then pulled the covers out from underneath him, so as not to get them wet. She studied his face for a moment. *So handsome.* Look at those eyelashes. *Unusually long nose for English gentlemen, but it fits his face.* Her eyes moved to his torso. *Oh, the tight muscles all lined up perfectly. Hard not to stare at him. Stop it.*

With a bowl of hot water on the nightstand, she rubbed his skin with the wet cloth vigorously, starting with his arms and shoulders, working her way down towards his hand. She covered the damp skin with the sheet as she worked, sighing when she felt his skin cooling. "Wake up now, Dane. Please wake up." She touched her fingers to his forehead and gently moved the damp strands of hair away. She had wanted to touch his face many times but wouldn't have dared, naturally. "Oh…" she whispered, knowing that she cared, really cared for him, and more. How much she wanted to touch him. His chest. His … *Good Lord. What makes a girl want to touch a man?*

The ringing of the phone interrupted her thoughts. It was Joel asking for an update.

"I think he is much improved. I'm just finishing the second go 'round, and then I'll go make the soup. Thank you, Joel."

After reheating the water, she hurried back to her patient. As she leaned over him to work his midsection, she fought the urge to stare at the obvious bulge beneath his shorts, but her eyes kept drifting downward. She covered him up and tucked him in tightly, studying his face while he slept. Mrs. Danbury's harsh words came rushing back: *"Don't be fooled by the 'andsome face or the charming manner. He will never marry, an' 'e will never love."* Her heart sank, knowing she would never feel his lips on hers, then fingered her lips thinking of his kiss in Barclay's car. She understood now why Priya allowed herself to continue to see him, even though she knew he would never be hers. *Other men don't look like this, nor are they as generous or kind. Priya had said he was sweet and tender with her. Pleasure, she had said.* The pictures from the particularly interesting book in the family library fresh in her mind, she swallowed hard. *Time to make soup.*

She found all the ingredients she needed and, after tasting it, she set out two large bowls and some day-old bread for herself and Ellis.

As she gulped hers down, Ellis remarked, "What's your rush?"

"Oh, Dane isn't feeling very well. He's just taking it easy today. I'm going to bring 'im some soup. *Him* some soup."

Ellis smiled. "You take very good care of us, my dear. Thank you. And you are doing very well with your speech. Good girl."

They smiled warmly at one another as Katie filled a third bowl, anxious to get back upstairs with the soup.

The fire had died down a bit, and Dane was shivering when she re-turned. His teeth chattered through his moans; he was unaware that he had thrown his blankets off the bed.

She sucked in her breath. "Oh, my God!" Setting the soup down, she put more logs into the fire, moved Dane onto his side, and started rubbing his back vigorously, covering him with his blankets, and throwing herself practically on top of him.

Without warning, he reached his arm up and pulled her down into the bed, adjusting the covers on top of them both, pulling her close, his front to her back. "Just for a second, love. Till I warm up," he whispered, his body still convulsing.

She gasped, her eyes wide. *Oh my God.* He scooted closer until every inch of his heated bare skin pressed against her. His warm breath soothing against her neck, his arm draped over her with his hand resting under her breast and his thumb resting upon it.

"Don't leave me," he whispered.

And then silence. *Is he asleep?*

"My beautiful, wonderful wife. How will I ever let you go?" The words were slurred, but his grip tightened once more.

Katie sucked in her breath, his words gripping her heart. Her exhausted body screamed for rest, and truth be told, she couldn't bear to leave. His arms around her as he slept, his hard bulge nudged against her behind, and the thumb upon her breast...*Thrilling! What was the hurry? Just a few more moments,* she thought, sliding off her slippers.

·♥·♥·♥·♥·♥·

KATIE GASPED WHEN SHE opened her eyes, the sun's rays bursting into the dark room through the slightly opened drapes. *Goodness, I slept the night in his bed! Good thing neither Mrs. Macklin nor Mrs. Danbury are here. What would they think?*

As she pulled herself up, his arms tightened around her. "Morning, love." His voice was deep and hoarse. *He's awake. Blimey.* Needing the for-mality, she said, "Oh, please, Mr. Wellington, you must release me."

"Not until you tell me how you came to be in my bed, me in my briefs, and you ..." He lifted the sheets to check. "Oh, thank goodness. And what time is it? Or rather, should I ask what day is it?"

"It's morning, January 2. You've had the most awful fever. You slept all day and all night. Quite delirious, you were. Are you feeling better, then?"

"I feel like I've been run over by a rubbish lorry." He tried to focus and lift himself on his arm, but he couldn't manage. "Have you been here all day and night taking care of me?"

"Yes. And I made your gram's soup, but you were asleep."

"Oh, thank you, love. I'm starving. And quite thirsty."

She lifted herself up, reached for the glass on his nightstand and handed it to him.

"Ah, thank you," he said. A wave of dizziness caused him to fall back onto the bed as he tried to sit up.

"Let me help." Sitting up further, she brought the glass to his lips. The intimate moment did not pass without both noticing. "I'll get you some soup," she said, returning the glass to the nightstand.

As she started to exit the bed, he held her arm. "First, you must tell me. How did you come to be in my bed?"

"I...I rubbed you with the wet compress, then I and covered you. I lit the fire too, but I'm afraid you must have gotten a chill. You were burning up something awful and muttering quite daft things. I tried to warm you. And then, you just grabbed me and tucked us both under." She didn't dare tell him how close he was, or which of his body parts she felt.

"Good God. I didn't know what I was doing. You must forgive me."

"Of course." He released his grip, and she stood up. "I...I...In truth, I could 'ave left." She covered her face with her hands and mumbled. "It's not actually all your fault. It was ...warm...and I... My body kept you warm. You were asleep, and I knew nothing was going to happen. And then I fell asleep too. I didn't mean to stay the night."

"What daft things?" he asked.

"What?" Grabbing the soup bowl she had brought up the day before, she turned away.

"What daft things did I say?"

"Oh." She shook her head. "No. Never mind. It doesn't matter."

"Come now, what did I say?"

She paused and looked into his eyes, her heart racing. "You said, my beautiful, wonderful wife. How will I ever let you go?"

Dane froze for a second and gulped. "Oh, dear. Did I say that?"

She nodded. "I'll bring up a fresh bowl."

He considered, then laughed. "Well, that's not so bad, is it, now? I mean, you are my very beautiful, wonderful wife, in truth. Oh, bloody hell, I was delirious. Let's not analyze what I said." He laid back down and closed his eyes. After she left, he said. "Me and my big bloody mouth. I am going to hell."

·♥·♥·♥·♥·♥·

WHILE DANE RESTED, KATIE and Ellis played chess, and although she was getting quite good, she was not good enough to best her teacher. After a few hours, Ellis retired to his room for a nap, and Katie headed to the parlor to listen to her records. Swaying to the music, her wide skirt swayed like a bell as she moved from side to side.

Hearing the music, Dane made his way downstairs, and stood, resting against the doorway, arms crossed, watching her move. He enjoyed watching her.

Katie spun around and they locked eyes. "Oh, I didn't see you there. I love the new records! Thank you!" she said. She pranced around the room, as though she was waltzing with a partner. "And I see you bought *The Nutcracker*! Tchaikovsky! Wonderful! I love it all! I do love to dance!"

"I'm aware." *She has joie de vivre,* he mused. He contemplated waltzing with her. Looking into her eyes, holding her close. *Bloody Hell.*

"You feel better now?" she asked.

"Much, thanks to my nurse. Mademoiselle, je te suis reconnaissant," he bowed.

She froze and stared at him. "Oh my goodness, you speak French? Of course, you do. What did you say?"

He stepped over to her and whispered, "I am grateful for you."

She stared, and then, the smile.

Her smile lit up the room. They stood grinning at one another like idiots, their shared affection reflected in their faces. *Good thing she will be back at school tomorrow. What a face! Priya was right.* He tore his eyes away. "Thank you for bringing the soup earlier. But, I'm still very hungry, love. And I can't stand here much longer, or I will collapse. Will you keep me company in the kitchen?"

She nodded and followed him.

"So, how did you enjoy *The Nutcracker*?" she asked.

"It was, well, a lovely ballet, I suppose." He recalled his little daydream during the ballet. "Ballets are not my favorite, but I do enjoy the music."

"Did Priya enjoy herself?"

"Oh, Priya enjoyed *attending* immensely. Mostly the dressing up, the people watching, and people watching her. I hate to admit it, but truthfully, if you ask Priya next week what it was about, or even more certainly, who wrote the music, I doubt she'd be able to tell you."

Katie laughed. "Tchaikovsky, of course."

He nodded his approval. "That's my girl." *My wife.*

They shared another moment.

He felt a sudden twinge of guilt. "I should not say that about Priya. She isn't ignorant. She has a good head on her shoulders. She just isn't interested in culture or art, or ..." he shook his head, frustrated at her lack of interest in just about everything, except shopping, dancing, and dining. And of course, sex.

Mrs. Macklin had placed a bowl of Katie's soup in front of him, along with a hearty slice of turkey with mustard on fresh bread. Dane caught her smiling as she watched their interaction.

Dane clasped his arms in front of himself, sighing. "I'm afraid I'm not strong enough to drive today, love. George will have to take you back to school."

Katie laughed. "I'm not due back until the sixth. I have several more days!

Dane's eyebrows furrowed. "Oh dear. I hadn't realized that. I am off to Paris on the fifth."

"Paris? How wonderful! Will Priya be accompanying you?"

"Good God, no. Priya in Paris? Wouldn't dare. All she would want to do all day is shop and then sit and rest at outdoor cafés. I would be terribly bored and quite a bit poorer. No, thank you. I am meeting friends there, actually. We did a year at school there, you know, and we travel together yearly."

When they were alone, Dane leaned in. "I want to apologize for pulling you into my bed. I should not have done that."

She bit her lip. "It's alright."

·♥·♥·♥·♥·♥·

DANE AND JOEL SPENT the next evening together, catching up on the latest events. There was a lot to review; New Year's Eve, reactions to Christmas presents, the engagement, *The Nutcracker*, Dane's illness, and his unconscious night-time cuddle.

After hearing about the latter, Joel laughed, "Good God, man! I'm going to win our wager sooner than I thought! I knew it. She's too pretty to be living under your nose. I believe you are smitten, big brother." He pointed his finger at Dane. "You might as well admit it. She has already slept a night in your bed. It won't be long now, to be sure."

"Why must you taunt me so?" Dane said, shaking his head. "I will not touch her. Truly. But I cannot believe I pulled her into my bed. And she stayed the whole damn night, admitting she could have left but fell asleep instead! I must be more careful."

"That's your subconscious, indeed. It happened because you both wanted it to happen."

"Nothing happened. I was ill. I must admit, though, I'm noticing that the difference between them is night and day." Dane said, shaking his head.

"Yes! That's correct. Your wife for day and your mistress for night." Joel laughed, slapping the table at his joke.

"Oh, sod off! Will you cease your games? Please."

Joel's face softened at his brother's pleading. "Priya is simple-minded. Not interested in anything but herself, unfortunately. Your wife, however, is remarkable. Sharp, witty, sensitive, loving, and selfless. Night and day, just as you said. I'd say you have less than a year, brother. After that, you will lose Katie if you don't act. And mark my words, it will be the mistake of your life."

"Hmm. Father has said the same." He flashed on waking to find his arms around her.

"Well," Joel said. "Let's talk about my wedding, shall we?"

Chapter 17

A MAN REVERED

JANUARY 1957

R ETURNING TO SURREY AFTER a week in Paris, Dane's gaze fell upon a terrifying sight, an ambulance near the entrance of their home, its rear doors open. A bone-deep sense of foreboding, like an icy hand squeezing his chest, gripped Dane, sending a frigid chill coursing through him.

Rushing in, he found his father being rolled toward the door on a stretcher, an oxygen mask covering his face. Dane's heart sank, and he instantly regretted not having been present when he was so needed.

"Heart attack," the doctor at the hospital said. "He will need to stay several days, and after being released, a daily nurse will help him regain his strength."

Dane's conversations with his father's doctors over the next week painted a grimmer picture; his father's strength was waning, the cheerful energy replaced by listlessness and fatigue. As Dane watched the once strong, vibrant man slowly deteriorate, he couldn't shake the feeling of unease settling in his stomach like a heavy stone. With each passing day, a growing sense of helplessness and fear seemed to hang in the air, making it hard for Dane to think clearly or even breathe deeply. He had work to do but could not concentrate on anything.

Dane worried about his father's strength, but Ellis's focus now was on his son, preparing him to carry on with both business and life. Dane felt the burden and urgency of his father's words.

As Ellis spoke, a wave of warmth and gratitude washed over Dane, causing his eyes to well up with tears, knowing these were the last days he would have to hear his father speak. Grateful for this precious time, his hands trembled, a newfound determination gripping him—he would not only listen carefully but would strive to live up to his father's unwavering belief in him.

"You are already an extraordinary human being, and if my vision becomes a reality, you will one day be a wonderful husband and father. It is my utmost wish for you to follow that path, my boy. My dear boy. And you are well on your way. Most young lads would not have taken the burden you did with the girl. I'd say well on your way." Ellis, typically uncomfortable with sentiment, took Dane's hand. "And son, I know I don't say these things much, but I love you. You are the most wonderful son."

Dane's heart was full. His father's words wrapped around him like a comforting hug, important for him to hear, even though he didn't know it just then.

Ellis also took this time to address his failures, especially regarding Dane's mother. Ellis's sorrowful tone told Dane this was as hard for his father to say as it was for Dane to hear. He closed his eyes. "I candidly regret failing your mother and sometimes, you as well. I did not know how to be a father to a young child nor a good husband to a young, energetic wife. All I knew was work for me and boarding school for you, and that's where you were shipped. I regret sending you there so terribly young."

Ellis forged ahead, his eyes downcast. "However, my greatest regret is not being there for your mother. You know, she went home to her parents, as she could not manage here by herself. I could have taken her back and raised Joel as my own, but I did not. I let her go, and in the process, you lost your mother. And towards the end, when she was ill and returned to be with you both, I could have helped. But I did not. I failed her in so many ways, and I realize you suffered those mistakes."

Dane gripped his father's hand.

"I was angry at her. Hurt. Prideful. Foolish," Ellis continued. "I should have helped them. Could have done so, easily. I was wrong and I deeply regret it. It goes against everything I stand for. My very core beliefs." Ellis placed his other hand on his son's arm. "Sometimes it takes a lifetime to get it right."

Ellis closed his eyes, and Dane left him to rest, ringing Katie. Returning a while later, he found Ellis lost in thought. His face brightened upon seeing Dane.

"I've sent George to collect Katie," Dane whispered.

"Ah. My girl," Ellis chuckled. "Perhaps I wasn't such a dreamer after all? Perhaps there is some force we cannot comprehend regarding us three. Fate has surely played its part many times over." He paused, and Dane knew he was going to recount the story of Katie's illness again. Dane, appreciating this precious time with his father, let him continue. "George and I were heading home that stormy evening. Not scheduled to stop at the Clarke's. Something... told me to go. And she was at death's door, son. Would not have survived the night." Ellis shook his head to make the point. "I believe I was sent there...perhaps by God. She was saved ... for you."

Some force? Saved for me? He shook his head. *How could it be? I don't believe in fate. But the day I married her, wasn't that fate? I showed up just in time, as he had done all her life.*

Ellis squeezed Dane's hand. "I don't know *how* I know. But I have loved her since I first laid eyes on her, and I've no doubt you will love her evermore," Ellis paused, then added one final thought. "I am at peace knowing you will have love and purpose in your life."

Dane had the utmost respect for his father and knew him to be a disciplined man with sensible and honest ideas about the world. He trembled silently, his mind resisting the notion that his marriage was his destiny and that his life, as he knew it, would change.

Dane heard Katie barging into the house and met her at the entrance to the conservatory, holding her arms as she tried to push her way through the door. "What's happened? Is he alright?" she trembled.

"No. Katie, he's not getting better. He's weakening. He's peaceful, and so must you be. Be strong, love."

Focusing on Dane's arms around her, she took a deep breath and nodded as she walked into Ellis's room quietly. A profound sadness enveloped her, bringing tears to her eyes as she gazed at him. She rushed to his side, and for the next several hours, she tended to him, speaking softly and holding his hands.

·♥·♥·♥·♥·♥·

A FEW DAYS LATER, a knock at his bedroom door startled Dane awake. "Come in."

"I'm so sorry, sir," Mr. Macklin said. "Looks like Mr. Wellington has taken a turn. Might be pneumonia. The doctor has been called, said it might be a while before he can get here. Shall we take him to hospital, sir? I can call an ambulance."

"I'll be right there," Dane said, throwing his trousers on. Stumbling to his father's bedside, alarmed at Ellis's struggling breaths, Dane reluctantly concluded his father had nothing left. *This is it,* he surmised. It was surreal. *How could this be happening?*

Ellis was barely conscious. "Not hospital, son. Here," he whispered wearily.

Dane nodded, the thumps so heavy coming from his chest, he placed his hand over his heart, surprised at the intensity. "Mr. Macklin, wake Katie, will you?"

Dane placed a cool compress on his father's forehead, holding his hand as he moved in and out of consciousness.

Katie and Dane sat by his side, and when Ellis regained consciousness, he reached for both their hands, sandwiching his own between theirs. When Ellis closed his eyes, she cried, dropping her head on Dane's chest, his arm wrapped around her.

Their hearts heavy, Mrs. Danbury, the Macklins, and George surrounded the bed, holding hands as they prayed. Joel arrived shortly thereafter, along with Dr. Schultz, Ellis's long-time friend and doctor.

"I'm so sorry, son," Dr. Shultz said to Dane. "He has been a close friend for over fifty years. I came as soon as I could." The doctor checked

Ellis's vitals. "His lungs are filled with fluid, and his breathing is laboriously difficult. We could make him more comfortable at the hospital, but it is unlikely he will survive this. His body is simply too weak."

Dane whispered, "He told me he doesn't want the hospital."

Doctor Schultz nodded, then took Ellis's pulse and held his hand. "Then we'll let him pass in peace, surrounded by those he loves and who love him, in his own bed and at his own time. It is my honor to stand by this great man's side as he passes."

"No!" Katie wailed, sobbing into her hands. "Oh, please, he can't die! Please, No. Oh, Dane, he can't be dying! Why? I don't want him to die!!"

Dane reached for her, pulling her close to him as they cried.

The entire group held hands, and one by one, said their goodbyes to their dear employer, father, guardian, mentor, and friend. As they spoke and cried openly, their hearts ached with the weight of their emotions. Each goodbye felt like a physical rending of their souls, leaving them raw and exposed in the wake of their shared grief.

Just before dawn, as both Dane and Katie held his hand, a chill swept through them as Ellis Wellington passed.

With the promise that he would make the arrangements with the undertaker, Dr. Schultz left the family to grieve. One by one, the staff returned to their quarters, and Joel left for home, leaving Dane and Katie alone with Ellis's body.

"Why do people have to die?" Katie said, her eyes red and swollen. The question hung in the air, unanswered.

Dane sat with his elbows resting on the desk, hands clasped at his lips. "I didn't appreciate this before, but all that is left is the love you have shared and perhaps the legacy you leave, the lessons you have taught. And he taught me a great deal. When I was young, he taught me to drive. Later, about finance and real estate, and throughout my life, he encouraged me to do good in the world. My head is filled with his lessons of life, and now I wish to God I had paid closer attention, and more importantly, been more appreciative."

"Dane, you have been a wonderful son to him, and he was so proud of you." Katie's face was red and hot, her fists clenched, as her body heaved with the intensity of her anguish. Living in his home was a dream come true; he had been a father to her. "I have loved living here with him, watching the love and respect the two of you shared. But, it wasn't long enough. I want more time. And I didn't get to play my Chopin Prelude for him."

Locked in an embrace, they tearfully watched as the undertaker removed Ellis's body from the house.

Dane placed his hand on her cheek. "Let's get some sleep. We have a difficult day ahead of us." Dane led her to her bedroom, pulled back the covers, and she crawled in.

Grabbing his hand as he closed the covers over her, she whispered, "Will you stay with me until I fall asleep?"

He settled himself on top of her covers, closed his eyes, and left before she awoke.

By noon, the group was in high gear, making lists of the people to be informed, and dividing the tasks among Joel, Katie, and Dane.

Although Priya's condolences were sincere, and she made it clear that she would have attended the services, Dane, as he beheld Katie, knowing she would need his attention and comfort, thought it best if Priya were not present for the funeral. *Indeed, she would not like the physical closeness that has developed between Katie and me over our mutual grief.*

･♥･♥･♥･♥･♥･

T EN DAYS LATER, THE funeral was a solemn yet impressive affair. In attendance were several dignitaries, socialites, government officials, friends, tenants, bankers, partners, other landowners, and members of the various clubs to which Ellis belonged. Dane hired a violinist who played the classics Ellis loved, and hundreds of people came to the church to bid farewell to the man they revered.

Ellis, dressed in his black wool suit, lay with his hands crossed, holding the ribbons and awards that had been bestowed upon him. Draped over the casket was the King of England's war flag, a poignant tribute to the generous gentleman. Father Lionel conducted the service and spoke personally about Ellis and the stories he had heard from his parishioners.

When the vicar concluded, Dane took the podium. "I want to thank each of you for being here today." Dane touched his chest. "It is quite an honor to see so many people paying their respects. My father was a formidable businessman, a respected veteran, and an exemplary employer. But I realize now that the reason you are all here to commemorate him is because of his gracious heart. He touched each of you personally and implored me to follow that path, repeating his mantra often. 'Be extraordinary. Rise above and do good for others.' And he was that man. Magnanimous. Philanthropic. A great friend. A wonderful father."

Dane paused, breathing deeply and wrapping his fingers tightly around the podium, he steadied himself before continuing, determined to regain composure and get through his speech without losing his voice or breaking down.

"Many of you have conveyed your special stories about him to me today, some I had never heard before. I thank you all for that. Now that he is gone, I realize how precious time actually is, and how much of it I have wasted. He taught me well, and I am aware of my purpose and will forever strive to fulfill his hopes for me. I invite you now to take the podium, if you will, to tell your special tales. Thank you."

George reached to take Dane's arm as he stepped down, then replaced him at the podium, his heartfelt words and the revelations he shared almost breaking Dane. "I was a boxer when I first met Mr. Wellington, an' I 'ad lost a fight, badly. Mr. Wellington 'eard the doctor say I couldn' fight no more. I might 'ave died. That was when Mr. Wellington insisted I end me boxin' days and come work fo' 'im, as 'is driver. He 'elped me gain back me pride an me health." He paused for a moment, gaining the courage to continue. "An, most people don' know this, but I 'ave a son. Was born when his ma and me were just children ou'selves. I didn' know 'im. Wasn' part of 'is life until Mr. Wellington bade me to see 'im. 'Make a go of it,' 'e said. An I did. 'e's a fine boy, an I'm proud a 'im. We are mates, and I am part of 'is life now. Mr. Wellington is the best man I eve'r known. I owe 'im me life."

Mrs. Danbury and the rest of the staff also told their stories about earlier days, Ellis's generosity, and how he had shaped their lives.

Katie's parents and many of the other tenants from Leatherhead were there, as well. Norma seized her daughter in a tender embrace. Words yet unspoken, their deep affection reflected in their eyes, Katie sobbed on her mother's chest. "I know 'ow much ye loved 'im. What a'good man 'e was. He 'as been good t'us all."

Lord, how will I get through this day? Dane thought, holding his aching head. Joel caught his arm, noticing his brother's unsteady stance. Dane hugged him tightly. "Thank God you are here. I want you to know it was Father who suggested you be brought into the business. He was ashamed he had not helped you and mum more when you returned home. It was one of his greatest regrets."

Katie came and took Dane's other arm, and sandwiched between his wife and his brother, Dane smiled, mouthing the words '*Thank you*' in her direction, grateful that he was not alone.

The funeral progressed to the gravesite, attended by only the closest family and friends. Pastor Lionel recited a few more prayers and then Psalm 23. The sky was miserably dark and although there was no storm forecasted, booming thunder interrupted the vicar several times. Katie and Dane shared a questioning look, wondering if it was a coincidence, or if some force was voicing grief as the pastor spoke of the loss of the revered gentleman.

As the polished mahogany casket lowered into the ground, Dane, gathering his strength, threw a fistful of fresh dirt over it. His voice cracked as he spoke to his father one last time. "Thank you for being the best father a man could have. If not for you, I would be nothing. I will forever strive to follow your lead, to be extraordinary, to be generous and humble. You have given me the tools and the education, but more than that, your wisdom and words will remain forever in my head. I only hope I become half the man you were. I love you. Until we meet again."

Dane wiped his eyes with his thumb, his heart breaking as he turned to Katie, her tears raining down her red blotchy face, her emotions ranging from fury to despair. With dirt-filled fists, she looked ready to punch the walls, preparing to slam a fistful of dirt onto the casket, rearing her arm back. Stopping herself, she held the dirt for just a few moments longer, finally letting it trickle from her hand.

"Goodbye Father. Thank you for saving my life, and being there when I needed you. Thank you for making me feel special, and for giving me your love and attention throughout my life. You were the most wonderful father. You gave me the courage and determination to reach for the stars, and I always will. I will forever be grateful for your faith in me, your unending generosity, and your unreserved love. You will rest in my heart for my life to come."

Dane, filled with emotion as she spoke, recalled how the two greeted one another each time they visited, her joy over the piano Ellis had purchased for her when she was young, and his father's anger when he learned she was not in grammar school. He had truly loved her.

And he said one day I will love her too. How could he know? Was he right?

"What a most terrible day," Katie said, dragging her body into Ellis's cherished car. She scooted closer to Dane, laying her head on his shoulder as he wrapped his arms around her in comfort. "What will we do without him?"

Once home, without saying a word, they trudged to their rooms. Katie, hugging her pillow, watched her clock tick through the minutes, then hours. There would be no sleep.

At about half-past three, upon exiting the washroom and noticing Dane's light on, the door ajar, Katie whispered, "Are you awake?" She pushed the door further, as he hadn't answered. She stood in the doorway, her sad, swollen eyes staring, pleading.

His eyes locked on hers as her body heaved intermittently from crying. Closing his eyes for a second, knowing he shouldn't allow it, he lifted the edge of the covers, silently inviting her to slip in. Her bare feet scurrying, she lowered herself onto his bed, her back to his front. He pulled her close, their sorrowful, aching bodies connected. Closing the covers around them, his hand rested just under her breast, his thumb ever so slightly upon it.

They were asleep seconds later, and she left his bed before he woke.

Chapter 18

ON SHAKY GROUND

FEB 11, 1957

A LOUD RAPPING ON his bedroom door jarred Dane to consciousness.

"Mr. Wellington, sir." Mr. Macklin shouted through the door, knocking louder. "Your brother is on the phone for you, sir. Says it's quite urgent."

"Alright, I'm coming," Dane growled. Rubbing his eyes, he crawled to the edge of his bed, donning his slippers and robe. He picked up the phone in the hallway. "Yes?"

"I just heard there's been a devastating earthquake in Derby, near our flats in Nottingham. Radio is saying many buildings have collapsed, and roofs have caved in. Few deaths, but hundreds of buildings destroyed. Our man, Grayson, is doing what he can, but his home is damaged too."

"Is there phone service? Are we able to contact any of our tenants?" Dane asked.

"Phones are working, but most of our tenants still do not have phones, or they have shared lines. One of us will have to assess the damage in person to decide how to accommodate them."

"Alright, I will go. I have known many of them since I was a young lad, and of course, I want to help them. You can help to coordinate from the office. It's in our best interest and theirs to help them while they are scrambling to find accommodations. Can you see if you can find me a room? Not too close. Maybe twenty minutes away. I will call in a couple of hours." Dane hung up the phone and turned to Mr. Macklin.

"Mr. Macklin, you heard, no doubt? There's been an earthquake near our flats in Derby. I need to get there to help our tenants. Would you please gather any surplus blankets and pillows we have and ask Mrs. Macklin to prepare some food and drink so I needn't stop unnecessarily on my way? Thank you."

Hearing the commotion in the hallway, Katie opened her door. "What's happened?"

Dane told her the news and his plans to leave immediately.

Her heart sank. Still on bereavement leave, she avoided solitude at home. "Can I be of help? I can go with you. There might be families needing help, perhaps childcare."

Her pleading eyes, peeking out from the waves of unbrushed hair that cascaded past her shoulders, sealed his decision before he had time to consider more carefully. "Yes, I believe they will require considerable help. Pack some things, and we will be on our way," he said, instructing Mrs. Danbury to inform Joel to book two rooms.

They packed Dane's car with supplies and the basket of food Mrs. Macklin had prepared, and drove three hours towards Nottingham, encountering police directing traffic, closed roads, fallen trees, and gaping sinkholes.

The sight of the collapsed front wall of their ten-unit building stole Dane's breath; a mountain of rubble blocked the entrance, making entry and exit difficult. "Good Lord!" he shouted. The impact also damaged their twelve-unit building's side wall. When he saw it, he breathed, "Bloody Hell."

Since both buildings were evacuated, Dane stopped an auxiliary policeman who was guarding the homes from looters. "Where are the people who live here?"

"There is an emergency shelter at the school," the bobby answered, directing Dane.

The shelter was chaos, the air thick with the sounds of sobbing adults and wailing children. The feeling of helplessness and desperation was palpable as people clung to their loved ones, pets, and precious belongings. A line of men, women, and children stretched across the large school gymnasium as people waited their turn at the Red Cross booth. Katie clung to Dane's arm as they made their way through the sea of dazed faces. The Red Cross volunteer took down the names of their tenants and Dane and Joel's information. Waiting was all that remained.

They passed an area where several small children were being cared for by one ill-equipped male attendant. Katie touched Dane's arm and turned back towards the attendant. "Can I help you?"

"Oh, yes, please! I can't handle this! I don't know what to do," he flustered.

"Don't leave this area or I will never find you," Dane warned. "I will be back."

Katie nodded.

Someone directed Dane to a room with a telephone, and he and Joel coordinated with other landlords and friends willing to loan their summer homes and cottages. After locating and aiding several tenants, Dane rushed back to the makeshift nursery, finding it vacated.

Panic mounted after several volunteers shrugged their shoulders, until a young mother pointed to another building on the campus. He sighed deeply upon witnessing the gaggle of calm children surrounding Katie, some sucking their thumbs, clutching blankets and stuffed animals, listening to her animated voice as she read a story from a picture book. When the story ended, she found Dane staring at her, amazement and relief in his eyes.

As she sat in a child-sized chair, he leaned close and said, "I'm starving. Come with me. We'll be right back." He took her hand to help her rise and never let go until they reached the car.

Inside the car, they gulped down the food and drink Mrs. Macklin had prepared. Katie rested her head against the window, enjoying a moment of silence. "It's so loud in there. My ears are ringing!"

"Mine too. I spoke to Joel. He booked us rooms about twenty minutes from here, said we needed to check in soon, or they might be given away. All the inns are booked."

Dane walked Katie back to her nursery. "I'll be back in about an hour."

Three hours later, the scene in the nursery was quite different from the rest of the loud, unorganized shelter. Sitting on the floor with her back against the wall, Katie was asleep with seven sleeping children sprawled around her, tucked under blankets, pillows, and stuffed animals.

Mother Goose, Dane thought.

The volunteer approached Dane. "She took over and handled them all. I don't know what I would have done without her! Can she come back tomorrow?"

"Yes, of course," he sighed, viewing the calm scene. *I love my wife's heart.*

· ♥ · ♥ · ♥ · ♥ · ♥ ·

THE DARK CLOUDS MOVED quickly, bringing icy rain and relentless winds that whipped at Dane's Jaguar as they slowly navigated the slippery roads towards the inn. Trying to see the road through his racing windshield wipers, he assured both himself and Katie, "We are not too far, another few minutes."

Biting her nails, Katie said, "I hate storms like this. They make me nervous." She sank into the car seat, wrapping a blanket around her. "I've never been alone in an inn before. Hope the wind doesn't howl all night."

Dane shook his head. "We are not sharing a room! Don't even think about it."

"I know. Of course not," she said, staring straight ahead. Both were silent the rest of the way, the wipers' rushing rhythm matching their heartbeats.

The distraught clerk looked up from his desk when they entered the inn. "Are you the Wellingtons by chance?" Dane eyed the families sitting in the small lobby, their exhausted and frightened children clinging desperately to their parents' necks and arms.

"Yes, we are. Hopefully, you still have our rooms?"

The clerk glanced at the other families and said, "You hold the last two rooms, sir. These families have waited hours to see if you arrive."

One mother, clutching two of her three weepy children, stepped forward, worry and fear gripping her voice as she spoke. "Please, sir, there are no other rooms anywhere. We have nowhere else to go. Our home is destroyed. If you could make one room suffice, we would be very grateful."

Dane and Katie looked at one another. Katie frowned at Dane and shrugged. "Of course. We will manage in one room."

Dane sighed, eyeing the precious eyes of a sleepy little boy. As Dane signed them in, Katie covered her sly smile with her hand. Dane shook his head. *At every turn, I am being tested.*

They gathered their belongings from the car, and upon entering their room, they paused, both staring at the small bed.

"We need to use the loo now, before retiring. Don't go outside to use it alone without me." After washing up, changing into their nightclothes, and gobbling the last bites Mrs. Macklin had prepared, Dane built a fire, thankful there was one, and offering Katie the bed, settled himself on the floor nearby. He turned off the lamp and said, "Try to sleep, love."

"Goodnight," she said. But watching him squirm, unable to get comfortable, she said, "This is silly. You'll catch your death if you sleep on the floor. There is room for both of us. Not like we are strangers."

Dane sighed, knowing he would not fall asleep on the floor. "Alright." He climbed in, situating himself so that his back was toward her. Waking after a short while, Dane felt something tickling his face. *Oh, good God!* Somehow, they were back in 'their' position, his hand under her breast, and his thumb resting just upon it. *Bloody hell!* He lay awake, his breaths tightened, wondering if he should move away and if she was awake. He finally gave in, took a breath, and relaxed, not eager to disturb her.

He was up and dressed when she awoke; neither said a word about their night. After stopping for breakfast, they drove an hour to the second shelter, where they immediately connected with several of their tenants, finding them, and many other people, temporary lodging with Joel's help. Once all were settled, they traveled back to the first shelter, where Katie had offered to help with the remaining children. "Don't leave here," Dane warned. "I will be back for you." They shared a moment as Dane placed his hand on her arm.

When they finished for the day, Dane and Katie found an open pub and ate quickly, returning to their room by half past ten.

"You did well today. I'm so very proud of you. You have a brilliant heart," Dane said.

Katie jumped and froze when the howling storm sent tree branches crashing against the window.

Dane, already in bed, lifted the bedcover. "Come on." He had given up trying to stay away from her. She lay down. He inched closer, their bodies almost touching. "Try to rest," he said.

Suddenly, another violent shake rattled the chandelier and everything in the room.

"AH!" she jumped out of bed, unsure of what to do, certain it was another earthquake.

"No, love. I think it was just a truck passing. It's ok, come."

She scurried back. "I'm so frightened, I can't relax."

After half an hour, they were both still awake. She was curled up and shivering. Dane moved closer, tucked his face into the back of her neck, and pulled her close to his body. She reached for his hand and rested it just under her breast, and his thumb once again rested upon it.

Damn, he thought, but he couldn't help himself.

Once again, he woke before her, dressed quickly, and sat in the chair, gazing at her sleeping form, reviewing his actions and feelings. *This cannot happen.*

After a bite of breakfast, they made it back to the shelter, now much more organized. Dane had successfully arranged temporary accommodations for all their tenants.

"I believe we've accomplished our task. We need to be on our way, and I should drive you straight to school, unless you need to stop at the house." *We are getting much too accustomed to sleeping in the same bed!*

Katie shook her head, no. They spent two hours driving in awkward silence, Dane's mind a battlefield of conflicting thoughts.

He pulled off the road for petrol and a bite to eat, and after they ordered, he said, "Katie, I want to apologize. I keep finding myself lying too close to you and with my hand ... where it shouldn't be. Forgive me."

She sighed deeply. "Nothing to forgive. It's my fault, I think. I can't help it." She lowered her eyes. "I find it comforting lying next to you."

They gazed at one another. His knuckles glided tenderly over her cheek. Aware of his racing heart, he thought, *not until a year has passed, as promised.* He swallowed hard. *Good God! A year until consummation was the promise.* 'The subconscious mind,' Joel said.

Chapter 19

SOMETHING BREWING

L ULLED BY THE TRAIN'S locomotion as she headed home for spring
break, Katie checked her watch, then closed her eyes, counting, as
she often did, all the nights they had shared a bed. Mrs. Danbury's words
haunted her. *He will never love.'* The night at the inn during the earthquake
became a consistent dream. *What if it went further? Well, we would be truly
married. What's wrong with that?* As she stepped off the train, she waved to
George standing by the car.

The house was astir with preparations for Joel and Trisha's wedding
when she arrived. The couple was staying at the house to spend time with
Gram, who was arriving the following day. Dane had the painful task of
clearing out his father's bedroom to accommodate Gram, and Katie and Joel
exchanged glances, noting Dane's foul mood.

The conversation during supper centered mostly on the wedding until
Trish asked Katie about school.

"I have finished all my required courses, and am taking psychology
classes now."

"That's wonderful, Katie! Well done!" Trisha said. "Psychology is so
very interesting."

"And, you will be able to analyze all of us! Especially him," Joel said,
pointing to Dane. He laughed lightheartedly.

"Oh, I already have. I know exactly what makes him tick."

Joel crossed his arms and sat back. "Oh, I'd love to hear this."

Dane answered flatly. "Never mind. I don't want to hear all the reasons I am a nutter. What good is that, anyway? I can't change my past."

Katie repeated what she had heard her teacher say. "No. But you can change the way you think about your past. You can work on overcoming the obstacles you have because of your past."

They stared at her. Joel grinned and clapped slowly and loudly. "Quite profound. Well done."

"One day ... perhaps I'll be ready to listen," Dane sighed.

Progress! she thought, smiling at everyone. Joel and Trisha shared a glance as well.

The ladies spent the evening discussing the wedding plans, while the men filled the unseasonably warm night air with their pipe tobacco aroma, drinking gin, and toasting the groom.

· ♥ · ♥ · ♥ · ♥ · ♥ ·

"SHE'S GOT YOUR NUMBER, old boy," Joel said. "And she has her head on straight. I admire her. She is no silly schoolgirl anymore. Not that she ever really was."

Dane stared into space. "I'm aware."

"It's about time you stop fooling around and settle down. You are a fool if you don't act. Someone else will snap up her heart and that will be that. You have but a small window of opportunity, brother."

Dane studied his pipe, taking another puff. "I'm aware."

Joel looked at his brother and shook his head.

Dane looked around to make sure no one was listening. "Let me ask you something. You and Trish, you haven't been intimate... How do you know you will be compatible?"

"I don't have any expectations. I think we will be alright. She is loving... she takes care of me." Joel looked at Dane's tortured face and put his hand on Dane's arm. "Oddly enough." Joel re-lit his pipe and took a puff. "When you have that one person in your life you rely upon, and who relies upon you. To share difficult times, the joys of success, and, hopefully, one day, childbirth. One person, if it's the right person, is all you need or want, indeed." Joel explained further. "We both have this unspoken sense of 'what can I do for you?' It's brilliant, really. I believe you and your wife have it, too. You're just not ready to grasp it. Not all women are like our mother, you know. She was immature and bored. And the circumstances are very different. You think because of that, you can't trust women, but that's not true. Katie, will not disappoint you."

Dane considered his words until the girls interrupted.

"Ok, boys," Trisha said. "We have a question for you. Shall the band play ballroom music or popular music, or both?"

"I don't know, I don't dance," Joel said.

Dane put down his pipe, stood abruptly, snatched Katie by the waist and arm, and started waltzing around the entire length of the pond, humming "The Blue Danube," by Johann Strauss. "I think we should have a brilliant waltz or two, most definitely some foxtrots, and absolutely some popular songs. Why not? I love to dance!" he grinned.

Katie was laughing so hard she could barely breathe, her face alight with amazement. "Oh, my goodness! Dane. What a wonderful dancer you are. You love to dance? Why haven't you told me this? You know how I love to dance."

When he stopped, they were at the other end of the pond. He held her in his arms for a few extra seconds, and then dipped her low, holding her head so she wouldn't lose her balance. His face and lips were so close, taking Katie's breath away.

"Ah," she bubbled, catching her breath and staring at him.

He whispered, "You know why."

Katie lowered her eyes, blushing.

·♥·♥·♥·♥·♥·

T HE NEXT DAY, GEORGE took the girls to Harrods, the most upscale of London's department stores, where they shopped for last-minute things for the wedding and then stopped for tea at the café.

"Are you excited?" Katie asked Trish.

"Oh yes, dear. Terribly. A little nervy, too."

Katie understood her meaning. "Don't worry, Joel is sweet, and he will be gentle. I know he will."

Trish lowered her head and whispered, "I know nothing. Do you?"

"A little. I have learned a bit from Priya," Katie whispered, "and from a book I found in Dane's library."

Trisha's eyes shot up. "What? A book? What kind of book? You don't mean …? There are books about that?"

"Yes! I'll show you when we get home!"

A fit of giggles erupted between them as they looked at one another, Katie taken aback by Trish's naivete, considering Trish was twenty-three.

Trish's expression changed as she regarded the pretty girl. "Dear, I'm truly worried for you. Dane, I mean. He has had many women, of course. And he…well, he is not satisfied with just kissing." She grinned, holding her hand to her mouth.

"I know," Katie said, stirring her tea.

Trish put her hand on Katie's arm. "You must be very, very careful, love. You could lose everything in a blink. He won't marry, you know. I know he is quite a dish. The perfect male specimen, indeed. But, you mustn't give in to him." Trish clapped a hand over her mouth, stifling another giggle that ended in squeals of laughter from both of them.

Katie shook her head, looking down at her tea. "I won't. And he hasn't. He doesn't think of me that way. More like his little sister."

"And you … You want him to kiss you?"

Katie looked at Trish but didn't answer. Her desperate look said it all.

"Oh, dear!" Trish said worriedly, taking her hand. "You are much too innocent to be kissing a man like that. You best not encourage it."

Best not encourage it? Too late. I jumped willingly into his bed. Several times. But he did nothing but sleep.

Later that evening, the group watched television until Mrs. Danbury motioned to Katie to go up to bed.

"Well," Katie said to the group. "I'll leave you all now and say goodnight."

"Goodnight," they answered.

Once out of earshot, Trish said, "She is a darling girl." She looked at Joel, who looked at Dane, who looked away.

·♥·♥·♥·♥·♥·

GRAM, A STYLISH AND elegant American whose teased blonde hair resembled the American actress Doris Day's, arrived the next morning. Dane made the introductions, and Katie and Gram hugged one another warmly. Gram's vibrant orange suit and bold accessories matched her personality perfectly. Her laughter and colorful stories filled the house, as did her lingering perfume. Katie couldn't help but adore her. Even the staff delighted in her presence. Although her words were crisp and clear, she held onto her Eastern European accent, proud that her family had narrowly escaped the Nazis in Poland.

Once the group had settled in the parlor, Mr. Macklin announced a call for Dane from Priya. He took it in the study.

"Priya, darling. How are you, love? Is everything okay?"

"Yes. Everything is fine. I haven't heard from you for a while. Shall I ask you the same question?"

"Oh, yes. Well, actually, I have a house full of people. Family. Trisha and my brother will be married on Saturday, you know."

"Yes, I know. I had assumed I would attend the wedding with you. I'm a little disturbed that you haven't mentioned it. Was just wondering why?"

"Oh, well, it's just family, actually." Dane fumbled for the words. "Just a small crowd. Not a grand affair." He mouthed the word *"Blasted,"* to himself, pacing as best he could with the phone in one hand and the receiver in the other, the cord tangling around his legs.

"I suppose the girl is going?" Priya asked.

"The girl? Katie? Well, yes. She is … sort of family." Dane almost slipped, about to say 'my wife.' He rubbed his forehead. "I mean, she lives here, of course."

Priya was silent. Dane thought that she might be crying, and he closed his eyes waiting for her next words. "Priya?"

"Dane. I'm sorry. I thought I could handle this, but I just cannot. I believe there is … something. I know you are not intimate with her. But there is something, and I … well, she is beautiful, and quite charming. No, it's not that … it's more than that, actually. Your father adored her, and I believe it's just a matter of time … before you and she …" Her voice broke. She paused. Dane heard her take a deep breath. *"Oh, my God. I'm sorry, Dane. I love you. I do. And I've always let you have your freedom. But this is …"* she paused again. Now he was sure she was crying. *"Different. I believe I must say goodbye now. In truth, I cannot watch it develop into something that will utterly destroy me. Goodbye, Dane. Please, don't call me again."*

The line disconnected.

"Oh, Priya, don't be so melodramatic! Priya? Priya?" Dane yelled. "Bloody Hell," he shouted, slamming the phone. "And I thought my life would be the same. The hell it is," he shouted. Brooding in the study before returning to the group, he downed a shot of brandy and mulled over what had just happened. He considered calling her back, his hand remaining on the receiver. In the end, he did nothing but join his family. They were waiting for him to lead them on a tour of "The River Walk," a local park near the narrow portion of the Thames River, close to Wellington Manor.

As usual, the lovely day brought out the street musicians and cart vendors, as well as many well-dressed people strolling, walking dogs, and pushing baby carriages on both sides of the river's tree-lined paths. Children frolicked in the open park, and families gathered at the picnic tables. Katie adored this area, understanding why Mr. Wellington had chosen this spot to call home.

Gram and Katie walked arm in arm, chatting about school, as Gram had been one of the few female students at Philadelphia's University of Pennsylvania and one of the first to be admitted to the faculty. She, like Ellis, regarded education the key to independence, especially for women.

"I decided to move to New York City after my husband, Raffe, passed. I needed a change and a new life, really. New York has given me that life."

Katie spoke of her family and how she came to know Ellis and Dane.

When Gram asked why she came to the house when she was free from school, instead of home to her family, Katie glanced at Dane quickly, who was walking sullenly behind them.

"Oh, there's George," she said, waving to him, avoiding the question. As they squeezed into the car for the short ride home, they glanced at one another, silently questioning Dane's unusual mood.

When they stepped into the house, Katie asked Dane hesitantly, "You seem down. Is everything alright?"

He snapped back, "Oh, yes. Jolly well and good. Priya is done with me. To be expected, I suppose; a beautiful girl living in my house and all." He turned and left abruptly.

A wave of nausea washed over Katie, and she held her stomach, trembling. Flying to her bedroom unnoticed, she dove under her covers.

Joel pulled Dane aside. "What's wrong? Is this about clearing out your father's room?"

They headed for the study with a bottle of port.

Dane paced, then blurted, "Priya has left me. For good this time, I fear."

"What? Why?" Joel tried to appear supportive, clenching his jaw to prevent a growing smile.

Dane's face flushed with anger, nodding toward the upstairs. "I didn't invite her to the wedding. Or the funeral, for that matter. She has taken a back seat and doesn't like it. She thinks ... She thinks there is something brewing, and doesn't want to watch it develop."

"Well, it's understandable," Joel said.

"Blasted. I cared for her. I liked having her..."

"When you wanted her?"

"No! I'm not at all that bloody callus! I did care for her! I enjoyed her company."

"Indeed. You say that. But, may I ask, when did you enjoy her company? I mean, other than in the bedroom. Let me ask you, brother, would you take her out during the day, for instance, just to enjoy her company, with no intimate encounter planned for later? Did you spend time with her, going for walks, or sleep with her without sex, just holding her?"

The brothers faced off, Dane seething at his brother's challenge.

"Would she take care of you if you were sick, as your wife did?" Joel pressed. "I believe your enjoyment of her stemmed from the physical side of your relationship, and not enjoyment of her company! You confuse what your cock needs with what your heart needs. Sex and love are two very different things."

Dane sank into his chair, his head in his hands. "What we had was good. I've never felt what you describe. Love? I don't know what that is. I don't think it's possible for me."

Joel shook his head and pulled up a chair. "You just haven't allowed yourself to love anyone. I'm quite sure sex is totally different when there is a love connection. When you share your entire being." Joel shook his head. "You have had a million women, and perhaps the most erotic and lustful encounters, but you have never made love, brother. You keep your heart locked up deep in that fine chest of yours. Someday, I hope you let someone in, or you will surely be a lonely man with no one to worry about you. Tell me who worries about you, brother?"

They were silent again.

"Your wife does, you know, and she always will. There *is* something brewing...isn't there?" Joel kept pressing. "I know you don't want to admit it. She is innocent, and you have made promises. And that's all well and good. But I see friendship. And that's a bloody good start."

"No." Dane said. His fists in a ball on his lap. "I want easy. I want to be free. Priya is perfect."

Joel leaned forward and lowered his voice. "But, you didn't invite her. Truthfully, I'll bet you hadn't even thought of her. What might that mean? Open your eyes, man!"

Dane's jaw clenched tightly. He grabbed the port and drank from the bottle.

Chapter 20

AND SO IT BEGINS

D ANE, JOEL, AND GRAM, dressed and ready to go to the church, waited for Katie in the parlor. Trish and her mother had just left for the church to dress with Trisha's bridesmaids. Katie had spent two hours helping Trisha with her hair and makeup, replicating the methods the girls had learned at Harrods. Now that Trisha had left, Katie was free to prepare herself.

As Katie descended the staircase, a collective gasp arose. Her deep red chiffon gown, with its cinched waist and flowing skirt, shimmered with each graceful movement.

Mrs. Danbury, standing by the others, beamed with pride.

Joel whistled. "Wow. You look fabulous!" he said, offering his hand as she neared the bottom step.

"Brilliant! You are a sight for sore eyes, dear," Gram exclaimed.

Dane could neither speak, breathe, nor move. He couldn't remember ever having seen a more beautiful or more elegant woman. *Hours after Priya's devastating exit, the most exquisite creature emerges.*

Katie looked at Dane; his eyes were fixed on her in a silent, cold stare. The smile that had brightened her face faded, replaced by a sorrowful frown.

Glancing from Katie to Dane, Gram gave him a puzzled look.

He said nothing, but helped the ladies into the car, seating Gram in front and Katie in the back, next to him. Joel drove separately.

As the Rolls pulled out of the driveway, Dane let out a long breath, and leaning close to Katie, he whispered, "You are not supposed to be lovelier than the bride, you know."

"Wha—?" she said, sucking in her breath.

He looked into her eyes, his face void of humor, he was a man conflicted. "Just stunning." She had turned into an absolute beauty overnight. He was lost. He tried to force himself to keep quiet, to look away.

Katie took a deep, long breath, blinking back tears. "Thank you. You were so angry last night; I thought you hated me. Because of Priya, I mean. I'm so sorry."

"Of course not; it's not your fault you're so lovely." He tried to avoid her eyes, but he couldn't help himself. Their eyes lingered, far longer than a casual glance.

He shook his head, angry at himself for not being in control. He was captivated. Tortured, even. All he wanted to do was lie next to her in his bed. Though he turned to face the window, he saw nothing. *Good Lord! I think I am losing my mind.*

Dane introduced Joel's father to Katie, then excused himself, leaving her with Gram, to take his place next to Joel as Wagner's "Bridal Chorus" began playing.

Gram took Katie's hand as the bridal party sauntered down the aisle, beaming, watching her handsome grandsons in their black tuxedos, walking side by side. Dane stepped aside as Trish's father handed her to Joel. Holding hands, the bride and groom turned and faced one another.

From the altar, Dane studied his wife freely. *What was so different?* Her hair, piled loosely at the back of her head, accented with ringlets that fell around her face, created a soft, almost ethereal look. He had never seen her wear anything but a little lipstick, and usually not even that. *Now, her face and cheekbones seemed more angular, her eyes bluer and larger, and her pink lips fuller. Her figure ... stunning. Not that she wasn't stunning before. But now ...*

He tried to listen to the prayers and the passage from the Bible that followed, but his mind wandered. He pictured lying next to her as they had so many times before, kissing those lips, her neck, her ... Smiling to himself, he tried to focus.

The priest spoke about lifelong commitment and about love and honor. *Why am I breathing so hard? Good Lord!*

Dane caught Gram's smile as she followed her grandson's gaze to the beauty seated next to her.

The crowd roared to its feet, a thunderous applause erupting as Mr. and Mrs. Carrino, their hands clasped tightly, were introduced. They floated down the aisle, followed by Dane escorting Trisha's sister.

"Congratulations!" everyone shouted.

The reception at Trisha's aunt and uncle's stately mansion in Guildford started with the newlyweds' first dance as husband and wife. Their parents and then the bridal party followed. All eyes were on Dane as he whirled Trisha's sister, then Gram, then Trisha's mother, and finally Trisha skillfully around the dance floor.

When the song "The Way You Look Tonight," by Fred Astaire, began to play, Dane appeared by Katie's side, his hand out. "Foxtrot?"

She grinned. "Yes."

Her smile illuminates the room. He led with precision, their eyes never leaving one another's. Their energetic dance in perfect harmony, with grand steps and quick movements, created a feeling of magic and connection that enveloped them both.

"Well done, my dear," he said when the music ended, kissing her hand.

Although it frustrated him to no end, Dane obliged Trish's unescorted friends when they each asked for a dance. His irritation was clear as he passed Katie several times, each dancing with someone else. He wanted to dance only with her. When he was free again, Dane held out his hand for a waltz to "The Blue Danube."

Lost in the rhythm, she followed his lead, their bodies close, their fingers interlaced, and their eyes locked. She was the princess from her beloved novels, dancing with Prince Charming.

An applause from the crowd surprised them, as they hadn't realized they were putting on a show. Joel cheered, "Well done, brother!" Dane answered with a playful bow. Then Trish's sister asked for a dance, and he was gone, again.

When "Only You," by The Platters, started to play, he scurried to his wife just as Trisha's brother was leading her onto the dance floor. Dane quickly interrupted. "This one is promised to me, I'm afraid." Not waiting for an answer, he took her hand and led her to the edge of the floor. Seizing control of her, their conjoined bodies swayed skillfully to the slow, sensual ballad. Neither said a word. The melody and words filled their heads. As his face nuzzled her cheek, his hand held hers by her right side, while the other held her tightly around her waist, forcing her to follow his every movement. Her fingers rooted in his hair, drew him impossibly closer, and she inhaled his intoxicating cologne.

He heard a slight gasp as his manly package crushed against her, and he understood the arousing sensations he had awakened. Both became brilliantly alive, but they were barely moving. He lifted his head to study her eyes, and her lips, and then, without saying a word, leaned once again against her cheek. She was afraid to look at him or anyone else, wondering if they were being observed. When the beautiful music stopped, Dane stopped but didn't let go. He wanted to stand there holding her, and he did until it was awkward not to part. With a quick kiss on her cheek, he left her side, saying, "Excuse me." Katie watched him walk away, barely able to move. She wobbled dizzily to the seat next to Gram.

During the band's break, Dane stood up with a glass of champagne. "A toast!" He waited for everyone to pick up a glass. "To my dear brother, Joel, and his lovely wife, Trisha. May you always be as happy as you are today. Joel, you may be my younger brother, but you are always teaching me something valuable. And today, you teach us all about unconditional love, commitment, and the importance of family. I love you, my brother, and our growing family. To Joel and Trisha! Cheers!"

Everyone shouted, stomped their feet, and drank the last of the champagne.

When the band played pop hits like "School Days," by Chuck Berry, and Elvis Presley's "Hound Dog," Katie joined some of the other girls on the dance floor, enjoying the newer songs.

At a table nearby, Dane sitting with Joel, opened his tie and rolled his sleeves. Drenched and intoxicated, they watched the ladies dancing with one another, but Dane, seemingly in a trance, watched only one.

Joel, following where his brother's attention lay, quipped, "It's getting harder, isn't it? I think I shall win our bet, after all."

"Sod off," Dane replied, sourly. Plopping his head down between his crossed arms on the table.

Joel chuckled and slapped his brother's back. "My God! And, so it begins...I am going to enjoy your suffering."

"I don't know how I got here," Dane muttered. "I don't want anyone else. But, I'm in hell,"

As he exited the restroom, Dane spotted Katie waiting in a line. He quickly threw his hands against the wall, caging her in, his lips almost touching hers.

She could smell his whiskey breath. "Dane Wellington. You are a poorly sight. Piss drunk, and you smell like a wet dog. What do you think you are doing?"

He tried to focus. "I was thinking about kissing you," he said, stammering and trying to focus.

"Why would you think I would want you to do that? I'm not Priya, you know."

He reeled back. "Oh, that was harsh."

Katie gasped. "Oh. I'm sorry...I shouldn't have said that. I only meant that I cannot imagine why you would think it was alright to kiss me? You have made it perfectly clear you are not interested in staying married. That you don't want just one girl. I'm not like Priya, is what I meant. I won't share you...."

Dane tried to balance himself. "I didn't say I was going to kiss you. Only that I was thinking about kissing you. I made a promise, and I intend to keep it, hammered or not."

"Good! Keep it, then," she said, pushing her way out, leaving Dane to lean against the wall for support.

·♥·♥·♥·♥·♥·

I N HIS GROGGY STATE, Dane threw off his damp clothes and crawled into bed. Suddenly she was there in his bed. Her lips, warm and wet, her hands caressing his hair. He undressed her slowly, hearing her gasp. "My darling, wonderful wife. I cannot let you go. You are mine, now and forever." They turned, his hands caressing her breasts and her soft, subtle nipples. His head bent to suckle her nipple, and she groaned from the sensation. As his body covered hers, he told her again and again how much he loved her. He needed her now, needed to be inside of her, possessing her. His release came quickly, the encounter, exactly as she had described it in Barclay's car....

"Oh bloody hell!." He moved away from the wet spot on his sheet, turned over, and punched the pillow he was holding in his arms.

Chapter 21

SHE WOULD LOVE NEW YORK

WITH THUNDERSTORMS KEEPING THEM inside the following day, Dane, Joel, George, and even Mr. Macklin were ecstatic to watch the first-time televised football game while Gram, Trish, and Katie played cards at the dining table.

"It is high time I know what is going on between you two," Gram said to Katie.

Katie told the story from the beginning, including the multiple times Ellis had saved her, her piano, and the encounters with young Dane.

"My father is a drunk. Gambles almost all of his wages…an' he owed Mr. Barclay a small fortune. Mr. Barclay owns a lovely estate and land, and he has a good sum, of course. My parents wanted me married and settled. They pressured me to accept Mr. Barclay. They tried to convince me it was best." She paused a bit, thinking of the awful day he nearly abducted her. "But he is older, quite stumpy looking, and a bit of a bully, too."

"What?" Gram said, covering her mouth. "Your parents tried to marry you off?"

"Dane had discovered what was happening just in time. Rescued me."

"Might as well say the rest of it," Dane chimed in, now leaning on the doorway, listening, his arms crossed.

"What's the rest of it? You kidnapped her?" Gram demanded. "You took her from her home?"

Dane sighed. "Yes, I did do that. But first, we went to the church. Her mother signed the consent, and we were married. Then I took her home. And before you ask, no, not to *my* flat; I brought her here."

The shock on Trish's face almost made Katie laugh. "Oh, my God!" Trish said.

"Dane. Are you telling me Katie is your wife?" Gram shrieked.

Dane pursed his lips and nodded. "That's precisely what I am saying. But, we have not consummated the marriage. It's just for protection. In spite of what you might think, I am and will remain a perfect gentleman. I made a promise to my father, and intend to honor it. We will annul this marriage as soon as she is of age. I have no interest in being married, as you well know."

Hearing Dane's unequivocal words sent Katie's heart crashing, and a quick gasp escaped her lips. *After all this time, he still has not changed his mind.* She blinked back the sting in her eyes, remembering all the glances, gestures, and moments they shared...their dance last night...that gave her just the slightest hope that he might feel something deeper than friendship. *No, he is still shutting that door. That much is certainly clear. No interest...ever.*

Everyone in the room looked at him with shock on their faces, hearing his emphatic statement. All eyes then turned to her, waiting for her response.

Her voice cracked as she desperately shifted the focus to Ellis, a frantic attempt to disguise the pain that threatened to overwhelm her. "Mr. Wellington was overjoyed. He had wanted to send me to school long ago. He and Dane enrolled me in boarding school. Clothed me...oh, so many times. Summer, winter, and school clothing," she laughed, shaking her head. They all laughed as well.

"Mr. Wellington was wonderful, and I miss him so very much. Oh, what I used to sound like. They have both done so much to help me. My whole life has changed." She put her hand on her heart before wiping her eyes.

"Now, never mind all that," Dane said. "You owe me nothing. Father adored you. He loved having you here, as do I. All jolly well and good." Turning back to Gram, "She is away most of the time, but we spend some time together, and when we do it's perfectly ....wond ... ahhh ... pleasant."

They looked at him, catching his mistake. Eyeing their shocked faces, he said, "So, now you all know the truth of it. You can stop looking at me like that. I assure you, nothing sorted is going on."

Gram took Katie's hand while glancing at Dane's nervous leg.

"My dear girl, you have been through quite an ordeal. If you ever need someone to speak with, you must remember to reach me."

Katie smiled, blinking back her tears. "Thank you."

Gram leaned closer. "I saw that dance last night." Placing her hand on Katie's, she whispered, "He'll come around, dear. Have faith. It's beshert. The Yiddish word for it's meant to be.'"

"Can we please have supper now? I'm famished." Dane peered at Mrs. Danbury and Mrs. Macklin, who had each gotten absorbed in the conversation.

·♥·♥·♥·♥·♥·

AFTER SUPPER, GRAM TOOK Dane's arm.

"I know you, Dane Wellington. You are your father's son. You look at her the way your father looked at your mother. Who do you think you are fooling?"

Dane looked at his grandmother. "I haven't touched her."

"Not, yet, you mean," she said, eyeing her grandson sternly.

Dane caught his breath. It's all he wanted to do, truthfully. Touch her. Kiss her. His loins ached with the thought of her.

Gram shook her finger at him, warning him sternly. "If you finalize this marriage, you must be true to her. You cannot run around as you do now."

"I would never. And I will not finalize it. The marriage must be annulled."

"You mustn't take advantage of her. She needs time to blossom. To figure out who she is and what she wants for herself. Your mother should have had more time. She was twenty three but less mature than your girl."

"I know Father loved her, and she broke his heart. But I have long suspected Mother was pregnant when they married."

"Well, I suppose they might not have married, had they not gotten caught. Had they known one another better, maybe they would have realized they were not compatible."

"Why wasn't she happy?"

"He was English!" Gram's hand flew to her mouth and then his arm. "I'm sorry. I didn't mean that." But Dane already knew his grandmother blamed his father for his mother's eventual misconduct and ultimate disgrace. "He was considerably older than she. Proper. I'll give you that. Your mother was young and high spirited and quite infatuated with Ellis. She certainly was not ready to settle down with a child and a husband who had nothing but business on his mind. He wasn't interested in music or dancing. He had little time for fun. So, she occupied herself with music clubs and their drummers... He should have tried harder to make her happy. Taken her dancing. It would not have been that hard."

Dane placed his hand on his grandmother's arm.

Gram flashed her eyes at Dane, a thought occurring to her. "Maybe you ought to bring her to New York next time you come? Show her New York University and Columbia? We can introduce her to my friend in admissions at N.Y.U." They turned to regard Katie speaking to Joel and Trish.

He needed her far away. "New York. She would love New York." Dane looked at his grandmother. "Brilliant!" Dane nodded as he studied his wife. "Perhaps you are right. Maybe she needs to know a bit of the world before we spend any more time together."

Gram studied her grandson as he stared at his wife. "You must be honest with yourself, my dear. Would you really want her to go so far away?"

Though he didn't respond, Gram saw the answer in his eyes.

Chapter 22

THE DEBUTANTES

D ANE SAT AT HIS desk, trying to decide the most appropriate note to send to Katie for their anniversary. *Has it been a year already?* One after the other went into the trash. *What can I say that doesn't sound mean or condescending? "Dear Katie, although our marriage isn't real, you have been the best fake wife. Happy Anniversary." Good God.* Dane chuckled as he crumbled the paper into a ball and shot it into the trash. In the end, he wrote. *"I couldn't let our anniversary go unacknowledged, love. Thinking of you, Dane."*

Aware of his profound attraction, Dane was determined to keep the promise he made, occupying himself with work, only meeting Katie for daytime lunches or outings in the afternoons. There were no nights when they were both in the Weybridge home together. He encouraged her to invite her sisters to the house over her two-week summer break, as he would be gone to Bath and London a good deal of that time. And although he told himself he was looking to replace Priya, the truth was there wasn't an inkling of interest in any other girl.

My life is perfect the way it is, he tried to convince himself. Although, each time they were together, his body betrayed him; shaking, heating, sweating. He longed to hold her, to ... *Stop it. I must stop thinking about it!*

·♥·♥·♥·♥·♥·

Invitations to the Debutante Balls came in every season by the bundles, but Dane usually avoided them, as the young debutantes were there for one purpose only: to snag a prominent husband. He did, however, accept the invitation for a ball at the Harley House in Brighton, sent by the Earl of Oxford himself. Although Katie's non-noble birth prevented her presentation to the Queen, this ball, with its many guests and debutantes, would be suitable for her to attend as his guest.

As Harley House was close to Katie's school, Dane engaged George for the ride to and from Brighton, availing a drop-off at her school afterward. Knowing he needed to distance himself, Dane trusted that George's involvement assured him he would be back where he belonged by evening's end, no matter his level of intoxication.

He couldn't help but lose his mind, grinning like a schoolboy as he watched her emerge from her dorm, sauntering toward the Rolls in a breathtaking flowing ensemble of gold and beige silk. *That dress must have been designed just for her.* Her shawl, shoes, handbag and even shimmering stockings all coordinated perfectly, accentuating her waist and almost bare shoulders. The dress's full skirts billowed out from the waist with layers of chiffon, ending just above her slim ankles. She was the epitome of fashion and elegance.

George shot Dane a look, almost smirking at Dane's obvious pain.

"How absolutely brilliant. You are stunning," he said, kissing her cheeks and opening the car door.

"Good evening, Dane. Thank you. Hello George!"

"Hello, Miss. You look lovely, Miss."

Katie giggled.

With only minutes to have her all to himself before the inevitable onslaught of men vying for her attention, he savored the quiet moment. He tried not to stare, but it was no use; he was in over his head. Taking her hand and kissing it, and noticing the flower basket necklace resting just above the barest hint of cleavage, he allowed himself a few moments of unchecked longing.

"You look very dapper in those tails," she said, staring right back.

Harley House was a grand estate set on six acres of rolling hills overlooking the ocean. There were indoor and outdoor pools, tennis courts, several cottages, a pool house, and stables scattered about the grounds.

A few of Katie's friends were debutantes this season, including her roommate Lizzy. A hush fell over the crowd as an awestruck Katie watched the girls curtsy to the Queen and Prince Philip. Dressed in white, one by one, they made their way to the Royals in a most regal spectacle.

Lizzy hugged Katie afterward. "I'm sorry you couldn't be presented."

Katie shook her head. "It doesn't matter. I'm standing in the same room as the Queen. My gosh."

When the presentations ended, the six-member band began to play classic ballroom music. Much to Dane's chagrin, as predicted, many men were competing for Katie's attention, and he found it difficult to secure many dances with her. But the ones they danced together looked well rehearsed.

She was the perfect height for his large frame, however, it was their elegant attire, the way their eyes never left one another's, and their body language that attracted the attention of everyone in the room.

Chapter 23

SEASONS CHANGE

WHEN THEY RETURNED TO the house, Mrs. Danbury said, "Your neighbor, Miss Lucy rang. She was askin' if you would mind 'er little one tonight. Here is 'er number."

"Thank you, Mrs. Danbury." Katie took the phone number and went to the phone. When she returned, she said, "Lucy's husband is here on leave for the weekend. They would like to go out for a while and asked me to sit with Lilian. I said I would. Hope that's alright with you."

"Yes, of course. I'll walk you over." On their way, they shuddered at the darkening sky and fast-moving rain clouds. "Please call me when you are ready to come back, it will be quite a nasty storm."

Lucy's husband, Henry, was tall, with short reddish-brown hair, and a sweet, oval face peppered with red freckles. Katie loved the way they looked at one another and thought about the hardship Lucy endured, with her husband being away in the military. Katie greeted Lilian with a hug as their excited pup, Buster, danced around her feet. Lucy gave Katie some instructions about Lilian, and Katie distracted the little girl as her parents slipped out. After supper, a bath, two children's books, and a bottle, the little one was off to sleep.

Back in the living room, tucked under a throw with Buster snuggling close, Katie relaxed with the television on—a welcome treat because the school allowed only the news channel in the main room.

She did not notice the weather worsening until a vicious, windy gust shook the windows, startling her and sending Buster into a barking frenzy. A torrent of rain began pounding the roof, and Katie recoiled as crackling thunder shook the house. Huddled on the sofa hugging Buster, she watched for the next lightning, counting the seconds until the thunder struck. "Don't worry. It's only a storm," she whispered to Buster, petting his ears.

Suddenly, all went dark. Katie gasped, kicking herself for not searching for the candles and matches when she saw the lightning. She cowered under the throw instead, wishing she had lit the fireplace.

"Katie!" Dane's voice rang out over the howling storm. Buster, barking wildly, scurried to the door.

Katie caught a glimpse of a figure with a flashlight, and darted to the door. "Dane!" Though he was soaked, she clutched him fiercely, pulling him into the house. "I didn't know what to do. I don't know where the matches are."

"I figured." He grinned calmly. "I brought matches and a flashlight." He shook his trench coat and hat.

"I'm so happy to see you!" she sighed with relief. "Again, you came to my rescue."

"Well, there is nothing magical about noticing a blackout. I just guessed you wouldn't have known where matches and candles were."

"And I appreciate your thoughtfulness. Thank you for coming."

Katie watched as Dane transformed the darkness, igniting a stack of old newspapers, their edges crackling and curling as the flames spread to the logs. He removed his wet shoes and socks, placing them close to the fire.

"Your pants are wet too," she said.

Grinning, he cocked his head. "I don't think I will take off my pants. I'll just sit by the fire."

Blimey! She blushed, grateful that the ring of the phone interrupted her thoughts.

"Hello?"

"Katie, this is Lucy. I take it you have lost electricity as well? Are you alright?"

"Yes! Dane is here with me, and Lilian is sleeping. We are fine."

"We were just finishing our supper at The Savoy when the lights went out. We are thinking of taking a room here. Would it be too much of an inconvenience for you to stay the night? If it is, we could likely make it back by midnight, I suppose."

"Let me check with Dane." Katie covered the mouthpiece and glanced at Dane.

Dane threw his head back. "Let me guess. They want to spend the night."

His sarcastic remark troubled her, but she awaited an answer.

"Fine. I will stay." He threw his hands up in concession.

"We will be fine. Yes. It's my pleasure. Ok. Yes, Goodnight." Furrowing her eyebrows, she thought, *Is he angry?*

"Bloody hell!" he said under his breath, running his hand through his hair.

"Dane, I'm perfectly fine here. Really. I was only shaken because I was in the dark, but you've fixed that. You don't need to babysit me. Leave the flashlight with me and go home."

"You must be mad," he barked. "You think I would leave you here all alone, with no electricity?"

She shook her head, no. The sudden, deafening crack of thunder shook the house, sending her bounding over to the fireplace where he sat.

"I know you don't want to be here. The thunder is only jarring. I'll be ok, really; I'm twenty next month! I'm not a child. But, thank you, again, for coming."

He shot a look to her but then softened his gaze and his tone. "I wouldn't think of leaving you."

"Thank you." She didn't have time to consider the possible long-term meaning of his words, as Lilian was whimpering, likely startled by Buster's barking. They sat quietly, waiting to see if she would settle. But when another booming thunder shook the house, she woke in earnest.

Katie sighed. "Oh, I'm sorry."

Settling Lilian on the cushions Dane had placed on the floor, Katie lay down next to her, humming a lullaby while stroking her head.

Dane watched with amazement as the child fell into blissful slumber. "You will make a wonderful mother one day," he whispered.

They shared a glance, and she took in the moment. A warm fire-lit home, candles flickering, a dog lying peacefully, a child sleeping. It was a scene she loved, and she knew he dreaded.

"And I think you'll make a wonderful father one day, too. I know you don't think so. But, you're wrong."

He looked away from them, brushed back his hair and sat holding his knees to his chest, lost in thought.

He didn't have a mother who was there to soothe or comfort him. How sad. "I think I can put her back in her bed now."

Lilian back in her crib, Katie came back to the living room, seeing the two separate beds Dane had made on the floor near the fireplace, each with pillows, blankets, and throws from the sofa.

"You can sleep here, or you can go into their bedroom. I'm sure they won't mind under the circumstances. I will stay here."

"Thank you. I'm sorry you have to stay. I feel awful."

A silly grin lit him up. "It's all well and good, love. I found a bottle of vodka and some orange juice. Sound good? I doubt vodka is the answer, but ..."

"It's worth a shot," they said in unison, laughing.

"My pop tells that joke." They stared at one another, their laughter fading. This time, Katie broke the moment. "I'm a bit hungry. I better not have any vodka without eating first." She went to the kitchen with the flashlight and returned with some biscuits, butter, jam, cheese bits, and two sliced apples. They had a picnic near the fire.

"Dane, may I ask you a few questions? I have no one else to ask." She could not look at him.

"Are you going to ask me about sex again?"

Katie gigged. "The girls you are with. You are not afraid they will get pregnant?"

He swallowed hard. "They won't. I use protection."

"Protection?"

"Sort of a very thin sheath." They both looked away uncomfortably. *The book did not mention any protection.* "Everyone has told me that I must be careful. Especially with you. The women you court, they haven't saved themselves for marriage. Why not? And, more importantly...Do men really care? I mean, if Trisha had not been whole, would Joel have cared?"

"I honestly don't know the answer to that. Many men do care, I'm afraid." Squinting at her, he said, "And, who has been telling you to be careful with me?"

"Never mind!" she giggled. "But that would suggest it would be far more advantageous to remain a virgin. So, why are all the girls you court ... not?"

"Well, good question. I don't know the answer. Everyone has their own reasons, I suppose. Priya, for instance, cannot have children. Most men will not want to marry her for that reason. Other girls I know are innately promiscuous. I did ask Joel how could he marry, not knowing if they will be compatible."

"What did he say?"

"He said their love is extraordinary, that they already live the life of giving so completely, that he had faith all will be well.

Katie gestured with her hands to her heart. "Aw."

"There is no easy answer. This is a recent conundrum. With birth control becoming more common, women have more freedom, and abstinence is now not as necessary. But society hasn't changed their opinions, of course." He paused and looked at her tenderly. "I don't think you'd like that sort of reputation." They shared a long moment. "And frankly, some men are not as trustworthy as I."

She gave him a puzzled squint.

"The protection only works if you use it. Every. Single. Time," he said with a sly grin.

She giggled again, allowing herself to look at him for a second. His eyes were already on her. She looked away shyly.

"Thank you. I appreciate you answering my questions." She lay down on her blanket, studying his broad back as he turned towards the fireplace to add two more logs. "What does it feel like? I mean, kissing? Is it like what we see in the films? That passion? Is it like that?"

Dane paused for several seconds. Katie thought he might not have heard her question. "Yes," he whispered.

Was she imagining it? She thought she heard him curse. Oh, how she wanted him to turn around and take her, the blazing fire and darkness surrounding them setting the stage for a heated exchange.

"Come now, no more of this. You are much too interested in sex, young lady. I sincerely hope you are not asking me to kiss you!" He swiped his hand over his face, still facing toward the fire.

She adjusted her pillow and turned away from him. "No, of course not." She thought quickly. "It's only that I fancy a boy I know," she heard herself say. She bit her lip and closed her eyes, apologizing to God for telling a lie.

Dane attacked the fire logs with a vicious poke and snuffed the candles.

Warm and sated, they soon settled down into their makeshift beds. The heavy rain calmed to a soothing rhythm and the aroma of the burning oak and the snuffed candles filled the air. Buster was already fast asleep on his little blanket.

"Goodnight, love. Try to sleep." He reached his palm to the top of her soft head. "Bloody hell," he said under his breath, shifting himself in his very uncomfortable state. Turning onto his back, he bunched the blankets under his knees, trying to get comfortable on the hard floor.

A hair-raising crack of thunder shook the house again, and Katie lurched, throwing her throw over her head.

"Oh, Lord, not again," he mumbled, closing his eyes, his fingers pinching the bridge of his nose. "I know what you are thinking. Honestly, we mustn't sleep all cuddled up. I'm trying desperately hard to keep my distance. You are not making it easy."

"I didn't turn off the electricity!" she mumbled.

He sighed. "I know. For two people not courting, we certainly do sleep together quite often. What do you make of that?"

She giggled.

"Seems a conspiracy. Perhaps it's something predetermined, as Father mentioned. I'll have to speak to him about it again."

She gasped, uncovering herself and turning to face him. "You speak to your father?"

"Yes."

"Does he answer?"

He laughed. "Yes. In his way. Yes."

She sighed, tears pooling, thinking of Ellis. "Please, tell him hello from me. And that I miss him terribly."

Dane's eyes softened at the thought. "I will, but you ought to speak to him yourself."

They stared at one another for a few seconds. Their silence, deafening.

"Oh, Bloody hell! Turn over." He untucked his blankets and hers, pulling her close into the fetal position, cradling her with his arm, one hand just under her breast, his thumb slightly upon it. Moving her hair out of his face, he took in her scent, inching closer to her neck. He adjusted himself, but his slacks did nothing to hide his uncontrollable smoldering shaft, which he tried, unsuccessfully, to keep from digging into her behind. "Happy now?"

·♥·♥·♥·♥·♥·

THEY WOKE TO LILIAN whimpering and Buster licking their faces in the bright morning light.

"Oh! How beautiful it is outside!" She opened the door to let Buster out, then grabbed Lilian, changed her diaper, and brought her out to sit with Dane as she prepared a bottle.

Buster came running back, his little paws wet. He rubbed his back on the rug, begging for a belly rub. Lilian petted her sweet puppy gently. Dane marveled how tolerant and sweet Buster was with her, while Katie noted how sweet Dane was with Lilian. He had told her several times he didn't want children. But now, watching him play with her, new hope surged through her soul as they shared another moment. She noted the way he looked at her, at Lillian, and the calm, almost resigned look in his eyes. *He feels something. He is re-considering!*

Finding eggs, a loaf of bread, cinnamon, and powdered sugar, she grabbed the matches and lit the gas range. Dane watched his very capable wife take charge, and soon the house smelled of her delicious concoction. Little Lilian ate all that was on her plate, dipping her finger into the leftover syrup. Buster was going crazy smelling the plates, thrilled to get a few leftover pieces that he gobbled up within seconds.

Lucy and Henry arrived an hour later, immensely grateful for the time they got to spend alone together.

Lucy handed Katie a large wad of cash.

Katie shook her head. "Oh, this is too much!"

"No, it isn't! We got to spend the entire night together, alone!"

"Thank you." Katie said, taking the money reluctantly. *And I got to spend the entire night wrapped in Dane's arms, thank you.*

Chapter 24

NEVER BEEN KISSED

A FTER SETTLING IN THE conservatory, Dane's eyes, topping the edge of the Saturday Times, regarded Katie's reading material as she sat near the fireplace. *A school book?* As he watched her covertly, he saw she was turning pages inside the larger book. When she left for the loo, he got up to investigate. He chuckled to himself. Sure enough, it was the sex book from his library tucked inside the larger history book.

Upon her return, she saw him holding both books and gasped, covering her mouth with her hands.

"You are such a little devil! Why are you reading this? Good God, girl. Is that all you think about?" He bit his lip to keep from laughing out loud.

Her eyes widened in mortal embarrassment.

He shook his head. "It can't happen. You can read all you want. But it can't and won't happen as that would consummate our marriage."

She sighed. "I know. Before coming here, all I knew about sex was that it was something women must do to please their husbands. Now I believe there is more to it. So, yes. I want to know more. A lot more. Doesn't mean I want to do it, certainly not anytime soon. And, not with you. You are too old." She bit her lip as she said, "And as I said before, I have met someone I fancy."

He studied her, trying not to admit that his jealousy over her interest in someone else was real.

Seeing Dane's soured, indignant face, she said, "OK, maybe you're not that old."

"I'm just twenty-six in November."

They both chuckled, although his was forced.

"My friends and I, we talk about what it's like to kiss." He could hear her frustration in her voice. "I am twenty next month and I've never been kissed!"

"Don't you realize that one thing leads to another? Kissing starts the engines, and men are looking for more than kissing. And I am a man young lady. I am accustomed to taking it, well, further."

"I know." She sat quickly, picked up a different book and stared at the words, unable to focus.

He took a deep breath and exhaled, thinking, *She really knows nothing. I do indeed want to kiss you, love. Very much.* Shoveling his hair back, he shook his head. *Don't say it. Don't do it.* Instead, he took a seat next to her and calmly explained. "It's just a natural thing. When you kiss, your body releases hormones and sends signals to your brain to make you desperate to take it further. That book explains it more succinctly. All species, really, have an innate need, and that need, when fulfilled, creates life and secures the species. It's a need we all have, and kissing starts things rolling." He rubbed his temples. "I made a promise to my father. I cannot break that." *Oh, good lord. The year has long passed.*

"I don't want you to kiss me. You asked me why I was reading the book. It's not about you. Are you that conceited that you think all girls fall at your feet?"

He pursed his lips.

Just then, the song "Cheek to Cheek," by Fred Astaire, started playing on the radio. Dane could not resist, and a sly grin crossed his face. "Oh! Such a wonderful Foxtrot!" He held out his hand, helped her up, and started dancing and singing the words. She giggled, grinning from ear to ear. He showed her a few steps she had missed at the wedding, twirling her around and kissing her on the cheek when the song ended.

She turned her face up to his. Dane knew that look. A look that said, *"Please kiss me."* His resolve was fading fast. Their faces so close. *She has never been kissed!*

"Lunch is ready," Mrs. Macklin said, surprise plastered on her face.

· ♥ · ♥ · ♥ · ♥ · ♥ ·

THEY TOOK OFF AFTER lunch to see *The Prince and The Showgirl* with Marilyn Monroe and Laurence Olivier. It certainly had the elements both loved... grand balls, lots of dancing, and physical comedy. Afterward, they stopped at a nearby pub.

"I didn't get a chance to thank you properly for all my new clothes. I'm sorry for the added expense."

"Nonsense. I like seeing you in pretty dresses. Buy what you want." He smiled at her, trying to maintain his external composure. The cheerful shouts of patrons, the vibrant music, and the general raucous atmosphere of the busy pub failed to distract them. They shared moments of silence with thoughtful stares and heavily beating hearts.

"My sisters are sick, so they are not coming tomorrow. I'm going with Lizzy to the fair, instead. You are welcome to join."

"I think I'll pass on that. Don't go to fairs much. Haven't been in years."

"You never took Priya?

"No. Only to a film or dinner, but not much during the daytime, unless it was absolutely necessary."

"Oh, That's sad. You didn't enjoy being with her, then?"

"In the evenings, you know," he winked.

She giggled, shyly. "You rake."

Both were silent during the ride home.

Standing at the foot of the stairs, Dane said, "Goodnight, love. I'm heading outside for a brandy and a smoke."

She stared at him. Her lips pressed together. "Goodnight. Thank you for a lovely day."

His eyes followed her up the stairs. With cigarettes and brandy bottle in hand, he headed outside, mulling over his circumstances.

Sleep eluded both of them, each ill at ease. They had spent not a moment apart that day. *Surely,* Dane thought, *if Mrs. Danbury wasn't in this house, she would be in my bed tonight. Oh, blasted. That's not likely. She is not Priya. A girl like her is all or nothing.* He hadn't really ever been with a girl like her, though. He suddenly realized he had a pillow in his arms again, holding it as he did her. *Hells Bells. How the bloody hell had this happened? Priya was right, after all.* Dane pulled the pillow over his face and growled into it.

In the morning, Katie hung up the phone and entered the kitchen, throwing up her hands in frustration. "There goes the fair. Lizzy is sick, now, too."

Mrs. Macklin brought Dane a few scones, butter, and jam, and caught his face as he observed his wife making her tea, still in her night-dress and robe.

"I'll take you to the fair," he said.

Mrs. Macklin turned to look at him, her face a mixture of stunned disbelief and pure thrill.

Katie, tea in hand, looked up, frozen. "Oh, no. I couldn't impose. You don't like that," she said, her heart racing wildly.

His face softened, and he bit his lip. He smirked and shook his head, as though he had just lost a fight. "Let's go. Go get dressed. And I'll take you to school directly, so take everything you need."

Katie stood staring, her breaths, rapid and stuttered.

"Go on!" he said. *Good Lord, what has gotten into me?* He caught Mrs. Macklin's knowing grin and shook his head.

Katie bolted to her room. She tried on five different outfits before she was satisfied, then styled and re-styled her hair three different ways, finally settling for a ponytail.

In the car, she said, "Thank you for taking me. I have only been a few times, mostly to help Mrs. Smith run the pie-eating contest."

"I think I was a boy the last time I went," Dane said, remembering going with his father.

They laughed the whole day and ate a mountain of fair food. He found himself wanting to kiss her. Several times, in fact. His eyes studied her lips when he removed a piece of pie with his finger. Their eyes met more and more frequently and lingered longer before awkwardly looking away.

Dane won the rifle shooting contest, and she chose a stuffed pink pig as the prize. They played around in the Maze of Mirrors and later relaxed with some ales and chips, while enjoying the Battle of the Bands. Checking his watch, he said, "We need to get you to school, are you ready to go?"

She nodded. "I had a grand time, thank you."

"It was fun, wasn't it?" *Good Lord. I have done something fun with a girl, all day in fact, without it turning into a sexual encounter.* Remembering Joel's words, he said, "Hmph."

When they got close to the school, he turned down a country road, pulled into a field, and turned off the motor. He could feel his heart racing.

"Why have we stopped?" she asked.

Dane could not stop himself from reaching over, pulling her head to his, and touching his lips to hers, slowly and ever so gently at first, and then with much more fever, finally letting go of the raging desire they both withheld for so very long. Their long-awaited embrace was finally being filled with indescribable hunger, filling her heart so that she soon had tears rolling down her cheeks from the pure joy she felt from his loving kiss.

Dane's reaction to the kiss was startling. Yes, there had been the heat between his legs, a usual occurrence when kissing, but there was something else. An emotion, along with a longing he was not quite familiar with. He kissed her again, and then again. Cupping the side of her face, his thumb traced the delicate curve of her neck and his fingers softly caressed her ears. With a passionate touch that made her swoon, he let his hand caress her neck, then chest, then under her blouse to her bare breast, knowing he probably shouldn't, while his thumb glided over her nipple.

"Oh!" she said. She cupped her hand over his, holding it there, as if to say, '*Don't let go.*' Again, his mouth smothered hers, and she breathed. "Blimey, what a miraculous feeling!" He saw her face flush a deep red and her breath coming in ragged gasps.

Tenderly, his hand back on her cheek, he forced himself into retreat. "So, there now. You have been thoroughly and properly kissed. I pray that will hold you for a good long while." *And me.* "And it changes nothing. We are not courting, not a couple. Not going to happen again."

Breathless and giddy, she nodded excitedly. "Oh my," she said dizzily.

"You see how one thing can lead to another? You are wrong that I don't want to kiss you, love. But, once you start, it's very hard to stop. If we were lying on my bed right now, I'd ..." *want to strip you bare.* He stroked her neck under her hair. She responded, closing her eyes to his touch. Noting her passionate response, feeling the familiar pang in his shorts, he sighed, knowing the need he felt would not be satisfied any time soon.

"I do see that. And, I did not want you to stop. The book describes the *how,* but it cannot describe the *feeling.* Thank you for showing me." Unable to contain her absolute euphoria, she began laughing and kicking the floor with both feet in girlish delight.

Dane laughed at her giddiness as he started the car, shaking his head. *She is a beautiful, incredibly passionate, wonderfully joyful ch– No, not a child. She's a magnificent woman, actually. Blasted.* And he was in plenty of trouble. Thankful to be taking her to school.

LIFE'S GREATEST LEGACY

A SINKHOLE THE SIZE of a bus caused considerable damage to one of their cottages near Bath. Dane had been there all week getting bids for reconstruction.

Whatever is happening with Katie would certainly take time. In his hotel room, he picked up the phone, asking the hotel operator to connect him with Michelle Dugan. As he waited to be connected, he flashed to the night at Lucy's and their tender cuddle. Reliving the passionate kiss in his car, he replaced the receiver and spoke softly into the room. "Sorry Michelle. I can neither imagine my arms around you nor kissing you. I am unable." *Bloody Hell. What is wrong with me?*

Katie, Mrs. Macklin, and Mrs. Danbury were busy with preparations for the birthday party Dane had arranged for Katie. As she helped with rolling the dough, Katie asked, "Mrs. Macklin, if you tell the same lie twice to the same person, does it count as another lie?"

The ladies looked at her and grinned at one another. "I don't believe it does, dear," Mrs. Macklin answered.

"Happy Birthday, darling," Dane bellowed. "And Mrs. Macklin, thank you for this wonderful meal. Best lamb stew I have ever tasted." Dane held his hands to his stomach.

Mrs. Macklin said, "I 'ope you left room for this," as she presented a chocolate crème cake with twenty candles. Katie's siblings and mother, joyous to be all together once again, sang birthday songs, and, later, danced in the parlor to Katie's rock and roll records. Dane chuckled, noticing the beautiful dresses her sisters wore, each vaguely familiar. *But not nearly as lovely as they had looked previously.*

At the end of the evening, George took Katie's siblings home, leaving Katie and Dane alone in the parlor.

"I don't have a birthday gift for you. There was an emergency, and I have been away. But, I wanted to purchase a pair of pearl earrings. Would you like that?"

"Oh, no. You have spent a fortune on me! My clothing bills alone must be dizzying! Don't you dare think of getting me anything else!"

They stared at one another. *Don't do it,* he told himself, forcing his feet to remain where they were.

"What I would love, however ..."

"What?" *A kiss, no doubt. Oh boy ...*his chest erupted.

"Would you consider taking me to New York for Christmas?"

Dane sighed, relieved she wasn't asking to be kissed. *She would love New York.* "Yes, I will consider it."

"Thank you. And thank you for such a lovely party." She stepped closer, their eyes locked.

"Goodnight, Dane." Up on her toes, her lips brushed his cheek. He stood perfectly still, his breath slow and steady, fighting the monstrous urge to take her in his arms and smother her with kisses.

"Goodnight, love." He turned towards his study to grab a bottle of whisky, which he brought to his bedroom without a glass.

·♥·♥·♥·♥·♥·

I N THEIR OFFICES, JOEL and Dane studied the plans for the reconstruction of the Bath cottage. Katie's birthday request hadn't left his mind for a second. He weighed the pros and cons. *She will see New York. Maybe she will want to go to university there. But do I want her so far away? Bloody hell, no.*

"Where are you? What's on your mind? Joel asked.

"What? Oh. Well, I am considering bringing Katie with us to Gram's."

"You are going to bring a girl to New York, whom you are not intimate with?

"She'll have a room of her own. Gram suggested it. I think Katie will love New York. I'll bring her to see the campuses of N.Y.U. and Columbia. Perhaps she'll apply."

"Fine with me. What's the worst that could happen? You consummate your marriage? Not so bad. I'd be thrilled, actually. Trish too. And, if that doesn't happen, at least she is good company. Trish will have a mate to go shopping with. And perhaps we can scoot out to play some ball." Joel gave his brother a playfully devilish grin.

Dane picked Katie up on her last day of school for winter break and they headed straight to Harrods. He followed her around the store this time, helping her choose the few items she needed. In the lingerie department, his interest peaked, playfully fingering a pink bra and panty set. She hit his hand and scurried away, giving him a nasty look. Dane bit his lip and tried not to think of her in it, admiring the slight change in her bustline.

When Dane playfully placed a top designer's fur-trimmed hat on her head, he gasped. The red wool hat with the black fox trim, the matching gloves, and fox muff were a must!

"Oh Dane, it's too much! You spoil me! I don't know how to thank you, truly."

She gasped at his seductive grin, understanding the look that said, *"I know how you can thank me."*

She hit his arm coyly and whispered, "Believe me, I know how to thank you properly, as soon as there's a bit of gold on my finger."

He chuckled at her response, a stark contrast to his previous aversion to that notion.

After shopping, they went for tea and then to see the blockbuster film *An Affair to Remember* with her favorite stars Cary Grant and Deborah Kerr. Inside the dark cinema, Dane studied her face.

"I've missed you, love," he whispered. Her brilliant smile lit up her eyes. He took her hand to his lips and kissed it, holding it through the entire picture.

During the show, Katie squeezed Dane's hand tightly, yelping when the female character was tragically hit by a car and paralyzed while exiting a cab at the Empire State Building, missing the Valentine's Day rendezvous with her love.

"Oh, how perfectly heartbreaking, and so wonderful! I couldn't stop crying! He didn't know she was there! She didn't think he would want her, but he did! Oh, my goodness...Oh! So brilliant! I loved it! I loved it so much!"

Dane laughed. "I love how you get so enthralled by these films and their stories."

"I hope to be in love like that one day," she sighed, holding her heart. "Don't you?"

"I don't know if I believe in being in love. I've always thought it was rubbish."

Staring at him, she shook her head. "Dane. How sad." Her eyes and face sank. "I believe that love is the only thing that's truly important in life and that everything else is just filler. Time spent gathering things and trinkets as if they were indeed important. But I think none of that matters. Love is life's greatest legacy. Haven't you heard that?"

He opened the car door for her, and after entering, she placed her hand on his arm. "Think of your father. All that he did, and all the people he helped, his business and all the time spent building it. And in the end, it was the love he shared, the people who mattered to him, and who he mattered to. That's what was important." The thought of Father brought a hot rush of tears to her eyes.

Dane took a deep breath, considering her words and the twinge of heartache she had wrung. "That's an interesting perspective," he said. *Perhaps she is right. My wife is a deep thinker.* He was beginning to enjoy letting her change his mind. Moreover, he was beginning to think of her more and more as his wife. *Good Lord.* "But I don't know. I believe lust is what drives men to marriage. Not love. Their need, especially when withheld. It's overwhelming, sometimes. Drives a man wild. And then the act of lovemaking creates a feeling of connection that they think is love. And marriage ensures men stay with the women who bear their children. I know very few men who are truly in love."

"But Dane. That makes no sense. You have been intimate with many women, and you say you haven't felt love or a connection? Are you immune? Or, perhaps it's because you have not met your match? Someone with whom you share common bonds and a truly special connection?"

He studied her. "I haven't felt a connection like that with any of the women I've been with. I don't know if it's possible for me."

She turned towards the window, unsuccessfully shielding her watery eyes as they drove home.

·❤·❤·❤·❤·❤·

LATER, WHEN DANE CAME into the kitchen nook for supper, he spotted a silver box resting on the table by his seat.

Katie, already at her seat, smiled slyly. "I bought you a birthday present."

"You don't need to purchase things for me, love. But, thank you." Dane opened the box. A pair of sterling silver cufflinks gleamed brightly, with a small ruby stone embedded in each of them. Dane looked at her, his heart warmed by her thoughtfulness. He pondered when he had last received a meaningful present. "Thank you. They are beautiful." He leaned over and kissed her cheek, lingering, wanting her lips.

During supper, Katie asked, "Dane, can we visit the Empire State Building when we are in New York?"

"Yes, of course." he laughed. "Great views from up there, you know. We have much to see and do in New York. Are you interested in visiting any museums?"

"Oh, yes. The Museum of Natural History. I hear it's grand. I love museums. I've been to a few on school trips. I'll bet the ones in New York are spectacular."

"Alrighty," he mused, loving her excitement and the fact that she liked museums, art, and culture! *Common bonds? Priya enjoys none of those things.*

As they finished supper, Dane snapped his fingers. "Oh, I almost forgot. I have something for you." He left the table and came back moments later, handing her a wrapped package. "A belated birthday gift, if you will."

"What's this?" She unwrapped the box. "A camera! Oh, Dane, what a thoughtful gift. Now, we shall have lots of pictures to remember our trip. I'm so excited, I can't wait to go." She was about to hug him when she noticed Mrs. Danbury staring at them.

"Mrs. Danbury...look...a camera. Isn't it wonderful?" she said, smiling.

"It's easy to use," he offered. "It's the Kodak Brownie camera. You no longer need to be a professional photographer. Pretty much point and shoot these days! You only need to learn how to put the film in."

"Maybe you can teach me after supper? Thank you, again," she said, her eyes dancing as she left the room.

Mrs. Danbury was still eyeing Dane. "Takin' her to New York with your brother and his wife, then?"

Aware of her disapproval, he explained, "Yes, Mrs. Danbury. My grandmother wants to see her again. And perhaps she will consider university there."

"I see," she said sternly. "Perhaps that would be best. She needs to be far away from the likes of you! And the sooner, the better."

Dane bit his lip. "Yes, indeed."

He lay on his bed considering the beauty down the hall, the peach lingerie she had chosen that he wasn't supposed to see, and how she looked in the dresses she had modeled for him in the store. But was it just how she looked that stirred him? Oh, he wanted her. There was no doubt about that. But why? Because a man wants what he cannot have? Or, was it something else?

In less than two days and they would be off. *Bloody hell. How in God's name will I be able to keep from kissing her again? Perhaps I will sneak away for an evening to myself. Oh, bloody hell, who am I kidding?* He counted how many times he had held her while they slept. Desire had taken hold, and it wasn't fun.

Chapter 26

A PRAYER AND A SPY

As she settled into her airline seat, she glanced at Dane, surprised to see his eyes fixed on her. "You are staring at me, sir."

"I'm admiring your red … lipstick. Red is your color, indeed." His eyes devoured her exquisite figure in the tight red dress.

"Is that so?"

"Hmmm."

Katie turned away so he wouldn't see her grin, not wanting him to know how much she enjoyed his attention.

A car was waiting to collect them at the airport, and for most of the commute into Manhattan, Katie, although it was quite cold, poked her head out of the window, taking it all in, first the bridges and then the incredible skyline of New York. As they traveled up Franklin D. Roosevelt Drive, which runs along the East River, Dane pointed out several bridges, the Empire State Building, and the Chrysler Building.

"I can't believe I am actually here! Oh, Dane! It's breathtaking! Thank you!"

Gram's apartment on the Upper West Side of Manhattan, at 75th Street, was located across from Central Park and featured two identical towers soaring twenty-seven stories. Ralph, the elder doorman, greeted the travelers and helped them with their bags, taking them up the elaborate wood-paneled elevator to the sixteenth floor, devoted to just one apartment.

Trisha, and Joel, who had arrived earlier, were with Gram to meet them when the elevator opened on the main level. Katie gasped at the size and expanse of it, insisting Gram take her on a quick tour. The light-filled living room rose twenty-five feet high, and the eight-foot windows, one after the other, framed in white, stood out against a navy blue wall. An assortment of pillows on the white chairs and sofas coordinated with the navy wall. There was a separate dining room with the largest dining table Katie had ever seen, and a connecting kitchen. "Oh! The refrigerator and oven are yellow. Fabulous. I love the decor. The yellow tiles." The tour continued to the butler's pantry, a powder room, a large office with a glass desk, and Gram's suite. Off to one side was a small room and bath designed for a live-in maid.

Polished to a high sheen, the dark walnut floors reflected the light, creating a warm, rich glow throughout the apartment. A wall-to-wall two-story bookcase stretched to the ceiling with an attached wooden ladder that moved along brass rails, ensuring that every book was within reach. In the corner stood a polished mahogany baby grand piano. Ornate molding adorned the ceiling around the two Swarovski crystal chandeliers, the epitome of luxury and refinement. A rustic stone fireplace, complete with mantle and hearth, warmed the room, and gold picture frames covered the mantle, with both Christmas and Hanukkah decorations hanging from it.

"Fabulous," Katie crowed.

Gram beamed. "Please make yourselves at home."

Dane led Katie down the curved wrought iron staircase to the four finely furnished guest rooms below. There were two sets of suites, each with a bathroom between them. Katie squealed at the baby-pink sink, tub, and toilet and adored the black and white checkered tiled floors. A sign that said 'UNLOCK THE DOOR WHEN FINISHED' was posted on each door so guests could access the washroom from their bedroom when needed and lock the other side when in use. Dane laughed to himself when the door adjoining his room squeaked. "I must fix that," he said.

"I'm so thrilled to see both of you girls," Gram said, all of them hugging one another.

"Thank you for having me. Your home is simply divine," Katie gushed.

"Thank you," Gram said. "I got lucky. This area was not very popular when I purchased this apartment, and its value has skyrocketed now."

Katie studied the photographs on the mantle, recognizing Dane and Joel as children immediately. Dane came to stand behind her. She felt his breath on her neck as he pointed out his mother, Rachael. "That's my aunt Sarah, and my cousins Anthony and Hannah. You will meet them, as I'm sure they will be here tomorrow. They live in Philadelphia still."

"I remember you when you looked like this." He was already tall, and his hair was longer in the front, almost over his eyes. Joel was considerably shorter, and his hair was lighter than it was now. But it was Rachael, their mother, that caught Katie's attention. She had an angular face, dark hair and dark eyes, high cheekbones, and a longish nose. "Your mother," she whispered. "She was half Jewish and half Italian? You have her nose. Her angled face. She was stunning and exotic! Of course, Father had been dazzled by her beauty, and she by his charm and elegance."

"I suppose. That's Gram and Pops," Dane said, pointing to an old black and white photograph. "Wasn't she beautiful when she was young?"

"Absolutely," Katie said. "What is her first name?"

"Dora. And Pops was Raffael Carrino. She called him Raffé."

"She's still beautiful. People didn't smile in photographs back then. Wonder why?" she said.

"It is because it took a while for the photo to set, and they couldn't hold their smiles long enough," he said, staring at her as she studied the photographs.

Each day they toured another area of the city: the Museum of Modern Art, the New York Public Library, the zoo in Central Park, and several museums. They strolled Fifth Avenue, popping into Tiffany's, Bergdorf Goodman, Cartier, and Rolex. Katie loved watching the ice skaters at Rockefeller Center. But when Joel suggested a horse and buggy ride through Central Park, Dane declined with no explanation. Katie sighed with a glance at Trish, almost unable to hide her disappointment.

Dane took note of Katie's reactions as she enjoyed the sights, often catching Joel watching him. The brothers shared a knowing look more than a few times; Joel, shaking his head, found humor in Dane's obvious discomfort, while Dane rolled his eyes and muttered curses under his breath.

Gram, Dane, and Katie toured the ivy-covered historic buildings of Columbia University, taking in the sights and sounds of the traditional campus. Gram's admissions counselor friend showed them around the N.Y.U. buildings, explaining the opportunities and cultural experiences the school offered. Katie was surprised to learn that the school didn't have an actual campus; instead, it was woven into the bustling, colorful Greenwich Village neighborhood, its buildings scattered like hidden gems among the city blocks. Dane grew increasingly anxious with the lively discussions and excited chatter. *Might she actually leave England?* His heart raced with the thought, though he knew he had no right to suggest she stay.

"I knew you would love N.Y.U.," Gram said. "Think about it. I will help you with decorating the dorm room and get you settled in. Of course, I have a motive for enticing you to come." She winked at Dane. "I think my grandson would be inclined to visit more often, if you were here."

"I will think about it, but I don't know if I have the nerve to do such a thing."

· ❤ · ❤ · ❤ · ❤ · ❤ ·

LATER, DANE SURPRISED KATIE with a treat: high tea at the infamous Palm Court, inside The Plaza Hotel. Katie, impressed by the elegant silverware and serving pieces, exclaimed, "My goodness, everything is so well presented. Look at these perfectly cut finger sandwiches, the beautiful pastries, and the assortment of teas. Thank you for bringing me here."

"This is one of the most extravagant and famous hotels in Manhattan," he told her. "The rooms have the finest French furnishings, and the view of Central Park is the best in all of New York. The park is over eight hundred acres.

"I'd love to see the rooms someday," she said.

"Stop that," he said playfully.

She giggled, dotting her lips with her napkin.

Once outside, Dane and Katie stopped to enjoy Christmas carolers dressed in old-world costumes singing on the steps of The Plaza. Next to them, also singing, were the festively dressed cabbies with their horse-drawn carriages garbed in red velvet Christmas coats and black top hats, anxiously awaiting riders. The carriages glittered with tiny lights, and the horses, warm mist exhaling from their nostrils, wore lighted reindeer headgear, Christmas bells, and red velvet coats. The air was thick with the aroma of roasted chestnuts wafting from nearby vendors.

"How lovely," she gushed.

"Well, I guess we must."

As Dane chatted with the driver, Katie giggled, snapping a photo. Soon they were in the carriage, bundled in blankets, enjoying a ride through the illuminated Central Park.

Dane took her gloved hand in his. "I declined this when we were with Joel and Trish because I wanted to be alone with you when we did it."

Katie's mouth opened, but she could not speak.

Dane pulled her closer, planting his lips on her cool, reddened cheek. A shared glance of pure exhilaration sparked between them before they fell into each other's arms. Their unrestrained, desperate embrace, a whirlwind of urgent, impassioned kisses. In an instant, the world ceased to exist, the warmth of his kiss sending shockwaves to her stomach and further down to her core. His soft lips on hers only made her eager for more, and the passion and craving he wrestled with was now as obvious as her own.

"Oh!" she whispered. Her happiness was infectious.

He chuckled, "I'm sorry. And I was doing so well. Until now. Forgive me."

"Nothing to forgive," she said, touching her heart. "I was hoping you would."

His lips brushed hers once more, tenderly, and ever so lightly. He wanted to keep kissing her, but he took her hand and kissed it instead, closing his eyes to calm himself into retreat.

Desperate to get his mind off of her lips, he announced, "I have a few surprises planned for all of us. The best one is the grand Christmas

Spectacular at Radio City Music Hall, where The Rockettes are performing. And, the film *Sayonara*, with Marlon Brando, follows."

"Oh. Thank you. What a fabulous trip! The Rockettes! They are brilliant I hear! They can kick their legs to their ears!"

"Yes, quite remarkable." He laughed to himself, picturing that.

As they walked around the shops near 59th Street, Katie popped into a souvenir shop, admiring a small set of chimes, hitting them a few times to listen to their music. She ran her fingers over its metal plate decorated with the Empire State Building and the city's skyline. While she was occupied with other items in the shop, Dane motioned to the clerk to wrap up the chimes, handing him some cash.

·♥·♥·♥·♥·♥·

G RAM HAD SUPPER WAITING when they returned, and after studying their faces, noticing their euphoria and reddened cheeks, she beamed at Trisha with satisfaction.

As Gram celebrated both Christmas and Hanukkah, she and the girls prepared a wonderfully festive Christmas Eve supper that included the entire family; Aunt Sarah, her husband Tony and their two children had arrived earlier in the day.

Thinking of her own family, Katie mentioned to Dane the stark differences of what previous Christmases with her family had been like. "More often than not, mum had only handmade gifts for us all, or something shared, like a bicycle."

Dane made a mental note to send gifts when he returned, kicking himself for not thinking of it sooner.

"And, please, don't you dare get me anything." Katie shook her finger at Dane. "This trip, and the clothes. I know I spend way too much on clothing. I cost you a fortune."

"Don't be silly. Your clothing bills are fine. Anyone else would take advantage; you most certainly do not spend too much. And, I enjoy seeing you well-dressed. Father did too. You have wonderful taste."

At 11:15 p.m. Katie, Dane, Joel, and Trish headed to a nearby church for midnight mass. Dane took notice of how the service and the soulful choir songs moved his wife. He stood behind her while she lit a candle, whispering prayers first for his father, and then remarkably, for him, barely audible above the organ music.

"Dear God, please bring peace to his heart and let him heal. Let him love. Amen."

When Katie pulled back her cover to enter her bed that evening, there was a small bag sitting on her pillow. "Oh my," she said, pulling out the chimes, fingering them lightly, listening to their sweet music until she fell asleep.

The following day, Dane surprised them all with Christmas Day tickets to the musical *West Side Story*. Throughout the performance, Katie's silent sobs and tear-streaked face revealed the depth of her emotions. The movable sets, designed to look like fire escapes and graffiti-covered walls, added to the intensity of the powerfully tragic violence surrounding the lovers. Sitting on the edge of her seat, worry etched on her face, she gripped Dane's arm as Leonard Bernstein's powerful music swelled to a dramatic crescendo.

Holding her heart, she cheered as they exited the theater, "Incredibly brilliant!! Thank you so much for this! I will never forget this night! The dancing and choreography, oh my goodness!"

In a moment of clarity, it suddenly dawned on Dane what it was about her that was so very special. Her passion. For everything. Not only for films and theater. *Everything she experienced touched her heart. Nature. Animals. Art. Music and dancing. She appreciated life.*

As engaging as the days were, the nights were torturous for Dane. *She is driving me mad. What am I going to do? I must put this nonsense out of my mind.*

·❦·❦·❦·❦·❦·

F INALLY HOME, AND AFTER a drink and smoke with Joel, Dane went down to his room, removed his clothes, and lay on his bed, waiting for Katie to exit the washroom. When she finished, he tried to open the door, but she had forgotten to unlock it from the inside. He went around to her bedroom door and knocked.

"Yes?" she said, opening her door.

Illuminated from behind, the silken white nightgown revealed her feminine curves, her golden blonde hair falling in waves around her shoulders, setting his mind ablaze. "The door. I cannot. Locked. Ummm. The washroom?"

"Oh, sorry. I forgot." She giggled to herself, closed the door, and went to the washroom, opening his side.

When he exited the washroom, the squeak of the door once again struck him. *I must remember to fix that.*

Once in bed, he tried to sleep, but naturally, the vision of her in her nightgown, her curves beneath her nightgown, the memory of their passionate kisses left him restless.

It didn't take long for him to take care of his need; his manly sword quickly reached its peak, and the pillow covering his face diminished his deep, masculine grunt.

Seconds later, he whipped his head toward the bathroom door as he heard it squeak in the still silence. *Bloody Hell. She had been watching. Good lord. What did she see? It was very dark, so she couldn't have seen much, only my hand moving, and she would have heard my groan. What should I do?*

The next morning, Dane downed a few sips of coffee and announced, "I'm going for a run."

"May I join you?" Katie asked.

"Do you have any soft-soled shoes?"

"These?"

"Come on then." He was quiet in the elevator, but upon reaching the street, Dane stopped and crossed his arms in confrontation. "So, did you have interesting dreams last night?" He bore into her face closely with an accusatory look.

She gasped, her face reddening quickly. "Oh...I'm mortified. I'm such a horrible person. I didn't mean to spy on you. Truly. I am so terribly sorry. I have betrayed your trust and wouldn't blame you if you sent me home. I only wanted to ... see if you would let me lie next to you, so I opened the door. I didn't mean to..."

"It's alright. No harm done. You couldn't have seen anything?"

"No," she shook her head. "But, I'm so embarrassed." She covered her face. "This has been the most wonderful holiday. I hate that I have spoiled it."

"You haven't spoiled anything," he grinned. "Just as desire is normal, so is ... well, releasing." He tenderly moved the hair hanging in front of her eyes. "You do seem to have a one-track mind. Not that I mind, actually." He grinned, playfully.

"Oh, you rake!" She hit his shoulder, lightly. They laughed. "I couldn't leave..I.. I was frozen." She could not look at him when she spoke.

"Well, to be blunt..." he whispered close to her ear, "You can do the same as I."

"What? What do you mean?"

"You want to know how it feels? You have a hand. Use it."

"Oh!" Her face turned red, and her eyes widened.

"Come on," he laughed. "You need some oxygen in those lungs!"

He started a slow run through the park. She tried to keep up, her eyes following his buttocks.

· ♥ · ♥ · ♥ · ♥ · ♥ ·

U PON THEIR RETURN, KATIE squealed to Gram, "I love New York, and I don't want to leave! I can see why you love living here. The energy."

"You are welcome to come and stay any time, dear. Perhaps apply to university. Send me your application, and I'll bring it to my friend. You can make your final decision later on. No need to make it now."

Katie sucked in her breath at the thought.

After a grand and leisurely breakfast of Katie's making, they headed out to Greenwich Village via the crowded subway. The lights flickered inside the train and even blacked out completely for an instant, causing Katie and Trish to hold their breath. Gram laughed and said it was a normal occurrence.

Gram seized the opportunity to speak to her grandson, linking her arm over his as they walked from the trains. "She is lovely, dear. I am hoping you decide to finalize your marriage."

Dane took a deep breath, said nothing, and looked straight ahead.

As the group made their way to the village, stopping occasionally to admire a storefront, they noticed some younger people dressed in rather odd attire.

"These are the Beatniks of Greenwich Village," Gram said. "There seems to be more and more each day. They live what's considered a bohemian lifestyle. It's a revolution of sorts. Sexual and otherwise."

Katie's eyes widened, and turning back, she saw Trish giggling and Dane shaking his head.

"They have some very good music venues here now, with rock and roll music, jazz bands, and big band music. You should come down here for an evening." Gram said as they walked. "And this place is interesting," she said, stopping in front of a chess store. Not only did this shop have an amazing array of unusual chess pieces, ranging from zoo animals to the Knights of King Arthur's court, but they had an ongoing tournament running inside the store. The clatter of time clocks punctuated the quiet intensity of the players studying the boards and planning their moves.

"Oh, Father would have loved this!" Katie shouted above the noise.

In Chinatown, they shared a few plates, enjoying the frenzied hustle of the Chinese immigrants, and then shared some Italian desserts in nearby Little Italy.

As they walked to the main street to find a cab, Dane stepped between Gram and Katie, taking each of their arms over his. "Two of my most favorite ladies," he said, planting a kiss on each of their cheeks.

Taking Gram's suggestion to heart, they all went to a club in the village that evening. The pop music blaring, the jovial patrons danced, some taking solo turns, while the group cheered. Several drinks later, Katie snapped photos of Dane's sexy solo dance, showing off his moves while the ladies yelped and waved their napkins. He reminded Katie of the popular singer, Elvis Presley, whom she had seen on the Ed Sullivan show.

Katie got Trish and Joel on the dancefloor, dancing the jitterbug to "Rock Around the Clock," by Bill Haley and his Comets, "Rockin' Robin," by Bobby Day, and "Mr. Sandman," by The Penguins. But when Dane seized Katie for Les Baxter's "Unchained Melody," eyes locked in an intense embrace, Trisha, Joel, and Gram all smirked knowingly.

Chapter 27

DANELAND

JOEL AND TRISHA PLANNED to spend their last night alone, leaving Dane and Katie on their own for the evening. Heading out earlier than usual, their first stop was the Empire State Building, the 102nd floor observatory. As they crossed the heavily trafficked 34th Street toward the entrance, Dane reached for her hand, enjoying the glee at the simple gesture. "Don't look up now!" Dane chuckled.

"I won't!" she giggled, knowing he was referring to the film.

Visitors squeezed into the glass elevator, listening to the elevator operator recounting the history of the building. "On a clear day, one can see in every direction up to eighty miles. Hundred and second floor," he announced, when the elevator stopped.

Katie stepped over to the lookout. "Goodness."

"You can gain quite an understanding of Manhattan from up here," Dane said, pointing. "That's where we were earlier ... see the Statue of Liberty? And there is the Chrysler Building, with its very unique dome. And there, over there is Central Park," he pointed, positioning himself close behind her.

His warm breath against her neck, she turned her face to him. "It's extraordinary," she sighed, leaning against him.

"I think *you* are extraordinary," he whispered. His resolve once again shattered, he smothered her lips with his. Embracing her head with his hands and with his thumbs upon her cheek, he teased and then enveloped her mouth.

A wave of dizzying delight washed over them both. Their delirious need for one another finally shared, their laughter echoing in the air, they found each other's lips once more. This time, their kiss was slower and more tender, each moment stretching into eternity. Their eyes remained locked, allowing their kisses and gazes to speak the volumes words were yet to express.

Throughout their journey, there had been countless moments he longed to take her in his arms. Now, restraint abandoned, replaced with an intense desire that left no room for doubt. Suddenly, everything was different. He was in uncharted territory: wanting her, needing her, *Only her. But that would consummate our marriage.* He was caught in a vise with no easy resolution.

Back on the street, Dane hailed a cab. "Tonight, I'm taking you to the East Village, to The Generation Club. You will love the music there."

After dancing for hours and a late-night bite, they returned home long after everyone else had retired.

"I'll let you use the washroom first. Go on now," Dane said, kissing her cheek.

When he heard her leave, he entered. And when finished, he whispered into her room, "Goodnight, love." He waited ... nothing. *Hmmm.* Back in his bedroom, he pulled back the covers. Big blue eyes stared up at him. He groaned, "Oh, love."

Her eyes gazed over his bare chest and the bulge in his briefs, and silently asked for permission to stay.

"Absolutely not! Are you mad? With them next to us, and my grandmother above us? Go to your bed. Please."

She shook her head.

He laughed. "Katherine, I mean it. Go."

"Just a few minutes. I promise I will leave soon." She bit her lip, not recognizing herself.

"Good God." He slid into the bed, unable to stop himself, fixing the covers over them. His hands around her face, he took her lips in his, giving in to his long, mounting desire. Daring to take the next step, he pulled the delicate strings of her nightdress, slipping his hand down her neckline, running his finger lightly over her breast, then her nipple, kissing her neck and chest, and finally taking the nipple within his lips.

A groan escaped her lips before she could stop herself, and they both laughed, hoping they were not overheard. She whispered, "Oh! I have longed to touch you." Her hand over roamed his chest, over his tight stomach and then further down over his hips.

Shocked at her boldness, he could not move. This inexperienced girl was moving her hand, resting it on his pulsing, growing heat, uncontrollably beginning to peek its head outside of his shorts.

"Oh, lord," she said in shock, as she felt his rigid shaft grow rapidly, pulsing to the slightest movement of her hand.

"Oh, love. Come on now. We cannot do this." He put his hand over hers. "Please. Stop. You don't want to do this." He was panting, delirious with desire, trying to fight his passion with sensibility.

Mesmerized by his heated state, she could not stop herself. "I think I do! I don't understand it. But I want to touch you. Please."

"This is wrong. Oh, God!"

"Please." Her hand moved over the length of him, continuing a slow steady rhythm, as he gained in size and width until the head and much else was well outside the confines of his briefs. "My God," she mumbled.

She can't know what she's doing. But she blindly proceeded as he throbbed beneath her hand, daring to slip her hand under his shorts, her breath catching in her throat as she cupped his warm, soft skin. Guiding her strokes until she understood the rhythm, he smothered himself with a pillow to muffle his deep groans, releasing in a torrent of thunderous convulsions. He lay motionless as his breath slowly recovered. "Bloody hell, that should not have happened." He closed his eyes. "But, thank you."

Her eyes wide with amazement, she breathlessly whispered, "Most fascinating, indeed."

After changing his briefs quickly, he snuggled back under the covers, pulling her close beside him, his tender kisses, sweet and lingering. Wanting more of his touch, she placed his hand on her breasts, giggling with delight while his tongue tickled her ears.

"Shhh, they will hear us!" he laughed.

"Oh, I love this," she heard herself say. "I love...Daneland," she murmured, giggling to herself.

"Just a few minutes more, then I'm sending you far away." He didn't want her to go anywhere, but he knew he must insist. His skin tingling at her touch, a sweet tremor running through his limbs, he gazed into her eyes; their deep connection was unlike anything he had ever experienced before. Lost in the exploration of each other's mouths, teasing, suckling, the intensity of the moment overwhelmed them. He was awed not only by her response, but by his own. His heart hammered his ribs before he forced himself to snap out of his dizzying haze. "Alright...you had better go now, or I am going to remove your nightgown."

"Oh! You wouldn't!" Her eyes widened with excitement.

He chuckled at her shyness.

With a sly grin, he said, "Go on. I believe we have had enough excitement for one night. And I am going to Hell for what just happened. Go!" He kissed her again and pushed her out.

"Oh, you are so mean!" she giggled, leaving through the washroom.

Dane beat himself up about what happened. He closed his eyes and shook his head. That was the last thing he could have imagined happening. *How had this happened?* He was doing so well, staying away. He wondered what Hell would be like.

As he drifted, he considered consummating their marriage. No. That would be doing exactly what he was afraid of. Marrying for lust. *She deserves more than that. She must marry someone who loves her.* His breath ceased for a moment. *Love. What the bloody heck is love?*

Chapter 28

NEW YORK SPECTACULAR

THE CHRISTMAS SPECTACULAR AT Radio City Music Hall did not disappoint. Lit for the holidays, its grand marquee towered above the city street with flashing neon lights. Inside, the sweeping stage, grander in both width and length than any theater worldwide, was visible to all patrons no matter where they sat. The high, arched ceilings glimmered with extravagant leaded crystal chandeliers while luxurious velvet drapery lined the walls, the opulent stage, and the sides of the private balcony seats.

The show was a masterpiece of awe-inspiring grandeur, the dancers and singers adorned in rich, elaborate costumes featuring feathered headdresses, risqué bodices with high leg cutouts, skin-toned stockings, and the highest heels. Technical highlights included clouds, fog, and rain falling onto the stage. Katie sat on the edge of her seat throughout the sophisticated and expertly choreographed production, often yelling and clapping for the glamorous Rockettes.

As always, the finale included the famous Rockette high-kick line. Each girl, over twenty of them, looked the same as the girl next to her, kicking to their ears, again and again, arms clasped together as one, perfectly in unison!

"BRAVO!!!" The audience members, now on their feet, screamed and cheered wildly, applauding vigorously for several minutes, and Katie, screaming along with them, loved every moment.

As if that wasn't enough, the film *Sayonara* followed, with handsome Marlon Brando playing a U.S. Air Force Major stationed in Japan. In the film, he was dead set against American military men marrying Japanese women, until he, in fact, fell deeply in love with one. The ending left Katie in tears, and Dane gave her his shirtsleeve to wipe her eyes. He wanted to kiss away her tears, but instead, they shared a meaningful, long gaze.

Outside of the theater, Katie remarked, "Seems a familiar theme. Men who refuse to marry, and then fall desperately in love."

Joel and Gram chuckled loudly. Dane grimaced.

Brimming with energy and enthusiasm, she added, "What a glorious evening! It was fabulous! Spectacular!" On her toes, she planted a kiss on Dane's cheek, forgetting they were not alone.

"A true love story, if ever there was one," Dane snickered.

"Oh, I loved it too," Trish said. Everyone agreed and thanked Dane for the lovely holiday gift.

Standing at the door to his room, Dane wrapped his arms around her waist and leaned in, kissing her deeply and tenderly, his tongue and lips teasing and tasting hers. He seemed to know what she was thinking. He studied her face, saw the desire and willingness, and felt her chest and breaths beating faster than it had after several jitterbug dances. He shook his head. "Soon, love," he said, kissing her lips, her nose, and her forehead. "Soon." Dane opened the door for her, kissed her again with more passion than he had ever felt before, and said, "I'm not allowing you to enter. We mustn't repeat last night's ... um, mishaps. So, goodnight, love." He caressed her head and her cheek and kissed her one more time before closing the door, cursing. He considered opening the door and giving in to their shared desire. *No. Not until I know without a doubt what this is.*

❤ ❤ ❤ ❤ ❤

I N HER BED, SHE repeatedly replayed what had happened the night before. *I felt him, stimulated him, and he had released! My God!* She giggled
to herself...She had been so bold. It was hard to sleep thinking of it. Her
body tingled with excitement in her lower region. She wanted to be snuggled
up next to him. Desire consumed her. Her heart, she thought, was going to
explode. She longed for him to touch her, to keep going, but for what exactly,
she did not know. *What makes a girl throw all sensibility out the window?*

He was so attentive, so wonderful. *Is it true, all that Mrs. Danbury had
said? That he will never be a one-woman man? I had better stop encouraging
him. I don't want him to feel trapped. And that's not how I want to be married,
either.*

With her pillows in her arms, she turned on her side, placing one against
her backside and the other close to her body with her hand cupping her
breast. She thought of Dane's words. *'You can do it yourself.'* Her hand
continued to massage her breast, then caressed her tummy, and then moved
further to the area she felt tingling earlier. She noted her breathing increasing, deciding she must be doing it correctly. As she found her inner core,
it amazed her at how clueless she was about her own body, even though
she read and re-read about arousal in the book. However, unaware of the
mechanics of release, she soon relaxed and drifted off to her most favorite
place, *Daneland*.

· ♥ · ♥ · ♥ · ♥ · ♥ ·

O N NEW YEAR'S EVE, Trisha and Joel stayed in with Gram, preparing
for their flight early New Year's Day. Dane had reservations at the
Copacabana for Katie and himself.

Katie's stunning, well fitted, black silk evening dress, a color that accentuated her face and hair, sported a thick white, low-cut satin collar, sheer long
sleeves and white cuffs. She looked elegant and refined, a stark difference to
many of the other women who came dressed looking more like the cigarette
girls in fishnet stockings and low-cut bustiers.

Several comedic and variety acts took the stage before the lights went
down, and the main eight-piece band took over. The band, playing all their

favorites, had them on the dance floor all night long. Dane held her close during the New Year's countdown.

"Happy New Year, love. So happy to be spending it with you this year," he said.

"Happy New Year, Mr. Wellington." Her face was beaming with joy and love. "Last year, you took Priya to see *The Nutcracker* and left me at home." She hit his chest with her finger.

"I'm sorry, love. Never again."

TEN, NINE, EIGHT, SEVEN ...Amid the cheers, clatter of noisemakers, and waving streamers, their kiss, with eyes locked, isolated them in their own blissful world.

"Ah, they are playing our song!" Dane said. Once again they swayed to "Only You," slow and close, just how she liked it. His skilled, sensual hips moving in rhythm with the music, and his left hand, low on her back, holding her against him, made her almost too woozy to stand upright. Her left and his right hands clasped by her side, his cheek nudged hers while her right hand hugged his neck and her fingers caressed his hair. Letting herself go, she concentrated on his hardened package pressing intimately against her core.

She whispered, "Oh, Dane. I'm so happy."

They left the club at 2:00 a.m. and were snuggled in Dane's bed shortly thereafter, in their position, his burgeoning rod pressed deeply against her backside, his hand cupping her breast, and her hand on over his.

Around 5:00 a.m., before he and Trisha headed off to the airport, Joel poked his head into Dane's room to say goodbye. He smiled to himself seeing them cuddled together, Dane's arm around her. "I believe I have won our bet!" he chuckled to himself.

Gram considered her grandson as he finally emerged after 11:00 a.m. "Well?" she asked. "Are you officially married now?"

Dane poured his coffee, and without looking at his grandmother, said, "We have done nothing but kiss a little." He flashed back on *that* night. Lying to his grandmother did not sit easy, but truly, she *is, in fact, still intact. I haven't touched anything more than her lips. Well, maybe her breasts.*

Gram furrowed her brows. "What in God's name are you waiting for?"

Dane did not answer. He could not answer. He did not know.

Chapter 29

CONVICTION

AFTER TEARFUL, HEARTFELT GOODBYES to Gram, Dane and Katie returned to a cold, empty house on the night of the third. With the staff remaining on holiday until the sixth, they refused to be parted, sleeping together as before. Just before fully awakening, Dane cuddled closer, moving his hand over her tummy and then firmly over her center. His hand and fingers cupped her with a possessive squeeze. Katie lay motionless, feeling the warmth spreading from his touch, her breathing becoming rapid until a soft moan escaped her lips. As he came to full consciousness, he suddenly realized his error, snatching his hand away and leaping out of bed in a panic. "Good God! I wasn't fully awake! Forgive me."

Katie was wide awake. "Oh, Dane! You are stirring feelings in me that I didn't even know existed until recently."

"You should have stopped me."

"I couldn't!" she laughed. "Besides, my nightgown is still on. No harm done."

They gazed at each other intensely.

"I should take you back to school today. We ought not spend another night together. You know I will not break my promise."

"Your promise was to wait a year, which has passed."

"A year until consummation. I ... I mustn't touch you any further if there is to be an annulment."

Katie nodded, turning her head to hide her crushing disappointment. Her jaw locked tight. With her head still turned, she shot back, "Just take me back now, then. I'll go get ready."

She raced to her room, obviously upset. Dane thought, *Did she expect to stay married now?* Whatever she expected, Dane did not want her leaving angry. They needed to discuss this now. Following her, he knocked lightly on the door.

"Katie. Let's talk about it."

She opened her door, and trying to hold her tears, she took a breath before speaking. "I know this isn't easy for you, and I haven't made it any easier. But I want you to know I am filled with happiness. I've had the most wonderful holiday, and being with you made it so very special. Thank you a million times for bringing me, for your restraint, your friendship, and...for...loving me. I know I should not say it. I know you push people away who tell you they love you. But I can't help it. I love you." She placed her hand on his cheek. "I do. I've loved you since the day you brought me the daisies in Leatherhead." A tear left her eye and traveled down her cheek. "I know that's not what you want, and I won't say it again."

Although normally this would have evoked a flight reaction, her words moved him to tears. Hearing her say '*it's not what you want*' hit him hard. Was that true? In the past, yes. But now? No, actually. In fact, his heart soared hearing the words '*I love you*' coming from her lips. "I had the most marvelous time with you as well, love." He bent to kiss her moist cheek, wiping away her salty tears with his thumb, which then brushed her soft, trembling lips. "Father believed this was destiny and perhaps it is. I care for you deeply, and I will be miserable until I see you again. I want you with every ounce of my being, I think more than I have ever wanted anyone. And, I'm in Hell, I'll admit. But you deserve more than lust. You deserve to be loved, and I know you want to be married to someone who has begged on his knees for your hand, not just married after a lustful encounter. Is this love? I don't know. I've never loved anyone before, nor said those words. I need time to figure that out. But I won't take advantage of you until we both know the answer." He kissed her tenderly. "Will you give me some time? I promise not to mention annulment again. Let's enjoy these last few hours we have."

She nodded. "Alright.

They spent the day curled up by the fire on his father's lounge chair in the conservatory, playing in the pool, and enjoying a comedic television show.

After driving to the school in silence, Dane pulled off the road near her school and turned off the engine. Clutching one another in a desperate embrace, their kisses conveyed the heartbreak of having to say goodbye after sharing so many wonderful days and nights together.

As she walked away, Dane felt a bone-deep shiver up his spine. Their necessary separation weighed heavily, but he knew it was a must, for any more togetherness would surely result in consummation. Never before had he felt the pain of being parted, especially after spending almost two weeks together. *Is this love?*

·❤·❤·❤·❤·❤·

A LONE IN HER SMALL twin bed, Katie was thankful for the solitude and peace, as the girls were not due back until the following day. Her heart was full of love and hope, and her head filled with newfound determination. She was in love with a man who was afraid to love. And she had fallen deeply in love with New York. *New York University.*

Mrs. Hughes jumped in to help her get the application packets ready for N.Y.U. and two Oxford schools for women.

·❤·❤·❤·❤·❤·

"I BELIEVE I WON our little bet. You owe me fifty quid, brother," Joel said when they were both at the office days later.

"Incorrect! I believe our wager was that the marriage will be consummated before she turned twenty, which she turned in October. She is still intact, actually. I was doing well, I must admit. Until just before New Year's Eve. But, remarkably, we have somehow ended up sleeping together now, and

I do mean just sleeping, I don't know how many times! At least five, maybe six times. Not doing anything more than a close, ah, very close cuddle. It's bonkers! Brilliant, but bonkers. And even more terrifying is that I don't seem to want any other company! I am in Bloody Hell!"

"I know. Came in to say goodbye before we left for the airport, and saw you two snuggled together. I am pleased to see this change in you. Love can be difficult at first."

Chills suddenly tickled Dane's head, neck, and arms. *Love?*

♥ · ♥ · ♥ · ♥ · ♥

Back at home for Spring break, Katie's peals of laughter bounced off the walls as she watched I Love Lucy, her smile widening impossibly further as Dane walked into the parlor. He chuckled at her as she lay on the floor on her tummy, her legs swinging in the air.

"Dane!" she rushed to him.

"Come here!" He bent down to kiss her, not caring who might be watching. They were not children. "I've missed you."

"It has only been a month."

"Come, let's go outside. It's a beautiful day." He led her by the hand to the lounge, seating her on his lap.

As they sat huddled together on the chaise, Dane said, "I want to tell you ... Except for my grandmother and Joel, you are the most important person in my life. There will never be a time when I won't want to see you. I have always thought myself a bachelor, love. I never thought I would marry. But now, I might be rethinking that. But, how can ask you to wait for me, if I don't know when, or if that day will ever come? I feel it will. I want to say things to you I have never said to anyone. But then something holds me back. Perhaps I need help."

The kiss, sweet and lingering, the gentle touch of his lips, told her this was something more, something deeper than mere affection. It was a beginning. It was hope. *But there I go again, hoping.* She laid her head upon his chest. *I love you too, Dane.*

After supper, Dane and Katie spent the evening outside on the lounges. The hour was late, but neither wanted to leave. They sat for a while and held hands, not knowing what to do next.

Katie finally stood. "Goodnight, Dane." One short kiss, and she went up to her room, feeling an ache in her heart.

Sitting on her bed in her nightdress, longing to be in his arms, she considered how much she wanted him to come to her. *If he wants me, he will have to step up. I will not be like the other girls he has had. I must take care of me.* She remembered the words, "*How can I ask you to wait for me, if I don't know when or if that day will ever come?*" *What if it never comes? How long am I supposed to wait until he can tell me how he feels?*

Father's words lived in her heart. "*Live your life with conviction and passion, and never settle. Stay the course until you get what you set out for. No matter what it is.*"

Chapter 30

OXFORD

K ATIE MENTIONED TO DANE she had applied to the universities in New York, as well as two of the female colleges that were part of Oxford University.

"Let me take you to Oxford. You need to see it." Dane said.

Katie and Dane boarded the train at the Weybridge station, switching in London to the Oxford line.

Following coffee and biscuits, they headed out to follow the tour that Maggie had prepared for them. The first stop was the architectural masterpiece, The Bodleian Library, one of the oldest, most iconic libraries in Britain. Dane explained that it is Oxford University's main research library. Katie marveled at the centuries-old stone walls and the majestic domed building of the most famous part of the library, the Radcliffe Camera.

"Why is it called a camera?" Katie asked.

"The Latin word for room is camera," Dane said, "and Radcliffe is the name of the gentleman who funded it."

She giggled. "Then, why is a camera called a camera?"

"I don't know, silly. But we are in a library; maybe we can do some research."

As they walked, they came upon the university's famous Sheldonian Theatre, the round architectural marvel built in the sixteen hundreds. Lady

Margaret Hall and St. Anne's College, the two Oxford University colleges Katie had applied to, were next on the list.

"It's like the entire city is intertwined with the colleges and campuses, separate but united. I just love the feeling here."

After visiting several other important landmarks, they strolled to the city's open-air markets, enjoying the warm spring air and the fragrant scents of the wisteria and lemon balm trees. They popped into a café for high tea and, afterwards, relaxed on a park bench near the softly flowing Cherwell River, musing about people rowing while standing in their boats.

"It's called punting. You balance yourself and row with the metal pole," Dane said.

"Have you ever tried it?"

"Oh yes. We used to have races, of course."

"This city is fascinating. So much to see and do. I can see why Maggie loves it here," she said thoughtfully. "Did you bring me here so I would fall in love with it?"

"Well, I knew you would love it. I support you attending uni. Any uni. Oxford would be more convenient, surely. I don't want you to go to New York. I can't imagine you leaving England. But New York is the most exciting city in the world. If you have the opportunity, I wouldn't blame you if you took it."

"Dane, if I am accepted, and I go, I will be very sad to not see you. Will you come more than once a year?"

"Yes, of course. I will come often." He lightly fingered her chin. "I haven't kissed you all day, come here," he said. She closed her eyes as he claimed her mouth in a dizzying kiss.

"Alright," he laughed, pulling away. "Let's find a place for supper." He clutched his empty stomach. "We must watch our time. The last train departs at 9:45."

The lively pub they found was the perfect setting for their romantic day's end, with a view of the river, a small bridge, and the beautiful gardens. The evening arrived so subtly that it went unnoticed amidst the joyful atmosphere; the patrons, many of whom had been there for several hours, now quite intoxicated, were laughing and singing to the recorded music.

Dane closed his eyes for a second, then glanced at his watch. "We must head back to the train station soon, love."

Katie studied her love's face and sighed, her heart racing, pounding her chest as she considered her next words. Lost in the throes of love, she disregarded all of society's rules and the warnings in her head: *Perhaps he will never marry. How does it change things for me? Am I willing to walk away without knowing what it is to love him fully? "Conviction and passion," Father said.* Conflicted no more, knowing what she wanted and who she wanted, she blurted, "Must we leave?"

Dane laughed at her silliness. "What other choice do we have, love? A hotel room?"

She stared at him until he straightened and leaned into the table. "You want to take a hotel room?" He cocked his head. "You shouldn't encourage me or test me so. I'm not made of stone like these buildings around us."

She pursed her lips, thinking he did resemble a Greek statue.

Their eyes locked. "Ah, I think it best we go home. We can get some coffee."

"Let's stay. Please. I want to be with you." She held her knuckles against her lips, not believing the words had just come out of her mouth. *I must be mad!*

"Oh, love." He leaned in closer, placing his hand over hers. "I'll not take a room so that I can go mad with desire. You must understand what you are asking. Are you sure you are ready for this?"

She paused, her breath hitching in her chest. Placing her other hand over his, she fixed her determined eyes on his and nodded.

❦ · ❦ · ❦ · ❦ · ❦

AFTER PURCHASING SOME NECESSITIES, they settled into a cozy room tucked away from the noisy street, the soft carpet a welcome relief for their tired feet. She was tense, shaking even. Plucking his jacket and sweater off, he took her into his arms, kissing her until she relaxed against him, and they fell onto the bed, laughing.

Up on his elbow, he played with her hair, twirling it with his fingers. "How do the curls stay in place, I wonder?"

She grinned.

"Don't worry, love. You will leave here still whole, I promise. Although not quite as innocent," he smirked.

She felt herself relax as he caressed her face with his nose and lips. She breathed in the last hints of his cologne, sighing contentedly in the warm haven of his arms.

His fingers traveled slowly over her face, down her neck and above her bra line, moving over her cleavage, exploring her soft mounds. He was deliberately slow, kissing her, softly, with much love and tenderness. "You are not like the other women I have been with. I won't take you fully. Not until I know what this is. We'll go but so far. I'm honored to be the one to share this with you, though." He carefully unbuttoned her sweater, lingering over each button, before gently sliding it off. His fingers continued to move ever so lightly along her neck, while his tongue explored the top of her bra.

The heat of his mouth upon her sent waves of chills down her arms, and her heart quickened with anticipation. His fingers tugging on her earlobes oddly caused a pulsing sensation between her legs, and her breaths deepened as his tongue delved deeper and deeper under the fabric until his mouth found her nipples, taking one and then the other. She let out a quick gasp as he suckled each breast and nipple, first tenderly and then a little harder until she yelped and giggled. She put her arms around him and felt the weight of him almost on top of her as he unhooked her bra with one hand, throwing it theatrically across the room like an actor in a play.

Giggling with nervous energy, she said, "Oh my. Quite skilled at that you are, Mr. Wellington."

His eyes burned lovingly into hers. "You are about to learn a good deal more about my skills. My father insisted I do things well, you know. And I have been perfecting them for a good long while. Just for you, Miss—Mrs. Wellington."

"Hmmm." Her fingers glided over his chest and torso lightly, but her eyes studied his stomach and hips. She longed to touch him again, replicating their encounter in New York.

Lowering his head onto her belly, he kissed and licked, unbuttoning and slowly removing her skirt, leaving her delicate peach lace panties in place. "My God, you are lovely," he whispered. Slowly, his tongue tickled her torso, moving further and further toward her feminine center, until his mouth came upon her panties, tracing the elastic edges just below her belly button with his warm, wet tongue.

"Oh, my," she whispered. The touch of his lips upon her skin, the anticipation, her body's fluttering response ... nothing like she'd imagined.

He lifted his head. "I can stop here. Stay above your waist. You decide. Or, I can keep going just a bit more, my briefs will remain where they are. You tell me when to stop."

Breathless within minutes, every inch of her tingling and alive with goosebumps and pulses she couldn't quite describe. She took his hand and placed it on her breast. "I want you to keep going. Please don't stop." She didn't know where she got the nerve, but her body seemed to be in charge and wanted more.

He lingered around her belly, kissing her tenderly, his hands caressing her hips as his heated mouth followed. Little kisses covered her until his lips reached the edge of her panties. His tongue probed underneath the elastic edge, ever so lightly, and she felt herself leaving the world behind, trying to keep her mind from wandering ... following his mouth in her mind, anticipating where his tongue would go next, as he inched further and further beneath her panty line.

He kept going, probing with his tongue, and then moved back up, devouring her mouth, stroking her hair, and nudging her ears and her neck, before moving back down again to the breasts, nipples, then down, to the panty line once again. With a quick assault, his mouth and heated breath encircled her mound completely, and again, she heard herself groan. The heat over her panties sent a wave of chills over her, and she saw herself in her mind's eye, almost laughing out loud. *Who is this* wanton *girl, naked and writhing about?*

Although his swollen, aching bulge remained confined within his slacks, his pleasure stemmed from her groans of delight, her excited, heaving body, bursting with desire. He licked around her panty line, each time going further past the elastic, inching closer and closer like a snake sneaking up on its prey, until it finally seized what it was searching for.

Katie kept repeating, "Oh my God," over and over, giggling as she heard herself, unable to say anything more.

Discovering her lush and now moist core, he traveled leisurely, tenderly, until his mouth enveloped her completely. The broad sweep of his tongue caused her to tremble and moan openly as her center pulsed. A sly smile curled on his lips as he peeled off her soaked panties. After circling his tongue around her supple skin several times, he swept over the length of her softness, causing a sensation that made her quiver and writhe with dizzying pleasure.

He repeated this until she felt something harder upon her. *What is that? His finger? No, one hand is on my hips. The other is on my breast! It couldn't be his stiffened member—he still has his trousers on.* What was this hardness she felt? His head was buried deeply between her legs; his mouth, wet and soft. And then, more pressure, a firmer touch, thrusting. *His nose! Oh, Lord!*

Both the tip and the flat of Dane's nose pressed against her intimately, paired with his mouth, tongue, and lips, each lick and stroke propelling her higher into a state of ecstatic delirium. "Oh, my God!" Gasping for breath, she raked her fingers through his thick hair, her body shaking with a desperate, primal intensity she could not comprehend or control, finally rendering one shuddering, pulsating contraction after another, culminating in a long, loud, strained moan. Breathless, her bare chest heaved beneath his open hand, while his face rested on her belly.

Trying to catch her breath and focus, she whispered, "Oh My God."

He came up beside her, kissing her cheek and lingering there, smiling at her exuberance and his triumph.

"That was brilliant! I can't believe it. What did you do to me?" She hugged him tightly, smothering him with kisses. "My Lord. I never imagined..." she laughed, kissing him with quick pecks all over his face. "It was like I was out of my mind! In another universe!" She was laughing...and then came the tears.

He tasted her salty tears. "Oh, no. Why the tears, love?"

"It was just so...brilliant! Thank you. Thank you for not making me wait any longer! Oh, my goodness!"

"I'm quite pleased you enjoyed that. And that's just a taste of what's to come, love."

"Good Lord. None of this was in that book in your library, the feeling of it, the intensity, the tingling. So much more thrilling and stirring than I could have ever imagined. I even thought of Priya's moaning a few times, and laughed out loud. Did you hear me laugh? And then I heard myself moaning too!" She covered her reddened face with her hands.

"And they probably heard you next door as well," he kidded.

"Oh!" she yelped, pushing him, giggling. Katie could not wipe the immense pleasure from her face, and Dane chuckled at how excited she was and how much she obviously enjoyed it.

"Ahh...Priya," Dane said, thinking of their last spoken words. "She saw something. And, she didn't like it," he reflected, shaking his head.

"What? What did she see?"

"She saw ... something between us. The way I looked at you. She said she didn't want to wait to watch it develop. That's why she moved on."

"Oh, I'm sorry. Do you miss her?"

"What? Of course not!" His finger traced the length of her nose. "Don't be silly. Unbuttoning his shirt, with his eyes fixed on hers, he continued, "But seeing your lover's eyes alight with love for another—the warmth, the tenderness, the unmistakable spark—is more than any woman can bear, I suppose."

Katie combed her fingers through the hair on his chest. *Did he say love?* She took a deep breath, reveling in that thought, before her mind returned to her guilt over Priya. "I'm sorry I caused her pain. I liked her. Didn't mean to hurt her, surely."

"There. There it is again. That right there is what makes you extraordinary. That empathy, and for a rival at that! Not that she ever came close."

He removed his shirt, then lowered himself on top of her, his lips on hers.

Her hand slowly traveled down, fingering his tight muscles, then to his belt buckle, unfastening it.

He held her hand to stop her. "Hmmm. We will get there. Don't worry about me."

"But I want to worry about you. Remove your trousers. Get comfortable."

"Have you been speaking to Joel?"

"What?"

"Nevermind. Just something he said." After removing his slacks, leaving his briefs in place, he murmured, "I need to close my eyes for a spot."

Cuddling close in their position, she felt her center pulse again as his bulging heat pressed against her backside. "I'm still throbbing. Like little aftershocks," she said, wiggling.

"Good," he breathed, his eyes fluttered shut as he nestled his face in her hair.

"I didn't think I would like it. I have only known know how my pop treated my mum when he came home from the pubs. But this was so different than I thought it would be and wonderful. I can't believe it. Daneland. I want to live in Daneland."

"What, love?" he mumbled.

·♥·♥·♥·♥·♥·

Not understanding what she'd said, he squeezed her to him, grinning to himself, thinking of how much more there was for her to experience, and how he longed to take her that very moment and make her his. But he also marveled that he was content in a way he had never been before. Even though his loins ached. As they fell asleep, he recalled more of his brother's wisdom. *"One person, if it's the right person, is all you need or want, indeed."*

THE COTSWOLDS

THE BOUQUET OF WHITE and yellow daisies and white roses was so voluminous that one could see only Mrs. Hughes's legs as she carried them into Katie's room.

"You have an admirer, I'd say!"

"Oh, my goodness," Katie squeaked, pulling out the card. Her eyes filled with tears as she read, "*Darling, On May 21, 1956, my life changed forever. You have filled my heart with joy and a purpose I will ever cherish. Happy Anniversary. It will forever be our special day. Love, Dane.*"

She hugged the note to her chest, repeating the words "*Love, Dane*" in her head, and took the flowers, leaving Mrs. Hughes wondering. She loved that he acknowledged their anniversary.

Turning her attention to her mail, Katie's hands trembled as she regarded the three packages on her desk. All acceptance letters. While her friends talked of parties and balls, she had big decisions to make. *Which college? Graduation. Leaving. Will I be able to leave him?*

That weekend, Dane and Katie read through the brochure about the Cotswolds, and Dane considered the hotel arrangements for Maggie and Troy's wedding. He read the description to her, "This magical, historic area, west of Oxford, encompasses untouched twelfth-century towns, Old English limestone cottages with thatched roofs, meandering streams throughout the villages, and idyllic wisteria-framed storefronts and cafes. Each picturesque town scattered about the quintessential English countryside is more breathtaking than the next."

She took the brochure from him and looked at the photos. "It sounds so lovely. I have heard many of the old castles and large stone manors are being converted to hotels and wedding venues. Do you want to stay at the Swan where the wedding will be?"

"Yes. It used to be a coaching inn for travelers with horses. I think it will look odd if we chose somewhere else. It will be convenient, but I must book two rooms."

Katie could think of nothing else but being in a hotel room again with Dane. That night she held the note Mr. Wellington had left in the piano bench. *'Reach for the stars, young lady.' I'm reaching, Father. I'm reaching.*

·♥·♥·♥·♥·♥·

K ATIE'S ENTIRE FAMILY, ALONG with Trisha, Joel, Maggie, Troy, Lucy, and Lilian made the trip to Brighton to attend Katie's graduation.

As everyone congratulated Katie after the ceremony, one person's words especially touched her heart. "I'm very proud 'o you, dear," Norma said while hugging Katie. "I see you an ye 'usban are doin jus fine. 'e's a man in love, plain t'see."

Katie sighed deeply, assuring her mother that Dane was a good man.

Meanwhile, back at the house, Mrs. Macklin prepared a Shepherd's pie and an apple crumb cake in anticipation of the surprise party Dane had planned.

After all the guests had eaten their fill, Dane lifted a glass for a toast. "I want to say, on behalf of my father and myself, congratulations, Katie. You have worked hard and have achieved something remarkable. I'm so happy that we were able to do this for you, and I know Father is as proud as a father could be. He wanted only that you become extraordinary, and so you have. Congratulations, darling."

"Thank you. I am forever grateful to both of you." She could only plant a kiss on his cheeks, as they were not alone. But, later, by the doorway of Dane's room, their lips would not be parted.

❤ · ❤ · ❤ · ❤ · ❤

A FEW DAYS LATER, they were off to Maggie's wedding in the Cotswolds. "Oh Dane! It's so charming here! Magical!" she shouted over the roar of Dane's 1957 XK120 Jaguar. When they came to a stop, Katie stood in the convertible, snapping photographs of the old stone cottages and the medieval churches that stood a million miles high.

Dane sighed with relief when he saw that their charming rooms were not only next to one another but connecting, no longer worried about being caught going back and forth between each other's room.

"It's like we have stepped back in time," Katie said, looking out the window. The rustic barns, their paint peeling and wood grayed with age, seemed untouched by the passage of a hundred years. A charming old church stood in the distance, with pastures beyond.

Katie jumped onto the bed. "It's perfect! I love it!"

"I figured. And I'm starving. Let's get some lunch," he said, pulling her up.

"Food is never far from your mind, is it?" she chuckled.

The town bustled with the morning activities of hotel guests and locals out with their dogs. Vendors made use of their horses, carrying tourists in old-fashioned buggies as they did during the eighteen hundreds. Katie and Dane found a lovely café with a canopy of wisteria vines to shade them while enjoying a leisurely, satisfying meal. Dane put his hand on hers as they gazed at one another.

"I don't think I tell you often enough how beautiful you are."

"Thank you," she said, her eyes gleaming. She longed for him to say the three words.

Holding hands, meandering through the quaint village, ducking into a little museum, a bookstore, and several shops along the way, Katie purchased picturesque postcards as souvenirs. Stopping to rest on a park bench overlooking the water, they shared an ice cream cone. She watched as he licked and sucked the cream, then held the cone to her lips, and playfully pushed harder than necessary, smearing the cream all over her lips. She licked them clean with embarrassment and laughter.

After high tea at the hotel, they headed up to their rooms to unpack. When finished, Dane came to Katie's room, plucked the bedspread and blanket off the bed, removed his shirt, and threw himself on top of the cool sheet.

"What are you doing?" she yelped.

"Appreciating the breeze from the ceiling fan. It's hot. And I enjoy watching you." His eyes followed her as she unpacked, placing her makeup and hairbrush on the dressing table.

Mesmerized, she watched him in the mirror. His arms raised behind his head; the ripple of muscle beneath his skin resembled a sculpted marble statue. "Dane," she said softly, looking into the mirror at him. "We are married. But not in truth. Are we courting? I don't know what to make of it. No one knows anything. I feel... I feel, well, we are nothing. And yet ..."

"We are everything."

She sucked in her breath, turning to face him. A tear fell silently from her eye.

"I promise you. I am working on it. Don't give up on me yet. I wouldn't have imagined it last year, but now ... well, I've already begun to see a therapist, love. Ironically, her name is Daisy. Daisy Mulligan!"

"Oh, my. Brilliant!"

"It has taken me quite some time to seek help. And I apologize for that. Most men choose to remain strong and silent. I suppose my fear of losing you is greater than my fear of therapy."

Her eyes gleamed back. *"Stay the course until you get what you want."* *Yes, that's it. I can't possibly leave him now. Not when he is trying so hard and making so much progress.* She moved closer to him. "What do you talk to Daisy about? I mean, you don't have to be specific. Or, perhaps I shouldn't ask."

"It's alright. We talk a lot about my mother, both parents, I suppose. And a lot about you. Your passion about the things you care about. How easily you and I talk about things. How you make me reflect...even question my own thoughts. And we talk about trust."

Katie snuggled against him, knowing she had made her decision.

The jarring ring of the telephone sliced through their moment, causing them both to jump. It was Joel calling to ask if they wanted to meet for supper.

"Sure, we can meet you. We are about to take a nap, so 7:00?" Dane said, hanging up.

"We are about to take a nap? Is that so?"

"Yes, it is. I'm quite sacked," he said. Tucking his arms under her, he pulled her down under him, kissing her tenderly. "I need to rest. Just a bit."

As they cuddled in their position, his arms securely around her, Dane whispered, "I love this."

She smiled to herself. *I love you too, Dane.*

They fell asleep for two hours, longer than either of them had anticipated. She woke to find him resting on his elbow, studying her.

"What are you doing?" she said sleepily.

"Watching you sleep."

The corners of her mouth turned upwards into a wide, bright grin.

Unable to take his eyes from her, he said, "What am I going to do with you?"

Whispers, soft kisses, and laughter filled the quiet room until the buzz of the clock announced the time to dress for supper.

"I wish I hadn't agreed to go out," Dane sighed. "We don't get this freedom at home. But I cannot cancel plans with Joel."

They dressed in their own rooms and met in the lobby. It was difficult for Dane and Katie to keep their distance from one another or their eyes from exchanging loving glances. Throughout the meal, Dane caught Trish glancing at Joel, knowing looks flying between them.

·♥·♥·♥·♥·♥·

W HILE ENTERING HER ROOM, Dane said, "I don't want to presume anything, love. I've stopped counting how many times I have held you while we slept. I'll be happy just cuddling."

"You must be joking," she grinned, as she unzipped her skirt, not taking her eyes from his.

He chuckled, threw off his clothing except for his boxers, and said, "Honestly, we need not do anything more, but I do love you being naked in my arms."

"Oh my!" Her breath hitched in her chest as he removed the rest of her clothing, slowly stroking her naked, silky skin, until they were asleep in a loving embrace.

·♥·♥·♥·♥·♥·

W AKING TO A SUMMER storm the following morning, Dane laughed heartily, "A great day to stay in bed! I'm very pleased!"

She giggled beneath him, squirming as he kissed her entire face.

He held her arms over her head and came down upon her soft mouth in a blinding, searching, hungry kiss. "Good morning, love." Feverish with desire, he caressed her breasts, kissing them and running his tongue slowly over her. She giggled from his tickles until his nose found the sweet spot she yearned for him to find. The giddy laugh faded into heavy, rhythmic breaths of passion, while her fingers caressed and entangled Dane's hair.

This time, the anticipation of what was to come drove her crazy with want; boldly giving him access and reaching out to touch him as he touched her. As her mind floated, she heard herself say "Daneland" out loud.

His tender, sensual kisses relaxed her like a narcotic that releases all inhibition, and she marveled at her own willingness to allow him to give her pleasure without shielding herself in shyness.

"I don't think I have ever wanted anyone this much, love." His flat tongue possessed her slippery softness, lingering and then swirling, and finally nuzzling his face into her as she shuddered and spasmed with convulsive gasps.

"Oh, love," she blubbered, as she slowly recovered from the wonder of ecstasy. "Dane...Your nose." She touched the length of it. "You used it...on me?"

"Yes. A little trick of mine," he chuckled.

"It was....surprisingly....erotic," she said, sheepishly.

"I'm glad you were pleased, ma'am."

"I'm tingling, just thinking of it." She was giddy and coy like a young schoolgirl. "But now I want to explore you." Her fingers brushing over his tightly muscled chest, then hips; a shiver tickled her neck as she took the length of him in her hand. Her eyes, wide and bright with excitement, a rising heat between them, she watched his aroused organ grow like a burst of fire.

Laughing, he pulled her hand away...."Oh, my lord. Later, my love. I need some fuel!"

"Oh, again, thinking of food!" she giggled.

"And you are always thinking of sex! Not that I mind, actually."

She giggled again, snuggling up naked in the bed, awaiting his return.

Despite the sheets of rain, Dane braved the storm to bring back food and drinks. Back in their room, they picnicked on the bed while listening to the crackling radio, first a hilarious comedian, then a famous playwright's dramatic voice reciting a scene from his play.

"This has been the most perfect day," he said, lying on his side. "Do you know this sonnet?"

"Shall I compare thee to a summer's day?
Thou art more lovely and more temperate:
Rough winds do shake the darling buds of May,
And summer's lease hath all too short a date;
Sometime too hot the eye of heaven shines,
And often is his gold complexion dimm'd;
And every fair from fair sometime declines,
By chance or nature's changing course untrimm'd;
But thy eternal summer shall not fade,
Nor lose possession of that fair thou ow'st;
Nor shall death brag thou wander'st in his shade,

When in eternal lines to time thou grow'st:
So long as men can breathe or eyes can see,
So long lives this, and this gives life to thee."
William Shakespeare Sonnet 18

"Darling, oh that was beautiful. Shakespeare. You memorized that?"

"I did. I learned it in school long ago. But I relearned it last week, for you. You know Shakespeare?"

"We studied a bit. You recited it so well. You do everything so very well."

"A trait my father taught me, you know.

"Yes, I know. Be extraordinary. I loved him, so." She could not think of Ellis without the tears.

"You have no idea what that means to me, love." He tenderly caressed her face. "I could not imagine building a life with someone who had not known my father, and the relationship you shared with him is, now, even more precious. And how he told me we were meant to be together." Dane's heart was full of love. Love and pain. Clenching his teeth, hating himself for not being able to say the words.

"Will you recite it again?" she begged.

He did.

"So, it's about eternal love, as they age," she said, trying to remember and decipher it.

"Yes," he said, still stroking her face. "Time marches on. 'So long as men can breathe, or eyes can see, so long lives this, and this gives life to thee.'" He held her head in his hands and stared into her baby blues.

Time ceased as they embraced, exploring one another's mouths, unable to part. Dane's breath, rapid and short, knowing that his father had been right, he stroked her back with his fingertips. "I made reservations at another inn in Bourton-on-the-Water for tomorrow. I will be quite restrained and occupied tonight at the wedding, I'm afraid. It's always like that once the women realize I can dance. And I must be polite and dance with them all at least once. But I want you all to myself tomorrow."

"Of course. It's no different for women. We mustn't say no to one man and then yes to someone else. I expect to be quite busy myself. I hope we can get at least one foxtrot and one waltz."

"And all the slow sways, of course."

She bit her lip and closed her eyes. *Well, he may not be able to say it, but he loves me. He just needs time. But how much time? How long will it take?*

Chapter 32

A FINAL DECISION

WITH A DELICATE TOUCH, Katie carefully applied the rouge onto Maggie's cheeks, then a second coat of mascara. "I'm so happy for you, Maggie."

"Oh, Katie, I am forever grateful you invited us to your holiday party. It took forever for him to call me and even longer getting comfortable for our first kiss. But, now, oh, we love each other so much," Maggie gushed. Inspecting her student turned friend, Maggie reached for Katie's hand. "Katie, you look positively smashing! You are stunning." She paused, studying Katie's face. "And you seem on a cloud! What a change I see!"

"Thank you," Katie giggled.

Maggie stopped abruptly, her fingers gripping Katie's arm. "Katie. Are you and Dane...?"

Katie shuddered, not knowing what to say. "We are headed in that direction. We have kissed, and a bit more ... Oh Maggie, I must speak with you. Not today of course. But soon."

Maggie's eyebrows gathered in a fury of worry. "Katie." Making sure no one heard her, she looked around. "You mustn't let him take you. It is of the utmost importance. You could, God forbid, get pregnant. It happens to so many girls. Women have been giving themselves to him for years! I knew quite a few at Oxford who knew him well, and Troy knew him too during their school days. Back then he had a reputation, dear. A forever bachelor with a different gal every weekend. Oh, I fear for your womb, as well as your heart, love. You don't want to know the pain of finding yourself pregnant, loving someone who will not marry you."

Katie sighed to herself, knowing Maggie was probably correct. "I know all. I will be careful. Thank you."

Back in her room, Katie washed and donned a navy, ankle-length silk dress, with a vee-shaped off-the-shoulder neckline and a cinched waist. Shimmering faceted rhinestones held the silky long slit sleeves together, showing off her slender arms. Designed to flatter, the dress emphasized her attributes with elegant simplicity.

Soft organ music filled the beautifully appointed hotel chapel as the ceremony began. Maggie's parents accompanied her down the aisle, kissed her cheeks, and handed her to Troy. The pair stood facing one another, holding hands as they said their vows.

Dane put his hand over Katie's as the priest spoke. Her heart quickened as she looked at his hand on hers, then raised her eyes to his, both remembering their hasty wedding.

Everyone stood, clapping and cheering for the newlyweds. When Maggie and Troy reached Katie, Troy shouted and pointed to Katie, "This was your doing. Thank you."

"I'm very happy for you both," Katie said.

Though there were many obligatory dances with Maggie's friends and relatives, Dane was free to dance more with his girl as the evening wore on. Towards the end of the evening, the band played the main title song from the film *An Affair to Remember* by Vic Damone. Katie had been standing with Maggie's friends when a gentleman she didn't know asked her to dance. She scanned the crowded room; not seeing Dane, she accepted his hand.

Sliding to Katie's side, Dane breathed, "I'm sorry. I believe this dance has been promised to me."

Katie giggled. "Oh, yes. I'm sorry. I didn't see you." She looked at the gentleman. "May I catch the next one with you?"

Joel, Trish, Maggie, and Troy shared stunned glances as they watched the couple practically make love on the dance floor though they hardly moved.

·❤·❤·❤·❤·❤·

BACK IN HER ROOM, they shed their clothes unceremoniously, kissed and cuddled in their position until they were almost asleep. Reaching behind her, she cupped her hand around him, tracing his thick girth, feeling his arousal reach its peak within seconds. Turning around, she pushed him onto his back.

"Oh, love," he said.

Recalling the tantalizing tease of his tongue, she traced hers at the edges of his briefs, delving further under the fabric with each rotation, finally removing them. *My God*, she thought, *the full extent of him is still so shocking.* Gathering her nerve, she took the tip of his hardness into her mouth, moving her head and her tongue slowly but firmly, remembering what she'd read in that book. His moans brought a smile to her heart, knowing she was pleasing him, possessing him with stimulating strokes. His quickened breath relaxed into a steady, slow-paced rhythm, and with his arm resting over his eyes, his mind lost in a sea of clouds, he soon exploded with one long, thunderous grunt, his body jerking in spasms over and over. She grinned victoriously.

"Thank you, love," he whispered in her neck.

As they were falling asleep, he murmured, "I brought you to New York so you would think about attending school there. To have some time away from me. Time to grow, perhaps even court other men. But now, I don't know what I will do without you if you choose New York."

Squeezing his arm, her eyes sparkled with tears. "Well, now, you don't have to worry about it anymore because I've decided to accept Lady Margaret Hall."

"Oh, thank God," he said, pulling her close and kissing her.

·❤·❤·❤·❤·❤·

THE NEXT DAY THEY drove north to Bourton-on-the-Water, another charming town with a meandering river flowing through its medieval cobblestoned streets. They spent a few hours in a paddle boat with a bottle of wine, some soft drinks, and some freshly baked pastries. They laughed, sang songs from *West Side Story,* and the popular song, "Unchained Melody," now sung by Todd Duncan. Dane's heart, for the very first time in his life, was full of love.

"I can't believe it, but I think I'm falling in love with you."

"Oh!" She flung her arms around his neck. "I've already told you how I feel."

'I think I am falling in love with you.' She repeated his words over and over in her head. *He almost said it! Almost.*

Chapter 33

SOMETHING MORE

J OEL NERVOUSLY TAPPED HIS pencil and glanced at his brother in the office as they prepared for the quarterly land manager meetings. "How are things going? With Katie, I mean?"

"I think well. I have engaged a therapist, believe it or not."

"That is wonderful news. Tell me, brother, does Katie bring a peace to you heart you have never known?"

Dane frowned, thinking Joel was being smug.

"I mean that sincerely. I wasn't trying to be smart."

"I believe she does. I'm content. I don't know why. When we were in the Cotswolds, we stayed in bed, talking, caressing, and kissing for almost all afternoon. It wasn't about sex because that hasn't happened. Not in full, anyway. I enjoy listening to her thoughts, talking to her about important things like societal issues and news." Dane reflected. "It's just so different with her. I feel like she knows me, truly knows me."

"That's good."

Dane got up from his chair and started pacing. "She is extraordinary. The difference between her and, well, any other gal I have ever known, is the difference between ... day and night. Just as you once said." He froze, then looked at Joel. "It isn't lust, is it?"

"No."

It's something more. Something spectacular. Love. "But, why can't I say the words?" Dane pulled Joel up and out of his chair. "Punch me in the face, will you? Knock some damn sense into me."

"I think I'll let your therapist do that."

"My father. He said I will love her evermore. How the heck could he have known that?"

"It is peculiar." Joel sat back down and smiled at him, his fingers on his chin, "You two look quite cozy together. Honestly, you aren't officially married already?"

"No. We are not. Have you been doubting me this whole time? No, you have not won our bet."

Joel crossed his arms. "I cannot believe that! You two are madly in love. It's apparent to everyone."

"She is still ... well, whole."

Joel became agitated and gritted his teeth. "You musn't ruin her. I mean, if you don't plan to stay married to her. Promise me you will not. She doesn't deserve that, for God's sake! You married her in the first place to protect her. You must continue to do that. And you know your father would have insisted, too." Joel shook his head in frustration. He took Dane's arm roughly. "I mean it. Promise me."

Dane ignored him, deep in his thoughts. "Love? I can't bring myself to say the words. I'm blocked. I am in bloody hell."

Joel stood his ground and stared, crossing his arms again.

Dane finally saw his brother's ire. "Alright! I promise." Dane sighed, thinking of the Cotswolds. *I didn't take her maidenhood, thank goodness.* "Why are you getting so cross?"

"Because you are a dammed fool. Now, can we go over these numbers before the others arrive? Or, would you like to just keep talking about love?" Joel quipped.

Dane flung his calendar at him, an attempt to cool his own frustration and wipe away his brother's infuriating grin.

Chapter 34

UNWINDING THE CLOCK

Dane's barrister, James Caldwell, confirmed that the twice postponed hearing regarding their marriage would not be postponed again. "We will have enough time after the hearing to get you settled in Oxford, darling."

On the day of the hearing, as George drove to them to the London courthouse. Dane, lost in thought, reached for her hand.

"What will they ask?" she asked.

Dane saw the fear in her eyes. "I'm sure they will ask each of us if our marriage has been consummated. Perhaps, even separately."

"What shall we say?"

"We must say yes. Unless we want the court to annul it. But more than that, if we say no, then we have admitted fraud. That we haven't married in earnest. Then the judge might annul it himself. My barrister will be there. Do not say anything unless the judge asks you a direct question."

She nodded, noticing he had not said he *didn't* want it annulled, and looked out the window to hide her trepidation.

After shaking Caldwell's hand and introducing him to Katie, Dane and the others entered the courthouse. Mr. Caldwell explained the proceeding and what the judge might focus on, instructing them to use the term "Your Honor" when speaking and only to speak when answering the judge's question. When it was their turn to enter the courtroom, they sat on the opposite side of Mr. Barclay and his barrister.

The clerk entered the court. "Silence. Upstanding in Court! God save the Queen. The Honorable Thomas Denford presiding."

Everyone stood as the judge entered and took his seat, the customary seventeenth-century gray wig upon his head as protocol demanded.

"Be seated," said the clerk.

The judge began. "Good morning. We are here in the matter of Barclay versus Wellington. Who represents Mr. Barclay?"

"Charles McKnight, representing Mr. Edward Barclay, Your Honor."

"Go ahead, sir," the judge said.

"Your Honor, Mr. Barclay certifies that he was betrothed to Miss Clarke, and both she and her parents agreed to the marriage and signed the contract. The banns were read in St. Peter's Church in Frimley, but when Mr. Barclay showed up for the wedding, the bride was nowhere to be found. Mr. Barclay and Mr. Wellington collided by chance the day before at the barbershop. When Mr. Wellington learned of the nuptials, he became violent, throwing Mr. Barclay to the ground. My client later learned that, in fact, Mr. Wellington raced to Miss Clarke's home and married her solely to avert Mr. Barclay's planned union.

"Mr. Barclay has endured great expense renovating his home so that his mother and new wife would have the privacy they needed, and he secured an alternate residence for his brother, which he paid for and furnished. Mr. Barclay declares he was deprived of his right to marry Miss Clarke and was terribly damaged by her absence on the day of the wedding. He also believes their marriage to be unconsummated and, therefore, void and fraudulent. Mr. Barclay is suing for Breach of Promise and Fraud and is asking for damages in the amount of five hundred pounds to cover his expenses, plus litigation fees."

"What?" Katie yelled. Caldwell reached out his hand to quiet her.

"Counselor," the judge said to Caldwell.

"Mr. James Caldwell, representing Katie and Dane Wellington, your honor."

The judge nodded.

"Your Honor, for clarification, I will be using the rightful name of Mrs. Wellington and not Miss Clarke. Mrs. Wellington's father owed Mr. Barclay four hundred and eighty-seven pounds, and rather than paying off that debt as one might expect, Mr. Clarke and Mr. Barclay entered into an agreement to wipe the debt clean if his daughter wed Mr. Barclay.

"While outwardly agreeing to the arrangement under pressure from her parents, Mrs. Wellington inwardly withdrew. The weight of her discontent finally led her to seek Mr. Wellington's help. Mr. and Mrs. Wellington were well acquainted with one another for years, and Mr. Wellington felt it fitting that he should offer marriage. They were married with parental consent of course."

Caldwell paused, then added, "I might add, Your Honor, that they are happily married and love each other very much. They do not wish for their marriage to end. I also might add that Mr. Wellington paid five hundred pounds through me to Mr. Barclay to clear Mr. Clarke's original debt.

"My clients demand to be left alone, and have filed a petition for Restriction of Proximity against Mr. Barclay and his associates. Mr. Barclay is the violent one. He and his musclemen appeared at the Wellington's home, forced them both into one of his cars, held Mr. Wellington down, and viciously tried to abduct Mrs. Wellington. They were freed only after Mrs. Wellington was outrageously forced to recount the intimate moments of their wedding night. God only knows what might have happened had Mr. Barclay and his roughnecks been successful."

"Thank you, counselor. I have read the declarations, and I have some questions for both parties," said the Judge.

"Mr. Barclay. How do you know Mr. Clarke, sir?"

"Mr. Clarke and I have played cards and bet the horses together for many years."

"I see, sir. And it's through the gambling that he owed you four hundred and eighty-seven pounds?"

"Yes, sir."

"And you agreed to marry Mrs. Wellington as a way for him to clear his debt with you?"

"No, Your Honor. I was seeking a wife, and he was seeking a husband for his daughter. I am a devout man and as you may be aware, a father often transacts a business arrangement for his daughter's welfare. I am a landowner of considerable means, and her father agreed that his daughter's life would be greatly improved with this union. And, as we would now be kin, I agreed to forgo his debt."

"I see," said the judge. "Isn't it customary for the father to pay the groom, and not the other way around? If Mr. Clarke owed you four hundred and eighty-seven pounds, and that debt was dismissed in exchange for his daughter, then you sir, have bought yourself a bride. I believe it is illegal to purchase another human being in this sovereign. Had you met Mrs. Wellington before making this deal with her father?"

"I met her and her parents at a church function before asking for her hand, your honor."

"I see."

"Mr. Barclay. As far as you know, was Mrs. Wellington in agreement to the marriage?"

"Yes, sir."

"Thank you, Mr. Barclay."

"Mr. Wellington," the judge said.

"Your honor."

"How did you know Mrs. Wellington?"

"Mrs. Wellington and I have been acquainted since she was about two years old through my father, with whom she had a special connection. The Clarkes are long-term tenants of my father's, and, now, mine."

"And how did you learn of Mrs. Wellington's upcoming marriage?"

"I was in the barbershop about to get my hair cut when Mr. Barclay was boasting about his upcoming nuptials to a very young and beautiful girl, bragging that her father was his debtor. From his description, I guessed who the girl might be."

"And how did you come to be married to Mrs. Wellington?"

Dane recited the entire account up to their wedding.

"You married her on that day?"

"Yes, sir. I mean, Your Honor."

"How? Without the banns having been read?"

"The vicar obtained a special license from the archbishop, Your Honor."

"Impressive," the judge said, his eyebrows raised in surprise.

"And, one last question. Has your marriage been consummated?"

Pausing for a second, he gulped a quiet, "Yes, Your Honor."

"Mrs. Wellington," the judge said.

"Yes, Your Honor," Katie said, her voice quaking.

"This has been quite an ordeal for you, hasn't it, young lady?"

"Yes, Your Honor."

"Do you agree with Mr. Wellington's statements as to how you met Mr. Wellington and the way you were married?"

"Yes, Your Honor."

"And when Mr. Wellington asked you to marry him, did you think it was because he was trying to help you avoid your marriage to Mr. Barclay?"

"Yes, your honor," Katie answered. Dane and Caldwell shared a glance, knowing she just admitted fraud.

"Mrs. Wellington. Why did you agree to marry Mr. Barclay in the first place?"

"My parents pressured me to agree. They thought he was a good man, Your Honor."

"I beg your forgiveness in asking this delicate question, but in keeping with the law, I must. Has your marriage to Mr. Wellington been consummated?"

She twisted her hands together, answering, "Yes, sir."

The judge sat back in his chair and crossed his arms, studying the couple. "Well now, that does present a problem, doesn't it? It certainly doesn't sit well with this court that a girl should be forced or, as you say, persuaded to marry any man for any reason.

"Nor does it please this court to find that a marriage has taken place for the sole purpose of avoiding a binding betrothal." Dane and Katie shared a worried glance.

"However, this court is not in the habit of breaking up marriages. What would happen if the court insisted on that and, six weeks hence, the missus finds herself with child? No, this court does not separate couples unwillingly.

"Counselor," he addressed Caldwell. "In chambers, if you please. Bring your clients."

They entered the judge's chambers and sat in the fine leather armchairs. The judge studied each of them.

"I cannot ascertain if this marriage has, in fact, been secured. I can only make assumptions. What I see before me is an innocent young woman and an honorable gentleman." He nodded to each of them as mentioned. "I believe there is something between you, but I don't buy that you are truly married. Now, then. A marriage that has not been consummated can be annulled by this court. However, you have both sworn under oath that your marriage is true. Therefore, you can no longer request an annulment. The only way this marriage can end is if you seek divorce. And one of you will have to admit adultery, intoxication, or abuse as the reason."

Both of their faces went pale.

The judge observed their silent responses.

"Mrs. Wellington. I have one last question for you," the judge asked. "If I could unwind the clock, remove the threat of Mr. Barclay and restrict his contact with you, would you choose for me to do so?"

Katie and Dane exchanged a glance.

"In other words, I can annul this marriage right now, and deny Mr. Barclay's request and order that he have no further contact with you or your family. Would you agree to that?" He gave Katie a moment to consider his question.

"Seems to me you are caught between two evils. Not that Mr. Wellington is evil, but you had no intention of marrying. And, Mr. Wellington, I believe you have given all that you can to save this girl, and that is highly commendable. But, now, faced with no possibility of annulment, this marriage could create serious and life-long consequences to you both. If you two are not truly a couple that share a marital bed, I suggest you end this farce and allow me to correct ALL the wrongs here. If you decide later to wed, so be it. At least then, it will be for the right reasons."

Katie looked at Dane, who was shaking his head.

"Your honor. May they have a few moments?" Mr. Caldwell asked.

"I will see you back in the courtroom," the judge said.

Caldwell led them into the hallway.

"Katie!" Dane held both of her hands firmly.

"If we cannot annul it after today, then we will have to stay married or file for divorce. Neither of us wants to say we are divorced." Tears spilled from her eyes, and her chin quivered as she spoke.

"I don't know. I'm willing, if you are… to stay married," he heard himself say, devastated that it had come to this.

Katie stared at him. "Willing to stay married?" She lifted her head. "Absolutely not. You don't want a real marriage, that's clear. And I deserve more than just someone who is 'willing to stay married.'" She bit her lip. "This is the right thing," she nodded, squeezing his hand. She didn't give him any more time to respond. She turned and walked back into the courtroom.

Dane's shoulders slumped, the weight of crushing despair pressing down on him, he fixed his gaze on the floor.

The judge was seated. "Alright. I would like to make a few rulings. As to the petition by Mr. Barclay. It is denied. Mr. Barclay has been paid back by Mr. Wellington, even though Mr. Wellington did not owe him any money. Mr. Wellington even gave him more than Mr. Clarke owed. As to the expense you have endured, Mr. Barclay, I don't believe Mr. Wellington owes you any sums at all. If you have expenditures, your agreement, written or verbal, was with Mr. Clarke, not with Mr. Wellington. Therefore, while you may have a claim to be reimbursed for those expenses, it is not Mr. Wellington's burden to make you whole. If you feel the need, you may petition the court to collect from Mr. Clarke, although I don't believe that will be a worthwhile endeavor.

"Furthermore, neither you, your employees, family members, or your associates may contact or come within thirty-five meters of either Mrs. or Mr. Wellington at any time. You are hereby barred by this court from attempting in any way to enter into any contract, deal, or negotiation involving Mrs. Wellington, or any of her family members, for any reason, marriage or otherwise. Do I make myself clear, Mr. Barclay?"

"Yes, Your Honor."

"And, may I add, I strongly abhor the practice of older men seeking much younger brides. I believe this is morally corrupt, and I fear this would damage a girl for the rest of her life. I hope, sir, you will take heed and find yourself a more suitably-aged companion. That is all. You are dismissed."

Mr. Barclay got up with his barrister and several of his associates and stormed noisily out of the courtroom.

The judge waited until they exited. "Now, you two. What is your decision? Are we going to annul this marriage? Mrs. Wellington, once the marriage is annulled, you will return to your parents home. Your parents will remain your guardians until you turn twenty-one unless someone else petitions the court for a wardship with good reason. And no, Wellington, not you."

Katie interrupted. "Would I still be able to go to university, sir? I mean, Your Honor?"

"That depends on your parents' wishes for you. This court cannot make any rulings on that. Your time is up. I need to adjourn this and get on with my day."

"I want to annul the marriage, Your Honor," Katie said in a low, hushed tone, her chest caving from lack of air.

"No!" Dane said, softly. They looked at one another, their eyes locked. Both were miserable that they were at this junction.

"Please stand before the court," the judge stated. "You will each swear before this court that your marriage has not been consummated."

"I swear," she whispered.

Dane paused and looked down, reluctant to say the words. "I swear." His voice matched his heart, ragged and cracked. He wanted to grab her and run. But he could not move.

"The court of Magistrates hereby grants an annulment to Mr. Dane Wellington and Mrs. Katherine Wellington from their marriage dated May twenty-first, nineteen hundred fifty-six. You are dismissed."

They both jumped at the crack of the judge's gavel. Though aware that annulment had been the original plan, neither was prepared for the devastating feelings that accompanied it.

Dane was frozen. Caldwell shooed them out of the courtroom, literally pushing Dane's shoulder to walk.

The silence in the car was thick with despair, their rigid posture reflecting the sorrow gripping their hearts. Dane's shoulders slumped, his jaws tense, and his breath was shallow and labored. Perspiration glistened on his forehead.

Katie's hands rested in a fisted ball on her lap, she looked down, visibly trying to contain her silent internal turmoil that was threatening to burst into a thundering rain cloud of sobs at any moment.

He took her hand, gripping it firmly. He avoided her eyes, fighting back his own watery blur. *No longer married. It is what I wanted all along. What I expected. Why do I feel so bloody awful?* "Let's go home, George," Dane instructed.

Katie ran to her room and dove under her covers.

Dane went into his study, grabbed the brandy bottle, and then proceeded to his room.

Witnessing their dark moods and silence, the staff wondered what had happened. George shrugged as they questioned him. Mrs. Danbury knocked at Katie's door.

"Go away," Katie shouted.

"Katie, it's me, dear," Mrs. Danbury said.

"Oh, I'm sorry. Come in," she said through sobs.

"What's 'appened?"

"The judge annulled our marriage," she cried, placing her head on Mrs. Danbury's lap.

"Good Lord." Shocked and saddened, Mrs. Danbury stroked her hair. "Do no fret, dear. You will find the perfect 'usband soon'nough. 'E's no the one fa ye."

A HURRICANE

KATIE SPENT THE DAY and night with tears blurring her vision as she thought about Dane's loving words from all their times together, especially sonnet he'd recited. The photographs of their trips spread across the bed like pieces of a puzzle that no longer fit together.

'Willing?' *It is my own fault. I was warned. Everyone told me he would never marry. He told me himself. Perhaps he just cannot love anyone. And he doesn't love me. If he did, he wouldn't have let this happen. He had the chance but didn't step up.*

Thinking of Father, *I reached, sir. I reached for the stars, but it was only a dream. A stupid dream.*

Mrs. Danbury's harsh words came flooding back: *'You cannot tame him. Each of da girls prob'ly thinkin' they could too, but they ain' gonna.' Why did I think it would be any different with me? And to think I almost let him take me.* Every time another thought popped into her head, the torrential sobbing began again, like a raging, unrelenting hurricane.

Reaching for a tissue on the shelf above her bed, her hand brushed the chimes he had purchased for her, and soon she was lost in their delicate music, hitting them lightly and continuously until her eyes grew heavy. As she turned, pulling the covers over herself, she swiped the chimes to the floor with a crash.

She had made some decisions as she slept, for she awoke with new determination. She would stand tall, as Father had instructed. As she packed up the rest of her belongings, she thought, *I will face adversity through strength. Gram. I'll call her immediately. See if she can run a late acceptance over to her friend at N.Y.U. I'll have George help me move my luggage to mum's, spend some time at home and be off.*

A few hours later, call to Gram completed, plane reservations made, Katie, dressed and ready to depart for her parents', stared into space with untouched coffee at her fingertips.

Dane kissed the top of her head when he came into the kitchen. "It's ok, love. Nothing has changed, actually."

She snapped her eyes at him. "Everything has changed! I mustn't be here anymore. George is taking me home," she said quietly, looking down at her lap.

"What are you talking about?"

"I have no reason to be here. I'm not your wife and have no business staying in your house. The judge even said I must go home."

Dane's face flushed red. "Katie. Weybridge is your home."

"You heard the judge. I must go home to my parents. I don't belong here. I'm *not allowed* to be here."

"Darling, I know in my heart that you are perfect for me. In every way. You belong here. Now and forever."

Katie sat on her hands, digging her fingernails into her thighs. She tried to stay quiet, trust his words, but she realized she was finished. "*Perfect for you?* What does that mean? Dane, I've given you everything, my heart, my love, my life. I had even given up New York for you. And of course, you've given me more than I ever could have imagined. Every material comfort, all the clothes, truly more than anyone could ask for. I will always be grateful to you for that. But you can't give me the one thing I need. I want you. I want your love. I want the fairytale. And until yesterday, I'd been foolish enough to keep hoping that might be possible. But now, I'm just so sad. Because you can't do it. You will never be mine the way I need you to be."

She paused, not looking at him. "I think I'm the one who needs a therapist now. Clearly, I've been a fool, worrying about you for these past two years. You have been my world, and I love you. But, how long can I just wait around? You may never be ready. I'm almost twenty-one. It's time for me to worry about myself."

Dane's eyes popped as he felt the sting of her words. And her torment. "Darling, you know—"

"Don't. Don't say a word, Dane." She looked at him, wiping the tear as fast as it came. "Willing? You would be 'willing' to stay married? Do you think that's what I wanted to hear? Do you think that's what any woman would want to hear?"

"But we... I am getting there. I know I am. What we have is so wonderful."

"Yes, it was wonderful, but now? When you came to rescue me from Barclay, you told my mother this wasn't the 1800s, yet you've kept me a secret. Even after we have been intimate. I assumed it was because you didn't want to tarnish my reputation." She laughed sarcastically and added, "But, in the end, I feel like a concubine. Your secret lover. You said I was perfect. Your *perfect little secret*, you mean. Not really good enough for all the world to know."

"Oh, darling. Don't say that. You mean everything to me."

"Not quite everything," she sighed. "Don't misunderstand. I know I encouraged it. And I have loved our passion. Would have given myself completely had you just nudged a bit. But, I think we both have to face facts. Your challenges are monumental. And I don't blame *you* for them. But, Dane, if you couldn't stand up yesterday and say what I know is in your heart, then when? I ask again, how long shall I wait? Another year? Two? Four? I just can't do it any longer, love. I have to let you go."

·❥·❥·❥·❥·❥·

AFTER KATIE HAD SPENT several days with her family, Dane came to Leatherhead to take her to lunch.

"I don't understand why you won't stay at the house. We only have a few days left before we leave for Oxford. Don't you want to spend them with me?"

With a frown and her head lowered, she said, "I've sent in my acceptance for N.Y.U. Gram helped walk it through."

"What?" Dane's face flushed red. "New York? You're going across the Atlantic? Oh darling, no."

"Yes, New York. I love you, Dane. But, I need to leave. You cannot give yourself to me completely. You cannot bare your soul and confess your undying love. You cannot tell me that I am yours forever. You are not committed to me like I am to you. So, I must stand on my own two feet. Get my degree. Get a good job, and stop relying on Wellington money for everything in my life." She saw in his desperate stare, a silent plea, a drowning man reaching for words he couldn't say.

"Katie, love." He took her hands across the table. "What do you mean, not committed? I haven't been with anyone else. I don't want anyone else. This is not about my remaining a bachelor or seeing other women. I am making progress with my therapist. I know I am. I am quite sure that you are my one true...." He hesitated, still unable to verbalize his feelings.

"But, it is about commitment. Don't you see that? You're unable to commit to me. You couldn't even finish that sentence."

"No. It is about trust. Trusting that the one person.... "

"Oh, Dane," she put her hand out. "I know all about your issues and where they stem from. But this is me. After all this time, you cannot tell me you don't trust me. I know you do. And I know you love me, yet you still cannot say the words. And this is the reason I need to go. Maybe one day you will overcome the obstacles that keep you stuck. But right now," she swallowed hard, "I need to leave. I need to do this for me. Do you understand? Coming back to the house is not going to do anything but make my leaving more painful. This is the way it needs to be."

Dane insisted on taking her to the airport. At the gate, he held her shoulders and said, "I'm not quite sure what you are thinking. Perhaps you want to court other men and don't want to tell me that. But, I assure you, I am working on being able to tell you how I feel. I know I have asked before. I'm not down on one knee begging for your hand, but I am standing in front of you begging you not to give up on me. And, please call me when you get to Gram's." Dane leaned in for a kiss, a wonderful, soft, loving, desperately heartbreaking kiss. And then came the lingering hug.

With a choked sob, she pressed her face against his neck, closing her watery eyes. She took a long, deep breath, inhaling his cologne for the last time, a treasured memory to carry in her heart, as she silently said goodbye, knowing that there was the greatest possibility that they would never be together again.

On the airplane, she allowed herself a few hours of misery. *By the end of this flight, I will be done crying over Dane Wellington. I will start anew and get my degree. I will make a new life and be independent, just as Father encouraged me to do.*

•♥•♥•♥•♥•♥•

S HE WENT DIRECTLY TO Gram, who helped her register for classes and settle in. Exhausted from furnishing the dorm room, Gram sat on the bed, her feet stretched on a chair. The underlying melancholy the girl was trying to hide had not subsided. "Come now, why don't you tell me what is going on?"

Katie took a second, then let her head fall onto Gram's lap, releasing the torrent of tears she had been holding back.

Gram put her hand on Katie's head. "Oh no! These are the same crocodile tears my daughter cried. Are you pregnant dear?"

"No. I'm still whole, although we were quite intimate. But, it's over. Our marriage was annulled by the judge. Dane said he was 'willing to stay married.'" She lifted her head to Gram's eyes. "Gram, I'm so in love with him. He knows what I want. I want the fairytale. I want him down on his knee, begging me to marry him. I want him to pour his heart out. Not just," she lowered her voice to imitate him, "'I'm willing if you are.' He doesn't love me, Gram. Has never said it. Never told me how he feels."

Katie wiped her eyes. "But he certainly told me many times that he will never marry and that he doesn't believe in love. And I tried to be patient waiting for him. But, he thinks... he thinks he will be betrayed. That his wife will leave him, as his mother left his father." She sobbed, then took a deep breath. "Oh Gram, he has to know I would never do that. But I can't keep hoping he'll figure it out."

Gram gasped. "Oh, good God." She stood up, placing her hand over her mouth. "I should have seen it. I didn't understand his reluctance to love. It's all very clear now." She squinted. "Katie, dear. It's important for you to stand on your own two feet. You don't want to rely on a husband for support. But, I'm absolutely sure he is in love with you. Believe me. I know my grandson. He may have his fears, but he loves you. He'll come through. You'll see. Now, come on, let's go eat as you look starved to death."

Katie, barely able to eat anything, sat with Gram at a local café, trying to think of and talk about anything other than Dane. When she returned to her dorm, she buried her head in her pillows and slept for the next twelve hours.

A REVELATION

"I'VE NEVER BEEN IN New York in September," Dane said, taking a deep breath of the fresh air. The afternoon sun on Gram's patio warmed their faces as Dane told her about his sessions with Daisy.

"She loves you, Dane. Very much. Go get her. Tell her how you feel, already, and make her yours."

Dane nodded, then paused, thinking about his recent revelations. "Gram, Daisy and I spoke a lot about Mum. Can you tell me why she went back to Philadelphia?"

"Rachael was ill, dear, for a long time. She needed special machines that cleaned her liver and kidneys. She came home because she needed help. Your father didn't know that she was sick. She didn't want his pity. She wanted to bring you, too. But, of course, your father would not let you come full time. Only for summers and on holiday. Once she arrived and began treatments, she could barely care for Joel. Pops and I cared for him. And Aunt Sarah helped, too."

"She was ill already by then? I didn't know that. Why did she return to England, then?"

"To be with you, of course!" Gram sighed as she looked at her pained grandson. "Oh, darling, she wanted to be with you before she ..." Gram reached for a tissue to wipe her teary eyes. "Your mother loved you very much. I know the pain you must have felt, not having her. Her absence left a gaping hole, and you have suffered for that, I now see. But, she did not abandon you, dear."

Dane looked away uncomfortably, his eyes drowning in tears. The ache swirling in his chest was almost unbearable. He needed a few moments to gather himself. After all this time, the pain of her loss pierced his heart deeply, yet the revelation of his mother's love began replacing the anger he'd felt over her abandonment, bringing him bittersweet peace.

"She made a mistake, and she paid for it. But she did love you and your father, too."

Dane took his grandmother's hand, realizing the pain she must have felt, her dying daughter leaving home so that she could be with her children. "Before he passed, father confessed it as his greatest regret, not helping her when she came back. He said it went against everything he stood for. He said, 'Sometimes it takes a lifetime to get things right.'"

"Well, that's good to know. He was a good man, after all. It's too bad they couldn't work things out. But, I believe Joel was a constant reminder, and your father couldn't live with that." Gram patted Dane's hands. "I wish we would have had this conversation long ago. I fear your perception of the past has misguided you. You were cherished by both your parents, dear." She kissed his cheek. "Now, go get that marvelous girl of yours before it's too late."

· ♥ · ♥ · ♥ · ♥ · ♥ ·

A FTER PACING OUTSIDE THE dorms for what felt like hours, Dane finally spotted the leggy blonde with a tall, well-dressed chap, books in hand, strolling across the street. Seeing Katie walking with another man, tossing her hair back and laughing at something he said, stopped him in his tracks. Eyeing the ground, he placed his hands on his thighs in a moment of defeat. Then he sprinted at full speed, calming himself as he came upon them. "Katie," he called.

They both turned. Katie froze like a panther ready to strike. "Dane?" she murmured.

"Dane?" Her companion's face paled. "*Thee* Dane?" he said, swallowing hard. The preppy young man's lips pursed, clearly sizing up the distinguished gentleman before him.

Not taking his eyes off his girl and still huffing from running, Dane said, "Guilty as charged."

Katie's breath caught in her throat. The unexpected vision of Dane standing in front of her, after weeks of emptiness, constricted her chest. Finally finding her voice, she said, just above a whisper, "What are you doing here?"

Dane cocked his head. "Can we speak?"

Katie looked at Dennis. "Dane, this is my friend Dennis."

Dennis stepped in front of her, protectively. "Well, after everything I've heard about you over the last few weeks, I think you deserve a knuckle sandwich. But if she wants to talk to you, well, I'd say you are one lucky bastard." Dennis touched her shoulder. "Later gator," he said, leaving them.

"Darling. Can we go somewhere to talk?"

She had played this scene in her head many times over the past few weeks. Almost nightly she dreamed he would approach her, just this way, get on his knees and profess his undying love.

"Please," he begged.

"No," she said flatly. "I have a study group at half past. And I don't want to be late."

He exhaled with a great sigh. "Will you come to Gram's later? Please?"

Katie paused, knowing she would, but she wanted him to squirm. She looked at the ground. "I'll consider it."

It was pointless to attend the study group, as her mind was solely on Dane, her stomach in a knot after not allowing herself to think of him these past few weeks.

RECONSTRUCTION

Dane and Gram exchanged glances, sighing with relief at the sound of the doorbell. His knew his pacing was driving his grandmother crazy. They had discussed the possibility Katie might not come.

They both greeted her at the entrance. After a quick hug, Gram said, "I'm so glad you are here. I'll leave you two alone."

Dane kissed her cheek. "Thank you for coming. Can we speak downstairs?"

She followed him down.

"Darling." Dane started as he sat on the bed, offering her the chair that he pulled closer so she could face him. "Please allow me to say all that I need to say." It was time to plead. "No matter what I did in my previous lifestyle, I have always been honest. Of course, there has been my insistence that I won't ever marry. And that I didn't believe in love." He closed his eyes, knowing there was more. "My mistrust of women, of course. And perhaps, my inability to express myself. Good God." He shook his head, hearing his own words. "I know you would not be here in New York had I been able to say what I feel. And I apologize for that. But my inabilities ... you know I did seek help. I hope I get credit for that? I'm here now, able to tell you. I've ... overcome ... those obstacles, as you so accurately pointed out. Because, darling, the thought of losing you is unbearable."

Dane paused, took a deep breath, and then, gazing into her eyes, he gently clasped her hands in his. "I am madly in love with you. You are the only woman I have ever been able to love. I feel a fool now, for I have known it for so long yet had not been able to tell you. There's a lot that I don't know, but I do know I don't want to live my life without you. I refuse to live my life without you. I cannot live my life without you. And I intend to spend every day of my life proving to you I am the man you deserve."

Tears at the corners of her eyes, Katie's chin quivered, and her rapidly pulsing heart vibrated every nerve. She had prayed for this moment for years.

Dane stared into her face. "What is that look? Am I too late? That chap you were with? Desmond, was it? Are you and he …" His face flushed with anger, and his fingers curled into fists.

"His name is Dennis. We are merely friends, although he is … waiting."

"For what?"

She wiped her eyes. "For my broken heart to mend, of course."

"Oh my God, I'll never forgive myself for breaking your heart. The one thing I never wanted to do was hurt you. I fought my feelings for so long. Couldn't admit to myself that what I felt was real. Couldn't say the words. But," he paused, taking her hand, "Katherine Clarke, I love you. I love you and everything about you. I am crazy in love with you. Since before our first kiss in my car. I had wanted to kiss you for so long." Tears gathered in his eyes, blurring his vision. His face, red and flushed, "Do you not love me anymore?"

Katie crumbed. "Dane! Of course, I love you." Her expression mirrored her voice, trembling with emotion. "I've told you before. You know I love you. Ever since the day you brought me the flowers. I think I've loved you my whole life."

He took her hands in his and kissed them. "And I believe I loved you back then, too. All those times I accompanied my father to the different communities each summer. It didn't thrill me to go. Except when I knew we were going to Leatherhead. Only then was I excited to go, anxious to see you. To look into your eyes and and make you smile." He grinned, cupping her chin, then leaned over and pressed his lips to her temple.

Dane took a breath, then continued, "I've learned that I was using my challenges, as you have called it, as an excuse. I always thought I'd be fine on my own, then you entered my life, and my heart. And when you left, I was devastated. But I knew that you hadn't abandoned me; you'd left because of my stupidity, my inability to tell you how I feel. And I am so terribly sorry. I love you, my darling Katie. I will always love you."

She wrapped her arms around his neck, whispering, "Oh, darling. When I left for New York, I was afraid I'd never see you again. I tried not to think about you. But I've been unable to think about anything else." She took his hand. "Thank you for coming after me. Thank you for seeing Daisy and opening your locked heart." She laughed. "I can't believe I'm finally hearing the words I have waited so long to hear. Words I never thought I'd hear from you." Her voice breaking as she spoke, she cried, "I know how hard it was. Thank you. I love you, too, forever and always." A thunderstorm of emotion shook her body as they embraced once more.

They held one another's gaze, finally breaking into laughter. "Never see me again? I'd have died. Come here, you." He lifted her to the bed, falling onto it with frenzied kisses, relief, and laughter.

His kiss, a telling, passion-filled strike on her heart, left her breathless and giddy. She breathed in his cologne, the scent a potent reminder of how deeply he was missed. They kissed again and again, each wanting to strip off their clothes and devour one another.

He loves me.

When they stood, he said, "You look awfully thin, love. I'll bet you haven't eaten all day. Neither have I, and of course, I am starving. Come on. Let's go have something to eat with Gram. She has been a nervous wreck over this, as well."

"There is the Dane I know and love. Always wanting to eat," she grinned.

Once upstairs with Gram, their laughter returned. Gram made a platter of meats and cheeses and opened some champagne. They stuffed their faces without taking their eyes off one another, laughing and kissing in between bites.

"So, how are you liking school?" Dane asked. "Do you still love New York as much as you did before you lived here?"

"Well, from what I've seen, I love it. And now that we have mended, I won't feel so sad. Perhaps I can get out more. Meet some of the girls. I have picked out many things I want to do and see while I'm here. Museums and plays and Off-Broadway shows, where I heard the actors are only three feet from the audience. For the first time in my life, I am really on my own. I can go where I want, do what I want." She stopped and considered her next words. "It sounds strange, but now that my heart is in one piece, I can enjoy being independent. I feel like I am finally growing up here."

"Like a bird who has left her nest, I suppose," Gram said.

"Then, fly you must," Dane said. "I love New York, too. It's exciting, and I know it's good for you to be on your own a bit." Dane forced a smile and tried to be as enthusiastic as she, but he could not hide his fear. "I just hope you don't fall in love with it so much that you won't want to come home."

Katie looked at Dane and said nothing.

A knot formed in Dane's stomach as his smile faded. He put down his sandwich, sharing and a worried glance with Gram.

Katie held a straight face for as long as she could. "Of course, I will come home," she teased.

Dane sighed, laughed, and devoured his sandwich.

As the doorman hailed a cab for her, Dane asked, "I will see you tomorrow?"

"Yes. I'll ring after I get my work done."

"Alright. Goodnight, love."

"Goodnight, my darling."

She returned his kiss with unrestrained gusto and passion, her lips warm and eager as she pressed her body against his, and he knew all was well.

Their time together during the next week and a half was just as it always had been. After dancing on Saturday night at a club in the village, neither wanted to part. Katie spent the night and most of Sunday morning wrapped in Dane's arms at the apartment. They met for supper every evening during the rest of week, and she was back at Gram's the following weekend.

"I hate leaving you," he said, smothering her with kisses, until Ralph, the doorman, appeared in the elevator. "I'll see you in nine weeks."

Hands to her heart, she watched the elevator door close, feeling grateful and blessed.

❤ · ❤ · ❤ · ❤ · ❤

HAPPY TEARS FLOWED FREELY as she read Dane's heartfelt letter, the first of the weekly letters he so beautifully wrote. *He must have written this the night he arrived home,* she thought. *It hasn't been but a week.*

"My dearest, darling Katie,

Although I am morbidly unhappy being parted, I cling to the hope that we will be together permanently in the not-too-distant future. I'm so sorry I couldn't stay long enough to spend your birthday with you. We will celebrate both of our birthdays when I return to New York in November.

I am grateful, now, for the distractions at work and welcome the challenges that come regarding our tenants and the properties. It keeps my mind off missing you.

Do not fret, my love. This separation is a fine lesson for me, for you can be sure I will never forget this anguish and guarantee that I will never stray or make you unhappy, for I can neither bear to break your heart again nor imagine my life without you in it.

I have already made the reservations for my flight on November 16th, for The Nutcracker *on December 19th, for all of us at Radio City again, and for the Copa on New Year's Eve. (Buy a new dress! Buy two! Something spectacular, of course.) I will stay through January 12th.*

I am counting the days until you are back, n——d, in my arms. "(Can you guess the blank word?)

All my love, forever and always, Dane.

She pressed the letter to her chest, giggling as the tears flowed.

TRUE LOVE

T HOUGH HER CLASSES AND schoolwork consumed most of her time, Katie cherished the stolen moments she spent strolling through the bustling, vibrant city streets, shopping for unique treasures, or even reading in Washington Square. She visited Gram on Sundays, usually for a bite and to see a show or play. There were a few parties and dances at a speakeasy near the campus to occupy her, and although she enjoyed dancing with others, she found herself wishing Dane would suddenly appear and whisk her onto the dance floor. Whenever she heard the song "Unchained Melody" or "Only You," no matter where she was or who she was with, tears would well in her eyes.

As November neared, she found it harder and harder to busy herself with friends. The anticipation of seeing Dane was almost too much for her.

Dearest darling,

Thank you for writing so often and for your loving words. My birthday flowers are brilliant and are still alive! I took lots of pictures of the bouquet. Thank you, love. Being twenty-one feels wonderful!

I miss you more and more with each passing day. Truthfully, I wish I hadn't chosen New York, now. As much as I love being here, it isn't worth the agony of our separation. I hadn't considered the possibility that we would mend. I wouldn't allow myself that hope. But now that we have, I am miserable that we are so far apart.

Everything I do feels empty without sharing it with you. I miss seeing your face and hearing your voice. And, as hard as the days are, the nights are far worse. I'm afraid I've gotten quite used to my pillow wet with tears each night.

I'm quite sure your lonliness is as profound as mine, and I am sure you have been counting down the days until you are here again, just as I am. I dream of you holding my face in your hands and kissing my lips, and when I close my eyes at night, I dream you are there.

I do have two consolations: 1) The fifty photographs I have of your face around my room! I can't turn my head without looking at you. I guess I have taken quite a lot of photographs! And 2) I purchased another set of the chimes just like the ones you purchased for me. I left mine at mum's. They are a soothing reminder of your love, and their sweet music chases my blues away, most of the time.

I cannot wait to be back in your arms... hmmm, yes, n-ked in your arms, my love, and to spend two whole months with you and your family.

All my love,

Katie

Finals over, she occupied herself with Christmas shopping for both Dane's family and her own. The New York City department stores were not only alive with colorful lights and holiday decorations, but each department was chock full of fascinating items for sale. She spent a full two hours in the lingerie department at Bloomingdales, discovering the one-piece corsets that slimmed and lifted in all the right places and the sexy sheer sets that included garter belts.

"What would Lizzy say if she saw these?" she giggled, missing her friend. In the taxi heading home to pack for Gram's, she reread Lizzy's letter.

Dear Katie,

Well, as you can imagine, I was absolutely bowled over reading the fabulous news about you and Dane Wellington! (He's SO HANDSOME!) I am giddy at the thought. Watching you two dance at the ball, I thought there might be something between you. The steam between you two was smoldering! You seemed so perfect together!

I'm very happy for you, and I want to hear much more about what it's like to be in love! (WITH HIM! Oh my God!)

How is New York University? I have heard it is terribly difficult. I don't know how you are handling the pressure, but you are such a hard worker. I have no doubt you'll do well there.

As for me, I am in nursing school and living with my aunt in London. There are no men I am interested in. Will there ever be? You must come see me when you get home.

Please let me know what happens with you and Dane, and if it happens as I hope it will, don't forget to invite me to your wedding! Please come home soon!

Your friend, always,

Lizzy

At Gram's, and after a much-needed glass of port, Gram motioned to the piano. "Play something for me, please."

Katie played the "Nocturne in E Flat Major," followed by "An Affair to Remember (Our Love Affair)".

"You play magnificently, dear. You have talent."

"Thank you. I am thrilled I can play. I had wanted to play the "Nocturne" since I was a young girl. Silly. I remember telling Father, that I would play it correctly next time he visited. He even bought me a piano. But, it took me so long to learn it, he never got to hear me play the entire thing. That makes me so sad." She lifted her head and, through her tears, she smiled. "But, I can play because of him."

·♥·♥·♥·♥·♥·

WHILE APPLYING THE FINISHING touches of makeup the following morning, Katie heard the commotion of Dane, Joel, and Trish entering the apartment, and then someone immediately on the steps. Her heart hopping like a rabbit, she waited.

"Hello?" Dane said.

She opened her door quickly, and they stared at one another.

"Darling," he grinned. Seconds later, Dane's hands held her face, his browns searing into her blues. "Tell me, now. Are you mine? Only mine?" he teased.

She nodded and sighed with a laugh. "Yes, of course," she melted into him, taking in his delicious cologne.

"No Dennis?"

"Of course, not, silly. Only you."

Dane sighed, "Oh, my love."

Their laughter, tears, and smoldering kisses exploded with euphoria, and all at once, she was twirling around and around in his arms. They tumbled to the bed, devouring one another's faces.

"I love you. I'm so happy, darling. I've missed your face." Dane whispered.

"I'm happy, too." They kissed again, more slowly and tenderly, their eyes open and locked.

"I want to stay here and make sweet love to you, but you know we are expected upstairs," Dane murmured.

"I know. Don't worry, I'm not going anywhere."

They delighted in their kisses until Dane lifted himself off the bed and held out his hand for her.

As they settled around the table laden with Gram's elaborate lunch, Trish clinked her glass. "We have an announcement!" She took Joel's hand and grinned happily at him. "We are expecting! In June!"

"Congratulations!" Katie and Dane said at once.

"Mazel Tov!" Gram said excitedly.

"Oh, my goodness! I'm so happy for you," Katie squealed, jumping out of her seat to hug Trish.

"I'm thrilled for you, brother." Dane patted his brother's back. "Your life is shaping up quite nicely, just as you wanted."

"Thank you, Dane. Your generosity has helped considerably. I still don't know why I was just handed such a generous portion of the business. I love you, brother. I'm grateful for you and quite thankful you don't hate my guts."

"Why would I hate you?"

"Because my birth ruined your life. You lost Mum because of me. I had a pretty happy childhood. You were left with an unaffectionate father, no mother, and boarding school."

"That's true. But it wasn't your fault, certainly, and I recently learned Mum did not abandon me. She loved us both, but she was gravely ill and needed care. I loved being with you and the family during summer and holiday. I have always loved you and always will."

"I love you too, *Uncle Dane*," Joel said, squeezing Dane's arm.

They clinked their glasses. Joel glanced at Katie, who was speaking to Trisha and Gram, and then back toward Dane. "How's it going with Katie?"

"Good. We are good."

Joel patted his brother's back. "I am glad of that. And, even though you brought it on yourself, you've been through enough anguish. It's time for some happiness."

"Well, Joel and I have an announcement as well," Dane said. "We have a new project. E.W. Holdings will be the name of the new children's wing of the Surrey Library." Dane was especially proud, knowing his father would be pleased. "We are working closely with the architects, and I am learning more about construction and design. It's been a challenge and a great deal of work, but we are thrilled about it."

Katie shouted, "That's brilliant! I've been hoping you were going to get the chance to do what you wanted to do. I'm so glad you are doing this. How proud your father would be to hear this. It's wonderful." She blushed at Dane. "Keeps you busy, too, while I'm away."

"Yes, it does. I'm exhausted when I get into bed at night." He winked at her, and everyone giggled at his meaning.

Katie clinked her glass next. "Alright, well if it's announcement time, I have one too, although nothing compared to yours," she said, smiling at Trish. "Being here has opened my eyes to England's unfair education system. Students from the U.S. have had access to academic schooling throughout their lives, no matter their parents' status. Children of working-class parents in England aren't given the opportunity to prepare for university. I have had a hard time here in school, throughout school, really. I am slower at my numbers than the others, and science is foreign to me. I want to teach students like me, who have the desire and ability, but who are held back by the system." Tears formed in her eyes, her passion readily visible.

"Oh, love," Dane gushed. "Father would be so proud of you right now, as am I. Look at you."

"I'm proud of you too, dear. I loved teaching. It's a noble profession." Gram said.

·♥·♥·♥·♥·♥·

A T THE END OF the evening, Dane led her into his room. "I cannot bear to be apart. I hope you won't think I'm taking advantage, but I can't bear it."

"Darling. Of course not. I've been waiting for this, too," she said, melting into his arms.

His delicate touch relaxed her instantly. He lifted her to the bed, laying her down gently. His shorts still on, he undressed her. "My love. Every night without you in my arms is torture." His fingertips gently caressed her face, as if he was trying to memorize every feature. She leaned into his touch, her eyes searching his. He kissed her forehead, her cheeks, the corner of her mouth, reverent and trembling. "I still cannot believe it. One look into your eyes, and I'm babbling like an infant, my head is screaming, '*I love you*,' as it has for so long, only now I can say it freely. I love you, Katie Clarke." He chuckled. "It's so easy."

"I love you, too." The distance and time that had stretched between them crumbled as their kisses and laughter swept them away. His lips slowly traced her breasts and then her nipples, a delightful tickle that resulted in soft groans. He lifted her slender leg and began, slowly and sensually, suckling her toes.

"Goodness. How could I be feeling that elsewhere?" she breathed. Reaching out to touch him, she slid her hand down his stomach and over his shorts.

"Not yet," he murmured, his lips continuing their sensual assault on her toes, then traveled up her legs to her moist center. Muscular fingers coupled with wet, soft kisses slowly teased and tickled her delicate pinkness. With deliberate slowness, he used his mouth and tongue to guide her body into a state of surrender, teasing her with varying pressures and bringing her to the edge of ecstasy before stopping, returning to her lips, then trailing down again, pushing her to the brink, and halting, again, pausing her release. Skilled hands and tongue danced around her, teasing her thighs, manipulating and driving inside her wetness, sending her further into a trance with his thumb, mouth, and finally, his nose. Her senses alive with greed and desire, he finally brought her to release with a single burst and a verbal shout. His mouth covered hers to silence her as multiple spasms followed.

Nuzzled against her cheek, he whispered, "When we finally do come together fully, that was the moment. Your climax will come moments after I enter you. How I long for that day, love."

Breathless, she nodded. "As do I. And now, it's my turn, and don't you dare tell me you are hungry," she giggled.

As he lay on his back, he lifted himself to help her remove his shorts. She positioned herself between his legs, taking his hardened, smoldering rod into her hands and then her mouth. He suppressed his groans with a pillow while she tantalized him with her tongue, leading to his pulsating erection trembling with release.

They shared a deep, loving moment, her skin warm against his as Dane held her close, cuddled in their position, naked in his arms, just as he'd wanted.

In the morning, after a few minutes of warm, delicious cuddles, Dane said, "I don't want to, but we have to get up, darling. I'm sure they are already waiting for us."

·♥·♥·♥·♥·♥·

ALTHOUGH IT WAS BRISK and windy, the five of them took in the sights of Christmas in New York over the next several days, enjoying the ice skaters at Rockefeller Center, to the Macy's Santa Clause, and of course the festively attired horse and buggy ride through Central Park. They saw the Christmas Spectacular at Radio City Music Hall, visited several museums, a symphony at Carnegie Hall, and, the pièce de résistance, a performance of *The Nutcracker* ballet, finally fulfilling a long overdue promise. Through it all, Katie continued to express joy at the spectacles, even the ones she'd already seen.

One afternoon, while Trish and Katie were shopping, Dane and Gram headed to 47th Street. Dane's eyes darted around, trying to remember the stall where he had purchased her necklace. Finally, getting his bearings, he found Moshe, who grinned at Dane as the two eyed one another.

"My friend!" Moshe said with his heavy Russian accent. The men shook hands. "How could I forget a most distinguished English gentleman such as yourself?"

"I might be English, Moshe, but I am also the grandson of a wonderful Jewish woman! This is Dora Carrino."

"Ah! And now I like you even more, my friend!" Moshe said, patting Dane on the back. As he took Gram's hand and covered it with his other, Moshe said, "Oh, Bubbe, a fine mensch, he is." Moshe said.

"A Dank," Gram said in Yiddish. "That means thank you," she said to Dane. "I actually have two fine mensches, she laughed.

"Vhat can I show you, today?"

"We are here to choose a ring, Moshe. For my girl."

"Mazel Tov." Moshe took out the trays, and Gram pointed to the ones she liked.

"This one is pretty," Gram said.

"I like that," Dane took the ring and put it on his pinky.

They studied a few more, returning several times to the 1.5 carat round brilliant diamond, held by six prongs, on a thin band with five small diamonds on each side.

"It's perfect. She'll love it," Gram said.

"Let's talk money. I don't like the haggling part, Moshe. Just give me the bottom line." Dane continued looking in the cases. "Oh, and throw in those pearl earrings too, will you?"

As they completed the transaction, Moshe held out his hand. "If za ring doesn't fit, please come back for sizing. I'd like to meet za lucky gi'l."

"We will. Thank you."

"And you, my dear," Moshe said to Gram, taking her hand. "Mazel Tov."

Chapter 39

LOVE AND PURPOSE

DECEMBER 1958

WHILE DANE AND JOEL were out playing ball, the delicious aroma of roasting turkey with vegetables and potatoes filled Gram's apartment as she and the girls prepared a special Christmas Eve supper. Aunt Sarah had called earlier to say they weren't going to make it, as both of their children were ill.

After enjoying the fabulous meal, Dane, Katie, and Joel walked once again to the church for midnight mass, leaving exhausted Trish and Gram at home. While lighting a candle for Ellis, a solemn moment passed between them. Dane took her hand and looked into her eyes. "When we were in Christ Church I wanted to tell you how sure I was that we will be married forever, but I couldn't say it."

"It's alright. You can say it now," she whispered, squeezing his hand.

·❤·❤·❤·❤·❤·

THE NEXT FEW DAYS were filled with more sightseeing, the Statue of Liberty, museums, shows, and lazy days. On the morning of the 28th, Dane took Katie's hand. "I'd like to make an photo album of our New York adventures. We have pictures of just about everything, but not all the places we have been. It's a nice day. Lets go take some photos around town today. We can start at the Christmas tree in Rockefeller Center."

After breakfast, they headed for Midtown. The giant Christmas tree at Rockefeller Center was indeed a wonderful photo opportunity, but it was only a stepping stone for the memorable day Dane had planned.

After snapping photos of the festive decorations and the ice skaters twirling at Rockefeller Center, Dane led the way down Fifth Avenue toward the Empire State Building. "Did we take photos from up there last year? Do you have any?" he said, pointing to the building.

"No, I don't have any, but I'd love to grab some if we have the time," she said.

Dane looked at his watch, suppressing a grin. "I think we can fit a quick trip in. Then we can get some lunch."

Holding hands, they entered the building and took the elevator to the 102nd floor.

Calm as a cucumber, Dane stepped off the elevator, led Katie to a viewing spot, then left her to speak to an attendant, handing him some cash and the camera.

Once back at her side, he said, "Here, stand next to me. He's going to take some photos of us with the city in the background."

Katie posed with her hand on Dane's chest and smiled at the attendant taking their picture.

Dane got silly and posed with Katie in various funny positions. The attendant laughed at their jovial play as he took snapshots. Finally, Dane held her for a moment, looking into her eyes, then pointed out a building far in the distance for her to try to identify.

As she considered the mysterious building, she felt his absence and turned to find him down on one knee, holding a blue velvet box.

With her hand over her mouth, she sucked in her breath, and high above the city, the world melted away. "Oh...my Lord," she shrieked, her eyes wide with shock.

He smiled and took a breath. "My darling, you said you wanted your man down on his knee, begging. Well, I would never have believed it in a million years, but here I am. You are my best friend, my true love, and the only woman I want to be with for the rest of my life. You are my heart, and you have my heart." He opened the box. "I promise I will always be true to you. I love you now and evermore, just as my father had said. Will you marry me, my darling? I'm begging you, will you please be my wife? For real this time?"

The crowd of people around them stopped to stare and whisper, awaiting her answer ... the entire floor, quiet.

With joyful tears and her heart bursting with love, she cheered, "Oh, Dane. Yes, I will marry you. I have loved you for so long. It would be an honor to be your wife. For real."

He put the ring on her finger, then rose and held her face, kissing her tenderly.

"Oh!" she cried, laughing through her tears, and hugging him tightly. He picked her up and whirled her around three times as the crowd cheered. A little girl came over to hug Katie and asked to see her ring. The attendant handed Dane the camera with a thumbs-up and a handshake.

Katie examined the ring. "Oh. Dane, it's absolutely gorgeous. I love it. And such a large stone. It's too large. You spoil me, again!" She paused for a moment. "Oh, my lord. How I have dreamed of this moment. All my life. This surprise, my handsome prince on his knee, begging? It was perfect; you are perfect. Thank you. I can't believe it" She jumped back into his arms, kissing his face, their brains exploding with fireworks and giddy laughter. "When did you—"

"When you and Trish were out shopping, Gram and I went to see Moshe. It fits?"

Katie looked at the ring on her finger. "Perfectly."

Dane grinned. "And now, my love, we have a date ... elsewhere."

After hailing a cab, Dane whispered to the cabbie before opening the car door for Katie.

They pulled up to the steps of the Plaza Hotel, and Katie squealed when she realized they were getting out. "Oh, Dane! Are we having lunch here? I love The Plaza!"

"Lunch, yes. I know, my love."

After a scrumptious lunch with much excitement, champagne, and enjoying watching Katie show off her engagement ring to their waitress and the people around them, Dane excused himself for a few minutes, returning with a giddy smile on his face.

"What is that grin for?"

As he paid the bill, he asked the waitress to pack up their leftovers.

"What are we going to do with that? We don't want to be walking around the city carrying food," Katie said.

"You don't have to worry about that, love."

Leaving the restaurant, Dane turned left towards the room elevators.

"I think the exit is this way, darling," she said, pointing to the exit.

"Not for us."

"What?" she giggled.

Dane pulled a room key from his pocket, dangling it playfully in the air. Katie squealed with delight. "You got us a room?"

"After you, my love." He graciously bowed to allow her into the elevator.

·♥·♥·♥·♥·♥·

D ANE HAD REGISTERED THEM as newlyweds, so the hotel immediately brought champagne, strawberries, and caviar, along with gold and silver balloons, to their magnificently furnished suite.

"Oh, my word," she cried, happy tears glowing on her cheeks.

Dane laughed at her blissful enthusiasm.

"I've tried to imagine what it might look like, but this is simply divine. Look at the chandeliers and the moldings on the walls. And these fabrics. My Lord." She touched the thick white towels and the polished marble countertops in the bathroom. She admired the faux fireplace adorned with green marble and the gold wall sconces that lit each side of the mantle. The brilliantly colored floral rug covering most of the floor in the living area in front of the sofa was thick and luxurious.

She sighed as she entered the bedroom, her eyes drinking in the intricately carved dark wood headboard and the crisp white-on-white elegant bedding. Dane was certainly correct in his description, as the suite on the seventeenth floor boasted the most incredible skyline views overlooking Central Park, Park Avenue, Fifth Avenue, and 59th Street.

"Dane we have no luggage. I have nothing but this dress."

"Don't worry. I've thought of everything, darling."

Moments later, the meticulously dressed bellman brought three large suitcases into their room.

"I had Trisha and Gram pack everything for you. Including your dress for New Year's Eve, your toiletries, makeup…everything. Joel brought everything over. We are here for the next three nights."

"Oh my God. You are…amazing. I'm so very happy," she giggled, jumping into his arms.

His face nuzzled her ears, "As am I. I love you."

"I love you too," she said, laughing.

"I want to look at everything, but of course, I cannot take my eyes from this." She gleamed, studying her ring, laughing like a child with a new toy. "I can't believe it. Dane Wellington. The one everyone told me would never marry. Oh, won't Mrs. Danbury be surprised? And Mrs. Macklin, and Maggie. And Trish! And Lizzy, too. Oh, my love, every day I went over in my head what everyone, and I mean everyone, told me. That you will never marry or love. I beat myself up because I let myself hope. Father supplied that hope." Her hand covered her heart as it often did when she thought of Ellis. "'Reach for the Stars,' he wrote."

"He told me to bide my time annulling our marriage. He said we would fall deeply in love. That you were the one. That he was happy knowing I would find love and purpose. How did he know that?" Dane asked, his eyes watering too.

"I don't know," she whispered. "I loved him so."

"I never told him how much I loved him."

She turned to hold his face in her palm. "Ahh, he knew, love. He knew."

"Oh, love," he whispered. "Daisy helped me see why I didn't believe in love. And Gram told me things about my mother that I wish I had known earlier. Might have…would have changed many of the things I believed," he said, reflecting. "It's just as Joel said. True love. We are everything."

Their eyes locked, and they felt a powerful surge of love, gratitude, and relief that resonated deep within their souls.

"I'm ready, my love," she whispered. "I want to be with you. In full. I don't want to wait any longer."

Dane sighed and then chuckled loudly. "Nor I, love. But, actually, I'm afraid I have made additional promises I must keep." He squinted and grimaced in apology. "To Joel. We must be married before we …"

"What?" she laughed.

Their faces pressed together, he whispered, "I've never wanted someone as much as I want you. I can't bear to wait until May. But, we must. I'm sorry. And, you know, both Gram and Father would have insisted as well. So, we will do as we have done before and go no further."

"May?"

"Of course. We must be married on our day."

Katie gasped. "But, Dane. Finals! I'll barely make it."

"We will make it work. Don't you worry."

They spent the night lovingly entwined in each other's arms, kissing, laughing, and holding one another closely. Lost in their love for each other, their frenzied need building, their bodies and minds severing the outside world, they wallowed in their all-consuming passion.

· ♥ · ♥ · ♥ · ♥ · ♥ ·

A s morning light filtered in, Dane filled the freestanding tub and carried her over to the warm water. Kneeling beside her, he washed her entire body slowly and tenderly, tilting her head forward to let the warm water pour down her back.

"Oh, how wonderful this feels. Won't you join me?" she coaxed, pulling his hand.

He hesitated.

"Come in here with me. Sit behind me and wrap your arms around me in this warm water. It's quite relaxing."

He did as commanded, sitting behind her, his arms around her, and taking in the intoxicating scent of her hair, they soaked until their skin wrinkled.

Katie watched as he stood to dry himself, her eyes devouring his statuesque frame. Once he was dry, he wrapped her up and lifted her to the bed, thankful she was no longer bashful, as their heated bodies melted into one. She marveled at how her naked body felt like it belonged next to his. His mouth on hers sent sensations to her lower core, and when his tongue slithered down over her belly, she submitted to him in hungered anticipation. As she reached to touch him, he held her arms above her head, smothering her with his mouth.

He whispered, "No no, my darling. You first, always."

"Oh my," she gasped. His tongue traced the outline of her delicate space once again, each time inching a little further, driving her mad with undulating pleasure. Skillfully using his warm tongue to awaken her senses, he pushed her to the edge of ecstasy before easing off and allowing her to calm. Then he repeated the cycle.

His warm, languid tongue flicked and skimmed over her soft, delicate, pink flesh. Long flat strokes sent her writhing until his nose and thumb took possession, working their magic until she let go with a quiet cry and thunderous pulses.

"Oh Lord," she said breathlessly. And the tears came once again.

"Are you alright, love?" He placed his warm hand over her center as if to signify a peaceful end.

"Yes! You are unbelievable! Thank you."

He kissed her tears tenderly. "Are you going to cry each time we make love?" he whispered.

"Yes, I think so," she giggled into the pillows.

He cherished those tears, he realized, her emotional response tugging his heart each time.

Through her happy tears, Katie studied his manly glory. "It grows so big! Just moments ago it was half the size!" She laughed, her hand over her mouth.

"I was in the water," he laughed.

She was anxious to send him sailing without water. Touching him more boldly than before, she coaxed him to lie down, luxuriating in his manly scent. What an empowering sensation it was, caressing him, stroking and licking him, as he eyed her every move. *He likes watching me.* Her eyes on his while her tongue danced around his hard shaft was indeed erotic. However, Dane eventually succumbed to his overwhelming need, closing his eyes and losing himself, his magnificent arousal raging until waves of pleasure washed over him. "My God," he said as he recovered, smothering her with kisses. "Thank you, love. Brilliant."

As they embraced in the afterglow of their lovemaking, they talked about the day and the engagement. Broaching the subject of their future married life, Katie asked the question burning in her mind. "Darling, children? I mean, not right away, of course. But, at some point?"

Dane laughed. "At some point. Yes, I suppose. I didn't think I wanted children, but seeing you with Lilian and the children at the shelter stirred something inside me that I didn't understand until recently."

"Oh, I'm so happy to hear that!" she cried. She clung to his neck and rained a hundred kisses across his face.

They spent the next three days making plans, visiting museums, taking long walks in Central Park, and dancing at some of the liveliest clubs, waiting anxiously for New Year's Eve.

·♥·♥·❦·♥·♥·

T HE HAZE OF PUNGENT cigarette smoke filled the air at the Copacabana. Dane felt the rhythmic pulse of the music in his chest as he observed the celebrities, the beautiful women, and the powerful Italian underworld bosses who seemed to radiate an aura of danger. He found himself utterly captivated, knowing without a doubt he was with the most elegant woman in the club. Her ivory satin gown, soft and luminous under the club's swirling lights, clung to her with effortless grace, while her swept up blonde curls shimmered like moonlight amid the darker dresses and suits of the crowd. Once again, they danced all night, swaying to the slow, sultry songs, waltzing, foxtrotting, and jitterbugging. They left the club exhausted, shedding their clothes and plopping on the bed, enjoying the taste of each other throughout the sleepless night.

Back at Gram's in time for New Year's Day dinner, Dane and Katie announced in unison, "We're engaged!"

"Mazel Tov!" Gram shouted! "I'm thrilled for you both and couldn't be happier. Katie, I love you as if you were my own blood. Champagne!" Gram handed the already chilled bottle to Joel to open.

Katie hugged each of them as they cheered and recited their parts in the well-executed engagement ruse. Gram told her how she met Moshe with Dane, and Katie touched her heart upon hearing Moshe was the jeweler who made her necklace.

"Thank you. I love you all, and am blessed to have such a wonderful family," Katie said.

"Well," Joel said to Dane, "I am thrilled, brother. Took long enough. I've been hoping our child would *still be a child* by the time you got around to it." Everyone laughed. "Seriously, I'm absolutely tickled for you both. Katie, I have known for quite some time you were the one. You are a match made in heaven."

Dane took Katie's hand. "The wedding is on May 21st. That is our day; the same day we were originally married." He took Katie's hand. "I'll make all the arrangements and check with you about everything." He took his grandmother's hand, too. "You will be able to make it, I assume?"

"If God allows me to stay alive, of course, I will be there," she grinned.

❣ · ❣ · ❣ · ❣ · ❣

AFTER ELEVEN MORE DAYS of blissful happiness, Dane's luggage by the elevator door, Katie buried her face deep within his chest.

"Leaving you is impossible," he said, kissing the top of her head. "I shall write a letter a week until I return in exactly sixty-seven days."

"Darling, your letters. They are divine! My heart soars when I read them. I love them all. Thank you for expressing yourself as you do. It means the world that you put so much time into them."

"I feel the same, love. Your letters keep me from going mad, and yet bring tears to my eyes," he said.

Katie hugged Gram tightly. "I don't know what I would have done without your love and guidance throughout my time here," she said, holding her tears.

"I'm here for you both. I expect our Sunday outings will continue? And, I want you to think about making amends with your father. Forgiveness is a great gift. You cannot harbor anger in your heart. It will eat you up. Bring all of those you love into your world and your world will be richer for it."

Katie pondered the wisdom of her words. *Older people know so much about life. They always seem to have all the answers.* "I will. Thank you. And yes, of course, I will see you next Sunday."

The new semester brought Katie much coursework, a welcome distraction. Occasionally, when she had spare time, she would sit by the window inside the popular Horn & Hardart Automat, a rather odd experience for a Londoner. Instead of waitresses taking orders, small glass doors, opening to small cubbies covered the walls. Behind each door was a different variety of packaged food, including sandwiches, salads, pies, and of course, their famous red jello cubes. After making her selection, Katie popped a nickel or dime into a slot, then opened the little door and took her food. She watched with fascination the food preparers behind the wall continuously stuffing the cubbies with packaged food. After munching on a surprisingly delicious tuna salad sandwich and enjoying her jello, she sat with a cup of hot robust coffee in her hands, watching the people outside race by. She admired the women's fashions, the fancy cars, and heeded the sounds of the yellow cabs honking their horns and the police on horseback blowing their whistles. *How lucky I am to have been able to experience this. An opportunity of a lifetime. Thanks to my father*, she sighed, *Ellis Wellington.*

As promised, Dane came for one more visit in March, and they spent six glorious weeks together. But, when he left, details of wedding plans swimming in both their heads, Katie felt the pang and loneliness.

Although Katie adored the vibrant energy of New York City, as her time there drew to a close, she knew in her heart everything that was truly important was waiting for her back home.

Chapter 40

LIFT A GLASS TO THE HEAVENS

MAY 21, 1959

WITH KATIE'S DETAILED INPUT, Dane arranged a beautiful May 21st wedding, complete with candelabras, cascading flowers, white roses and daisies, of course, at their quaint little church in Leatherhead, its aged stone walls echoing with the chatter of their guests.

As Gram and Norma helped Katie dress, Gram opened a worn velvet box, removing a strand of lustrous pearls. "These are the pearls Ellis gave Rachel as a wedding present. They are yours now."

"Oh my! Thank you. How beautiful. I will cherish them forever," she said, kissing Gram's cheek. Exchanging the flower-basket necklace for the pearls, she glanced at her reflection in the mirror.

Remembering her words long ago, she said to her mother, "Now, *this* is how I pictured being married. Thank you, Mum," she said to Norma, who was gazing at her through the mirror, tears welling in her eyes.

"I only wish I 'ad somthin' fancy t'give ye t'day." Norma reached into her small purse and pulled out a lace handkerchief with tiny blue and white daisies embroidered in the corners. A tear spilled onto her cheek. "I made this for ye; I 'oped ye'd carry it for ye som'thin' blue."

Katie looked at the delicate embroidery, took the hankie, and immediately used it to dab the tears leaking from her eyes before tucking it, discreetly, into her bouquet. She pulled her mother close and kissed her cheek. "Mum, I love it, and I'll treasure this more than any other present I will receive today. Thank you."

Their guests held their breath as they beheld Katie, a vision of dazzling bridal elegance in ivory silk and lace. With a fitted bodice highlighting her waist, the gown transitioned into a full ball gown skirt, supported by layers of crisp crinoline, a hoop, and several petticoats. Her hair, swept up with loose curls, was her crowning glory. Ivory kid gloves reached past her elbows, and she carried a simple bouquet of daisies and roses dotted with baby's breath.

Katie's beauty and grace took Dane's breath once again as he waited for her at the altar, his brother by his side, both dressed impeccably in black tuxedos with white roses on their lapels. Feeling both grateful and humbled, with one hand on his heart and the other wiping away tears, he marveled at the magnificent jewel approaching, escorted by her father.

Leading a heartfelt service, Father Lionel rejoiced that the couple he had hastily married years prior had, in fact, found love.

Tears of joy glistening on their faces, their friends, family, and staff watched the stunning couple recite their passionate vows, their voices echoing with emotion. Their hands and eyes held one another's, as Father Lionel finally said the magic words.

"I am thrilled to pronounce you man and wife."

"My darling, my wife," he whispered, kissing her boldly.

"Mazel Tov!" Gram shouted.

Joel and Dane embraced. "Congratulations," Joel said. "I'm so proud to be your brother and thrilled that you have finally found your way to this point. I know that you belong together." He paused, then leaned close to Dane. "You can tell me now. Did you keep your promise?"

"I did, you bastard," Dane joked, tapping his brother's shoulder.

Joel smiled. "Proud of you. I'll settle our wager later."

"I wouldn't have gotten here without you, brother. And after all you did to help me, let's consider it settled. Wanker." Dane answered, returning the brotherly embrace.

Dane took Katie's hand and walked her towards a mahogany upright piano. "Do you recognize it? This is the piano Father bought you all those years ago. I had it refurbished."

As she regarded the piano, memories flooded back. Katie's tear-filled eyes met Dane's. "Oh, God!"

Dane chuckled. "I thought it would be a nice tribute to Father if you played your Chopin piece now, and afterwards, I will send it to the cottage."

"What cottage?" Katie questioned.

Dane opened the piano bench and removed several photos, handing them to her. "The cottage I purchased in Burton-On-The-Water in the Cotswolds. My wedding present to you, my love. In case you ever need to run away from me, and I hope that never happens, you'll have a home of your own to run to. It's quite lovely, and of course it has a white picket fence and lots of flowers."

"Oh, my! Dane. It's beautiful! You are too much." Katie's hand covered her heart as she looked at the photos of the cottage and then at the piano. She reached into the open bench, lifting out Ellis's note, the sheet music for the Nocturne, and her grandmother's Bible, the dried daisies resting within. Overwhelmed with emotion, she kissed her husband. "Thank you. The cottage. The piano. My treasures. And you."

Katie's fingers danced across the keys, revealing a profound emotional connection to Chopin's masterpiece "Prelude in E Flat Major," the magnificent melody filling the room and all their guests.

"Extraordinary," Norma, remembering her child working so hard to learn that piece many years ago, shouted and clapped over the cheering audience.

Hearing that word, Katie looked at Dane, who already had his lips pressed together and tears welling in his eyes, thinking of Ellis.

A lavish reception followed at the exquisite chateau of Sir Henry Norman. Historic Ramster Hall was already renowned for its spectacular twenty-five-acre gardens, painstakingly cultivated by Lady Norman herself for well over twenty years. Over the years, Sir Norman had hosted several dignitaries and noblemen at the property and was honored to accommodate Ellis Wellington's son and his bride for their reception.

Gazing at all the people who mattered to him and his wife, Dane lifted his glass. "I want to say thank you. I am grateful to each of you, and I will thank you each separately, as well, for your help and interference, and for your unwavering love and support. I know each of you worried I would never marry. And each of you helped me get here today, indeed. To my brother Joel, thank you, for without your never-ending badgering, I would not be married to the love of my life today. Gram, for all your wisdom and guidance, thank you. I so wish my father was here to see this." Dane had given up trying to hold back his tears, needing a moment before he continued. "When Katie was a child, Father saw something special in her. Then, as we grew, he said I would love her evermore. He was bloody brilliant." Lifting his glass, "To you, Father. Thank you."

"To Mr. Wellington," everyone shouted.

The band began to play "Only You" for the couple's first dance. The newlyweds swayed as one, a breathtaking sight that held every eye in the room captive, keenly aware of the couple's eternal bond.

Once their dance ended, holding Katie's hand high in the air, Dane shouted to the crowd, "After all these years of bachelorhood, I am, finally, married to the love of my life. Well, that's not entirely accurate. Most of you don't know this, but Katie and I were actually married three years ago today. But, that marriage was never consummated, and it was annulled last August."

A loud ruckus erupted. Lizzy yelled the loudest.

Dane turned to face his wife. "I'm very happy to be your husband once again, darling. But, may we *please* consummate our marriage now? I believe I've waited long enough!"

Everyone screamed with laughter, and Gram covered her ears.

Katie pulled Dane close and whispered in his ear, "I wish we didn't have to wait until this party was over."

Following final farewells, Dane scooted Katie into the Silver Dawn.

"Where are we going?" she asked, noticing George was not heading toward Weybridge.

"Tonight, the honeymoon suite at a hotel near the airport. Tomorrow morning—the most romantic honeymoon spot of all—Paris."

"Oh, my God!" she shouted, kicking her feet.

"Mrs. Danbury packed for you. Whatever you are missing, you shall purchase there, but I assure you, you will not need much in the way of clothing," he winked.

Chapter 41

AND, FINALLY

S TUMBLING INTO THEIR HOTEL room, their heads dizzy from champagne, they wasted no time.

"Darling, oh, how I have yearned for this moment. Finally, we are here. I love you. Oh my God, I can't stop saying it. How I love you," Dane whispered.

With controlled urgency, he laid her naked body on the bed, his mouth passionately exploring hers with fervent desire. His fingers, lingering slowly over her nipples, down her torso, and over her hips, soon discovered the slippery evidence of her arousal. When his mouth left hers, traveling over her neck and then stopping to suckle her nipples, one then the other, she squirmed with anticipation, knowing where his tongue was heading. His fingers circled her curly mass as his warm tongue followed, lightly teasing around the edges. She lost herself in heightened need as his tongue and then nose found her delicate pink. An initial tickling with the tip of his tongue changed suddenly to a lingering, unhurried travel of her full length, driving her mad with pleasure and almost to the end. But, Dane was careful, taking her up and down, almost to the brink multiple times, her consciousness adrift, she trembled on the edge as he coaxed her higher with every stroke. Her climax seized her with unrelenting force, her body pulsing in waves as her hand gripped his hair and her moans shockingly wild.

Wracked with residual shudders, she lay breathless and immobilized. Tears of overwhelming passion filled her eyes, which he gently wiped away before drawing her close, kissing her face tenderly. She inhaled deeply, taking in his lingering scent, and basked in her unabashed nudity. As she calmed, feeling his kisses all around her, she admired the dark hair that framed his brown eyes. "Have I ever told you how handsome my husband is?" *And he's all mine.*

Her smooth fingertips traced the heat throbbing beneath his taut skin, a low groan rumbling from his lips as her tongue followed. Allowing her only seconds to taste him, he shielded himself before ensuring she was ready for his rigid maleness. His fingers and tongue caressed her until she was, once again, wet with anticipation, and inch by inch, her feminine sweetness along with her guiding hand answered with fevered eagerness. She felt a dull ache as the membrane detached, but he was gentle and wonderful, pausing for a moment to allow her time to adjust, then moved slowly, until her body responded.

"Oh, my darling, finally," she whispered.

After years of wanting, and years of denying, they unreservedly became one. Lost in one another's gaze, finally giving in to their long-awaited mutual release.

"Sex without love is nothing," he said as he watched her sleep. *Making love. Something I had never done before her.* The intensity of his connection with Katie was unlike anything he had ever felt. It was an emotional bond that transcended mere desire. He had saved her from a disastrous life with a fiend, and her love saved him from a lifetime of loneliness. They had saved each other. He crawled up next to her, turned her on her side, and assuming their position, held her close, smelling her perfumed hair. "My beautiful, wonderful wife. I could have never let you go," he whispered as he drifted off to sleep.

'So long as men can breathe or eyes can see,
So long lives this, and this gives life to thee.'
William Shakespeare, Sonnet 18

ABOUT THE AUTHOR

Sheri Sheldon, a New Yorker at heart, believes love is life's greatest gift and crafts characters who challenge readers' ideas about love and relationships, prompting self-reflection and new perspectives. Her writing reflects her rich life experiences and diverse career history.

Sheri lives with her husband in Orange County, California, and has traveled the world, but The Cotswolds, England, is her happy place.

If you enjoyed this novel, please consider helping this new author by posting a review on either Goodreads or Amazon. Good, authentic reviews are the **only** way a new author's work gets seen. Your input is appreciated.

For bonus chapters contact Sheri at AuthorSheri@gmail.com (Mailing list subscribers get free new EPUB releases)
http://sherisheldon.com